A
TIMELESS
Romance
ANTHOLOGY

Winter Collection

A TIMELESS
Romance
ANTHOLOGY

Winter Collection
SIX HISTORICAL ROMANCE NOVELLAS

Sarah M. Eden
Heidi Ashworth
Annette Lyon
Joyce DiPastena
Donna Hatch
Heather B. Moore

Mirror Press

Cover Design by Christina Marcano
Interior Design by Heather Justesen
Edited by Annette Lyon

ISBN-10: 1941145027
ISBN-13: 978-1-941145-02-9

Published by Mirror Press, LLC

http://timelessromanceanthologies.blogspot.com
E-book edition released October 2012
Paperback edition released January 2014

TABLE OF CONTENTS

OTHER TIMELESS ROMANCE ANTHOLOGIES

Spring Vacation Collection

Summer Wedding Collection

Autumn Collection

European Collection

Love Letter Collection

Western Collection

Summer in New York Collection

The Road to Cavan Town

Sarah M. Eden

Other Works by Sarah M. Eden

Friends & Foes

An Unlikely Match

The Kiss of a Stranger

Drops of Gold

Glimmer of Hope

Longing for Home

Chapter One

County Cavan, Ireland, 1864

*T*he roads leading to Cavan Town boasted a fine collection of young bachelors hying themselves to that gem in the midst of the lake county. They made the journey, not to conduct business, not to shop at market, not to worship. The men came to pay court to the belle of the county, each hoping to have a single word, a single glance from the object of their universal affection. Unfortunately for Alice Wheatley, she was not that belle.

Alice hadn't a particular taste for the attentions of hordes of men at one time. Her heart belonged to but one man, a certain Isaac Dancy, whom she'd met on the road to Cavan. He walked the dozen miles around the lakes from his home near Killeshandra every weekend to join the throng of besotted men. Alice walked nearly as many miles herself, returning home to Cavan from her weekday job as a maid-of-all work for a farm family of very comfortable means.

They'd struck up a conversation and a friendship quicker than a change of weather in autumn. He'd shown himself intelligent and thoughtful and kind. They laughed together and smiled together, yet their conversations were known to take serious turns as well. She knew his worries, and he knew hers. She felt closer to him than any other person on earth.

Yet he was making the weekly walk into Cavan to court another woman. Even knowing the reasons for his weekly journeys, Alice had fallen quite deeply in love with him. If her parents had given her a middle name, it likely would have been "Terribly Unlucky."

Still, as she followed the turn in the road that she walked each weekend and approached the spot where Isaac waited for her every Saturday morning, she didn't regret her lack of luck. He stood there as usual. Her heart smiled to see him. Unlucky she might have been, but she had his company twice each week and felt grateful for that.

"Good day to ya, Isaac Dancy."

"And to you." He rose from the rock he'd been sitting on.

Alice sometimes wondered if she'd ever grow accustomed to the sight of him. His hair could not have been a darker shade of black. Deep brown were his eyes, and full of intelligence and a love of living. And a life of working the land had left him broad of shoulder. What woman could help admiring the very sight of him?

"Have ya noted our fine view this morning?" he asked. "The last bits of autumn color are on the leaves."

She had noticed it. A fine prospect the lakes offered all the year 'round. Snow hung on bare branches in the winter. Buds of green brightened the landscape in spring. Foliage was lush and plentiful during the summer. She'd developed a fondness for the road in the two years she'd walked it. But the past four months, walking with Isaac, she'd hardly noticed the beauty around her.

"How went yer week, Isaac?"

Thus began their usual stroll. He spoke of having finished his harvest and preparing his home and land and animals for the coming winter. She spoke of her own work and the growing coldness at night, how her tiny closet of a room at the farmhouse hardly kept any of the night air out. He suggested she might want to begin bringing blankets with her as the seasons changed. She wondered aloud if the market would yet have apples or if the picking season had entirely ended.

'Twas always that way between them. Conversation came easily. They could speak on anything or nothing and thoroughly enjoy themselves.

In time, she told herself, he would recognize that for the wonderful thing it was. In time, he would give up his courtship of Miss Sophia Kilchrest and move on to higher pastures, as it were.

Sure, he'd been lured, like so many others, by Miss Kilchrest's lovely face and fine figure. He'd been pulled in by her flawless manners and twinkling eyes. He'd even found a bit of motivation in the dowry she'd bring with her, though, to his credit, he'd not mentioned that but once, and even then, as an off-hand observation. And, Alice had noted, having set his mind on the pursuit of such a highly prized treasure, Isaac had taken on a certain single-mindedness where Miss Kilchrest was concerned. Alice doubted he gave his pursuit much thought of late. He simply continued because it was a goal he'd worked on so long.

"Do ya plan to keep making this walk after the snows come?" Alice asked, praying and hoping and feeling generally quite desperate that he would.

"I don't plan to give over the progress I've made with Miss Kilchrest, if that's what ya mean."

'Twas not in the smallest bit what she meant. But life had taught her that men could be terribly thickheaded, and a woman had no real choice but to be patient with them.

"Are ya making progress, then?"

Isaac nodded. "She spoke to me quite particularly the last few weekends, though the other men vying for her attention were ready to rip me apart over it."

"And men enjoy that, do they, the look of violent loathing in the eyes of another man?"

Isaac grinned. "Indeed."

I will never understand men. Was it the loathing and the sense of victory Isaac liked, or was it the attentions from Miss Kilchrest? Surely he was intelligent enough not to court a woman simply out of pride. "And what did ya talk about during this jealousy-inducing conversation with Miss Kilchrest?"

He buttoned his coat against the growing wind as they continued down the road. "She spoke of her friends and fashion and the weather."

"Fascinating." Alice only just kept her tone less dry than she felt the comment deserved.

He laughed a little. "She and I aren't the friends that you and I are. We've not endless topics to discuss yet."

So stop trying to converse with her and start spending more time with me. She'd convince him one day; she swore she would. He'd realize Sophia Kilchrest was not for him. More important still, he'd realize she absolutely was.

"Can I let ya in on a secret?" he asked.

Alice couldn't help a smile. He'd shared "secrets" with her before. Sometimes 'twas nothing more than a teasing story, though on a few occasions, he'd told her of plans he had for his home and land. He told her personal things, important things, things she felt certain he hadn't told Miss Kilchrest.

He'd piece it together. He'd realize in time she was his match and not the Belle of Cavan.

"What's this secret?" she asked.

4

"This weekend in Cavan," he said, earnest excitement in his voice, "I mean to ask Miss Kilchrest if she'll consider me her exclusive suitor. I mean to see to it we're on the firm path toward making her my bride."

With that declaration, Alice Wheatley's world ended.

Chapter Two

*I*saac would never, as long as he lived, understand the female mind. He'd told Alice of his plans to move quite seriously forward with Miss Kilchrest. Rather than offer immediate congratulations or encouragement, she'd looked shocked. *Shocked.*

How could she have been even a little surprised? They'd spoken of his pursuit of Miss Kilchrest nearly every weekend since he'd first crossed Alice's path some four months earlier. She knew as much about his plans and thoughts as anyone on earth, *more* even. And yet she clearly hadn't expected his declaration.

Women will never make the least sense.

They reached Market Square, where the weekly crowd of men gathered to jostle for position alongside Miss Kilchrest as she wandered about the vendors' tables. Over the months Isaac had been at the task of courting her, he'd planned out his efforts quite meticulously. Those plans seldom needed review or second thoughts.

Alice, on the other hand, was near constantly throwing his understanding of her entirely out the window.

"Have we made good time?" Alice asked that question every Saturday as they came in to Cavan Town. She needed a timepiece of her own, she did.

He checked his pocket watch. "'Tis only just noon. Ye've time to reach yer grandparent's house for luncheon."

Her nod was one of relief.

"Have they taken a turn for the worse?" She'd spoken often of her grandparents and their failing health. They were the reason she returned to Cavan every weekend—to take over from a cousin the task of caring for them.

"No more than expected. They're growing old fast, is all." She gave him a sad smile, but with more than a hint of her usual optimism. He didn't like how it dulled her usually sparkling brown eyes. "I'd best not keep ya from yer efforts. There's a market full of men needing tripping up and pushing aside."

There was the laughing encouragement he was used to receiving from his friend. Perhaps she'd only been distracted earlier by worries over her family. That would certainly account for her unenthusiastic response to his news. 'Twas a logical explanation, something Isaac far preferred to confusion.

"Is there anything I can do to help with yer grandparents?"

"Bless ya, no. There's no immediate crisis, only the hardship of waiting and watching them fade."

He could appreciate that. "Ya know where to find me if ya need anything."

"Yes, I simply follow the crowd," she said dryly, with a bit of a twinkle back in her eyes.

"Indeed. And ye'll find me at the very front of it." He set his eyes in that direction, in fact. 'Twas time and past to get on with the weekend's goals. "Wish me luck."

She hesitated the briefest of moments. "I'll wish the best for ya."

There was some difference between that and what he'd asked for, though he couldn't put his finger on just what that difference was.

"Until tomorrow, then. Farnham Street after church."

She smiled. "I'll be there."

He watched her a moment as she made her way down Market Street, away from the square. She didn't attract the attention Miss Kilchrest did, but she was a fine-looking woman. Her light brown hair didn't capture a man's gaze the way a head of fiery locks did. But she didn't fade into the scenery. He'd wondered many times while walking at her side just why it was that no man had snatched her up yet.

His weekly walk to Cavan had improved drastically with the addition of her company and friendship. Even as the weather had turned colder, he'd not minded waiting at the point in the road where she always joined him. Her company was well worth the discomfort. She would certainly be the first person he told when someday Miss Kilchrest accepted his proposal. Likely only his mother would be happier for him, though she didn't live close enough for telling in person.

But he would have nothing to tell either of them if he didn't focus on his goal. The list of things to accomplish was clear and precise in his mind. He'd purchase a few foodstuffs to eat over the weekend whilst making his way to the coveted position at Miss Kilchrest's side. Once he had accomplished that, he would speak with her about furthering their connection. After her acceptance, he could see to some business he needed to undertake. While courting Miss Kilchrest was reason enough to come to Cavan, he found that justifying the time away from his farm was easier when he added business with pleasure.

'Twould be his most productive trip into Cavan yet.

He purchased a bit of bread and cheese from stalls along the market road. A few of the men he saw every weekend trailing Miss Kilchrest noticed him there. Their faces fell a bit upon seeing him arrive, a sure sign his progress with Miss Kilchrest had not gone unnoticed. She was a fine catch, to be sure. Her dowry was something any man would wish for, but her kind heart and gentle spirit even more so. That those arguments in her favor were combined with a strikingly pretty face and a fine figure had secured her more suitors than she likely knew what to do with.

She'd not have to worry over that long, though.

His sack upon his back and his eye on the thickest part of the bachelor crowd, Isaac set his mind to the task at hand. Some assertive weaving in and around tables and vendors and spectators set him within a few feet of his goal and well within sight of the lovely Miss Kilchrest as she walked at her leisure among the stalls. She did seem to take a great deal of delight in shopping and glancing coyly at the men who trailed her.

He'd thought it a very good sign during his twelve-mile walk from home that the last remaining autumn leaves were a shade of red that quite perfectly matched the color of Miss Kilchrest's hair. The glimpses of sky he'd spied between the ever-growing clouds reminded him of the brilliant blue of her eyes. A very good sign, indeed.

Today would be his day. Of course, first he'd have to actually come close enough to her to speak the words.

The past months had taught him to be more forward than he was by nature. Standing about waiting for Miss Kilchrest to notice him hadn't worked very well.

He stepped in front of one of the other men, moved around a few others. Miss Kilchrest was fully in his sight and lovely as ever she'd been. What man could help but notice her, especially when she wore a bright smile as she did in that moment?

The rising wind rustled the few curls she'd let hang loose about her face. She was sweet to everyone, charming them and easing even the most nervous of her suitors. The women, too, seemed happy to see her when she crossed their paths. At vendor stalls, she stopped to enquire after their goods and compliment their offerings, though she rarely made a purchase. Her friendly nature would make a good addition to his neighborhood.

He caught her eye in the next moment. She smiled welcomingly. 'Twas all the encouragement he needed.

Isaac slipped up to her side near a vendor's table with a small spread of braided watch fobs.

"A good afternoon to ya, Miss Kilchrest."

She laid a light hand on his arm. "How are you, Isaac?" She'd taken to using his first name, though he'd not felt comfortable calling her "Sophia." Perhaps after she accepted his coming request he would.

"It seems we are in for a bit of weather," he said.

She nodded, glancing briefly up at the sky. Her gazed returned quickly to the men standing about. Some held hats in their hands. Others stood with airs of confidence. Isaac had made a study of which men she gave second and third looks to. Those who arrived ragged or dirty she seemed less than impressed with. She preferred a smile to a somber expression.

The men who met those expectations were the ones to receive an invitation to call at the Kilchrest home. Isaac had seen at least a dozen men receive that coveted invitation. His turn was coming; he knew it was. After all, if she agreed to consider him her primary beau, his presence in her home would be a natural thing.

Miss Kilchrest, he had quickly learned, preferred to make the conversation than follow it. Isaac usually obliged her in that, but if he were to pose his question, he'd have to take control of their short time together.

"I wondered if I might have a word—"

One of Miss Kilchrest's particular friends arrived in that exact moment. Isaac stood back, waiting, while the women exchanged embraces and quick-paced words.

He looked over those men who hadn't yet given up for the day. O'Leary from Drumora, who'd received ample attention from Miss Kilchrest. Kelly from Pullamore Far. Others he'd not met in person but recognized from their many weekends jostling one another about. Malone and Sheridan, both Cavan men, who Isaac knew were his greatest rivals. They alone had been granted as much of her time as he. Others had, early on in Isaac's courtship, but they'd fled the field, apparently having been deemed not quite what Miss Kilchrest wished for.

Her friend moved along with one last wave goodbye.

Isaac began again. "Miss Kilchrest, I wished—"

"Buy a flower for the fine lass, will ya?" a little flower girl, likely no older than ten, implored with a bit of forward cheekiness, but wearing the dimpled smile of an angel.

He could hardly resist such a request, especially seeing the acceptance of the offering already hovering on Miss Kilchrest's face. Whether the flower girl had anticipated it or not, she'd made a clever suggestion. Given the sheer number of men still trailing after Miss Kilchrest, all the little girl's flowers were purchased and offered in a moment's time.

"Oh, I do love flowers," Miss Kilchrest said, her arms laden with blooms, likely the last they'd see in a while. The chill of late autumn hung heavy in the air.

A light sprinkling of rain began as it so often did. Usually, Isaac didn't even note it. But the timing today might actually prove helpful.

"There's an overhang just this direction," he said, motioning toward a nearby building. "If ye'll just step that way, ye'll be out of the rain."

"How thoughtful." She shifted the flowers into one arm. She offered a wiggly-fingered wave to the other men then slipped her arm through his.

Isaac took a deep breath as they walked swiftly away. His moment had come. Months of working to gain her notice were about to pay off. Soon she'd send the other men packing, and he could move on to the next part of his plan.

Safely under the overhang, he charged ahead. "Miss Kilchrest, I feel we've come to know one another these past months."

"Indeed." She smelled her flowers, obviously at ease with him. A good sign.

"I think ye've come to feel something of a preference for my company."

She touched his arm briefly. "Of course, Isaac. Who could possibly not enjoy your company?"

With that extra encouragement, he cut directly to the heart of the matter. "I wish to ask you, then, if ye'd be so good as to consider me yer beau, rather exclusively."

She did not appear nearly as shocked as Alice had, though perhaps a bit surprised. Her smile, however, remained serene. "You sweet man," she said. "I didn't realize you were so fond of me."

"Who could possibly not be fond of you?" He echoed her words of a moment earlier, thinking she might laugh at the sally.

Miss Kilchrest shrugged a single shoulder, returning her attention to her collection of flowers.

"I don't wish to press ya, but is there an answer to my question?"

A flattering bit of color touched her cheeks. "Of course there'll be an answer, I'm only uncertain what answer to give."

"Might I suggest 'yes'?"

She swatted at his arm. "You sweet man. Tis not a matter of yes or no."

"It isn't?" Isaac didn't think there was a third option.

"This is only unexpected, is all."

Unexpected? What did she think he'd intended with his four months of pursuit, if not an eventual proposal? The sensible assumption was that he meant just this, to further their connection.

She gave him such a heart-tuggingly uncertain look. "Can my answer be 'perhaps'?"

Perhaps. A third option, after all. "'Perhaps,' but not 'no'?" he clarified.

Miss Kilchrest looked quite pleased with that. "Yes, exactly."

Not no. He could accept that. For the time being.

And, he thought with some burgeoning hope, Alice would help him think of ways to win Miss Kilchrest over for good. Alice would help, and he'd have Miss Kilchrest's hand for sure and certain.

Chapter Three

Alice generally looked forward to her Sunday afternoon walk toward Killeshandra. For those few hours, she had sole claim on Isaac Dancy's time and attention. For that brief time each week, she could imagine he fancied her, that he thought her more than merely a friend. Walking the road as they wound about the lakes felt like coming home.

But, standing with her childhood friend, Billy Kettle, waiting for Isaac to arrive, Alice couldn't summon enough enthusiasm to even smile. Her favorite time in the entire week, and she was dreading it.

"Why do ya have to go, Alice? Can't ya stay here? We could have fun." Billy asked the same question and made the same arguments every week. He generally did so in the first moments after she left her grandparents' home and long before she left the street where both their families lived. He'd been more overset than usual that day and had followed her all the way to Farnham Street. "No one else will feed the ducks with me."

She patted his hand. When they were both little, she would pat his shoulder, but he'd grown far too tall. "The ducks have all flown away now. They'll not be back until spring."

"*Ducks* go away. *You* go away." His forehead creased deeply as he pouted. Though he had the look and build of a grown man, little else about him had changed over the years. "I don't like all the going away."

He kicked a pebble with the toe of his boot, his hands shoved into his trouser pockets. Poor lad. 'Twas the same difficulty, the same sadness every week. The only thing that changed was how easily he could be reassured.

She looked up into his handsome face and almost painfully innocent eyes. "I'll be back on Saturday as usual. We'll have grand fun then, we will."

"How far away is Saturday?"

"But six days. Not even a whole week. And yer da says he's found a bit of work for ya to do." She smiled encouragingly. "Ye'll be quite busy, and I'll be back before ya even have time to miss me."

His mouth twisted about, brow still furrowed. "I can miss ya fast."

He'd always been so sweetly loving, like a dear younger brother.

Billy's worried pout transformed instantly to a laughing grin. "Here comes yer beau."

He'd teased her about Isaac from the very first time Billy saw her arrive in Cavan with him. Billy gave her a quick hug, laughing like a child who'd heard a particularly entertaining tale. She couldn't help smiling at his antics. He rushed away, throwing grins back at her as he did.

She yet had a smile on her face when Isaac arrived at her side. Thank the heavens for Billy. She'd not have been able to greet Isaac with anything resembling cheerfulness without him.

"Who was that?" Isaac motioned with a small twitch of his head in the direction Billy had gone.

Had he never met Billy? Alice couldn't remember introducing the two. "He's Billy, m' dear friend."

"Yer *dear* friend is he?" Isaac's mouth pulled down, his eyes narrowed, still not looking at her.

Feminine instinct can be a wonderful thing. Useful, at the very least. The man, Alice realized on the instant, was a touch jealous. And if he could be jealous of her friendship with another man, he couldn't be quite as determined to court Sophia Kilchrest as he professed to be. Part of him, at least, must have some feelings for *her*.

Alice clasped her hands behind her back and walked slowly down the road, not looking back, but certain he would follow. "Aye, my dear, dear friend. He welcomes me to Cavan Town each Saturday and sees me off every Sunday."

Isaac caught up to her. "Why is it I've never seen him?" He looked back over his shoulder several times.

She shrugged. "Ye've been a bit distracted, ya must admit. Fighting off hordes of fellow knights in shining armor takes all the concentration a man can muster."

"But ye've never even mentioned him."

Aye, jealous he was, and no doubting it. "I'm certain I have."

She kept up her somewhat brisk pace, quickly leaving behind the outskirts of Cavan. That Isaac kept up with her without protest seemed a good sign.

Alice picked up a topic other than Billy. 'Twould do Isaac a world of good to let things spin about in his mind a while. "You were to have a monumental weekend, if memory serves. How did things go with Miss Kilchrest?"

She'd dreaded the conversation for two days but now found herself equal to it. Perhaps she hadn't lost her opportunity after all.

16

He buttoned his coat higher as they walked further from town, the chill of approaching winter stronger even than it had been the day before. "I had a chance to speak with her during that bit of rain we got yesterday."

Alice's heart stumbled a bit in her chest. She did her utmost to keep her expression and her tone light and unconcerned. "A proposal in the rain? Tis hard to set a more romantic scene than that. Perhaps if ye'd arranged for a dusting of snow."

Isaac yet watched her with creased brow. "Yer *dear* friend, he is?"

A smile tipped one side of her mouth. The situation wasn't entirely hopeless. "Never ya mind about Billy. Tell me how Miss Kilchrest answered yer question. Has yer courtship become etched in stone?"

Please say no. Please say no.

"Well . . ." He didn't seem to know just how to answer. "I asked if she'd consider me her one and only suitor and . . ." Again his face twisted in thought. "She didn't say 'no.'"

"Did she 'yes,' then?"

Isaac shook his head.

"Not yes, but not no." Alice took some comfort in that. "And ya mean to ask again, do ya?" But how soon? How insistent did he mean to be?

"I mean to go back and try my hand again." He gave her a quick but earnest look.

"Even if she makes that effort difficult?"

"The difficult things are often the most worthwhile." He nodded just off the path in the direction of the lake. "Like this here." He stepped off the path and bent over, plucking a bright yellow flower from the ground. "Blooming so late in the season is hardly an easy thing, and yet this daisy here has managed it."

"Tis a sowthistle." She smiled through the light correction.

The look he gave her was utterly amused. "Daisy. Sowthistle. *Colaimbín*. Ya can't expect a man to know the difference."

"Perhaps that is yer problem with Miss Kilchrest. Perhaps she's a flower expert and is disheartened by yer ignorance."

Isaac eyed her hair a moment. Her hair? What was the man about? He pulled a few low leaves off the stem of the sowthistle he'd picked and tucked the flower into her bun. Alice ordered her cheeks not to heat, but they only paid her the tiniest heed.

A tender gesture it was. A man couldn't be entirely indifferent to a woman and have such a thought even cross his mind.

Isaac didn't linger over the moment as Alice would have loved him to do. He simply nodded and continued on down the road.

"Ye'll help me, won't ya?" he asked.

Alice shook off her scrambled thoughts. "Help ya with what?" She lightly fingered the flower in her hair. She'd never look on a sowthistle the same way again.

"Help me work out just what will turn Miss Kilchrest's head? I'm all at sea in this."

He wasn't the only one. How could the man act so fond of her in one moment—acting jealous of another man, picking wildflowers for her—and determined to claim Sophia Kilchrest's hand in the very next instance? It seemed men were thicker in the head than she realized.

"Ya wish me to help ya win her over?" Her heart dropped at the thought.

He nodded enthusiastically. "What better person to help me than you? Ye're a woman."

"Noticed that, did ya?" she muttered.

"So what do ya suggest?"

Thickheaded, foolish man!

18

She picked up her pace, tension pushing her ahead. "I've no advice for ya, Isaac. Ye'll have to sort this one out on yer own."

"No advice at all?" He spoke from a bit behind her, no longer keeping pace. "Because ya can't think of anything? Or because ya don't want to help me?"

Not want to help him? He made her sound selfish, petty. Could he not even guess at her reasons? She was jealous and heartbroken. But she was also worried. She didn't know Sophie Kilchrest personally, but there was something about her she didn't like. But she *did* like Isaac, more than seemed advisable, in fact.

She slowed her steps enough for him to reach her side again. "Can ya tell me what it is about Miss Kilchrest that has captured ya?"

Something like relief entered his expression. He thought her question a sign she meant to help rather than a moment of self-inflicted pain. To know why she'd been passed over wouldn't necessarily help ease her regrets. She only hoped knowing the whys would lead to some degree of acceptance.

"Well," Isaac said, his tone filled with pondering, "she's beautiful."

There was no arguing that. Alice knew she was no beauty, though she'd not thought herself wholly plain.

"And she is genteel and sophisticated."

All things Alice knew she was not, and yet that ought to have been an argument in her favor. "What in heaven's name is a genteel and sophisticated woman going to do living on a farm?"

He shook his head firmly, eyes turned directly ahead. "Ya make me sound as though I live in a tiny crofter's cottage on a half-acre of barren soil."

"I said nothing of the sort." She'd learned over the four months she'd known Isaac Dancy that he could be a bit touchy about his land. "I know ya have some of the best land in all of County Cavan. And I further know ya've built a fine home for yerself. But in the mind of a woman like Sophie Kilchrest, who has lived all her life in a town the size of Cavan in a fancy house with all the comforts she must have there, the life of a farmer's wife will be entirely foreign to her."

Isaac didn't appear to even ponder her very logical argument. "She has a kind heart and giving spirit. Such a woman wouldn't turn her nose up at the life I have to offer her. I've told her enough of my home and life. If she hated the idea, she'd not have continued acknowledging me week to week. And she certainly would have answered my question yesterday with a no."

Alice wondered if Miss Kilchrest was simply stringing Isaac along. She couldn't prove it, nor make any argument that would likely convince him. Neither could she force herself to help the man who'd captured her heart win over another woman.

He'd long since set his mind to courting Miss Kilchrest. Though his determination and dependability were among the reasons Alice liked him so very much, his stubbornness could, at times, be so very frustrating.

"I wish ya luck of it, Isaac. I've a feeling Miss Kilchrest will not be easy to win over."

He shoved his hands once more into the pockets of his coat. "Then how do I go about it? I gave her flowers yesterday, but so did everyone else. My offering didn't seem to stand out to her."

Sophia Kilchrest is a fool. Alice once again brushed her fingertips along the petals of the flower Isaac had only just given her.

The road made its lumbering turn around the lake, a wind blowing off the water that made her shiver. She'd need to start wearing her heavier coat as the season turned.

Winters were not generally bitter in Ireland, but they were decidedly cold and, more often than not, wet.

"Do women have a favorite flower?" Isaac asked. "Perhaps if I chose better, she'd appreciate it more."

Isaac is a fool too, it seems. "Giving a woman flowers isn't about *the flowers*. A woman who really loves a man will love any flower he gives her, not because of the flower, but because of him. She'd not even need offerings. Simply being with him would be enough." Isaac had picked flowers for her now and then during their walks to and from Cavan, but she hadn't *needed* such things. He treated her kindly. He shared his thoughts and his worries. They'd found an ease with each other and, she thought, a closeness unique to the two of them. "If a woman really loved a man, she'd light up simply because he was nearby and think of him when they're apart. She'd be just as happy talking with him as she would be spending an afternoon in silence. 'Twouldn't matter in the least, so long as they were together."

She'd all-but bared her soul, nearly confessed what she never intended to. But did Isaac realize as much?

If his distant expression were any indication, he'd not made the connection. "I'm competing with half the men in County Cavan. I have to think of some way to stand out."

Alice shook her head, both out of frustration and sadness. How could he not see what was so obvious? "If she loves ya enough to marry ya, Isaac, then none of those other men would matter in the least."

He picked up a pebble off the road and skipped it over the rippling water. "Ya don't understand."

"What don't I understand? I'm a woman, like ya said."

He pulled his hat down more snugly on his head. "A woman, aye, but not one who has men clamoring after her."

The man might just as well have slapped her for all the sharp, immediate pain of that observation. No, she hadn't hordes of men desperate to enjoy the pleasure of her company. She hadn't even one.

21

"Billy likes me, so I suppose that's something." She knew if Isaac pressed her about Billy, she wouldn't be able to lie to him, but admitting the only man who thought her special actually thought of her the way a child did a playmate would only humiliate her that much more. She rushed her words, not wanting to give him a chance to ask questions. "I'm meaning to stop here a bit, spend some time at the lake before winter comes."

When she stopped, so did Isaac. Thoughts flitted across his face. His mouth moved without sound. She set her gaze out over the water, grey with the clouds hovering above. She'd rather look at the scene in front of her than see rejection in the face of the man beside her.

"You can go on ahead." As soon as the words left her mouth, she knew that "going on ahead" was what she desperately needed him to do. Being with him while his heart was elsewhere, listening to him sing another woman's praises, was more than her battered heart could bear.

"I can't leave ya all by yerself."

Ya already have. "I know my way, I assure ya."

"But—"

"Ya have animals to see to. We've spoken of them all, I'll remind ya." Indeed, she knew the name of his horse, both his cows. She knew exactly how many chickens he had, how many pigs. She knew just what was planted in every acre of his farm, despite never having actually been there. Sophie Kilchrest likely didn't know any of those things. Alice would wager Sophie didn't care, either.

"Ye're certain ye'll be fine here alone?"

Alice nodded. She needed to be alone. *Needed* it.

Isaac hesitated. "But ye'd have to walk the rest of the way by yerself."

She managed to smile at him, though her heart wasn't in it. "I'll be fine."

"Then, I'll see ya on Saturday, I guess."

Alice knew in that moment she couldn't endure another walk like she'd just had. Listening to him speak at length about his plans with Miss Kilchrest, hearing him tick off a list of how ideal she was, would be torture. Even making her walk in to Cavan alone would be better.

"Actually, I need to make the walk early this next weekend. But I know ya can't leave sooner than ya always do, what with yer chores and all. So ye'd best just make the walk and not wait about for me."

"But we always walk together."

That he would miss her, at least a little, was only small comfort. Her company was not dear enough to him to push Miss Kilchrest from his mind and plans. 'Twas best to make a clean cut.

"If ye're hopes for Miss Kilchrest come to be, ye'll not need to make that walk at all." She tried to look encouraging.

He asked a few more times if she was absolutely certain she wished him to leave her there. He finally seemed to accept her insistence and continued down the road alone.

In the silence he left behind, Alice sighed. She ought to have realized at some point in the last four months that Isaac was determined to continue with his courtship of Miss Kilchrest, and that no amount of wishing and caring on her part would turn his thoughts to courting her instead.

Alice pulled the sowthistle from her hair, spinning it about between her fingers. He'd given his intended flowers, but the woman hadn't cared. This tiny wildflower to Alice was a treasure. But it was also something of an arrow to the heart. He'd given it to her offhand, with no real meaning.

She stepped up to the lake's edge and set the flower in the water. It floated slowly away from shore. Alice watched it, wishing her heartache could drift away as easily.

She'd leave early for Cavan on Saturday, and Sunday return early to the farm where she worked. She would make the walk on her own and maybe, in time, learn to push Isaac

Dancy from her heart.

And on that thought, she watched Isaac's flower tip in the water and sink from sight.

Chapter Four

Alice didn't come to their meeting spot that Saturday, and neither did she meet him on Farnham road for the walk back. To Isaac's surprise, she didn't make an appearance the next weekend, either.

He had so many questions for her. Why, when he offered Miss Kilchrest another bouquet, one he thought was nice, didn't she seem any more enthusiastic than she'd been with the first one? Had Miss Kilchrest's collection of admirers diminished, or was he imagining it? Why did Mr. and Mrs. Kilchrest seem more inviting of late?

More important than any of the other questions, he wanted to know where Alice had gone, why she didn't walk with him anymore.

Late November gave way to earliest December, and still he didn't see Alice. She had to be avoiding him. They walked the same road twice a week. She knew exactly what time of day he'd be on that road. To not cross paths even once in weeks couldn't be a coincidence.

The maddening woman was clearly mad at him, though over *what* he couldn't say. They'd never had an argument in the months they'd known each other. They didn't always agree on everything, but those little disagreements never ended in anything other than smiles and continued friendship.

He hated that she had disappeared so entirely.

Walking down the streets of Cavan on the way to the Kilchrest home, Isaac stopped in his tracks. In the window of a small shop amongst a display of trinkets and jewelry and such sat a delicate lady's pin watch. Flowers of inlaid gold stood in contrast to the deep blue of the perfectly circular case. It hung on a bow-shaped pin leafed in matching gold.

Alice would love this. And, he thought with a smile, she'd not need to ask him for the time every weekend. He didn't know if Alice could read a watch, but he'd happily teach her how, especially if it meant seeing her again.

He slipped inside the shop and inquired after the price. 'Twas steep, more than he'd ever spent on a gift before. He made a comfortable living but wasn't rich by any means. The watch would set him back quite a bit.

I'd not have enough left to give Miss Kilchrest a Christmas gift. Not having a holiday offering for the lady he'd spent months courting made no sense whatsoever. And yet he wavered. Alice would love the watch. He knew she would.

He left the shop and the watch behind, but the question of Christmas gifts remained in his mind all the way to the Kilchrests' home. Odd that he knew precisely the present that would bring a smile to Alice's face, but couldn't begin to guess what Miss Kilchrest would like. He'd given her flowers on a few occasions, but the offerings hadn't made her gleeful by any means. He simply hadn't stumbled upon what she loved.

A stern-faced servant opened the Kilchrests' door. Isaac was not terribly accustomed to calling at a home where the owners didn't answer their own door.

"I'm Isaac Dancy. The Kilchrests invited me to call." He felt he ought to explain why he'd come, when, if truth be told, his position in the world was far more equal to that of a housekeeper than a master of the house.

He was ushered inside. Isaac had never been to the Kilchrest's home. He glanced about the entryway, with its fine furnishings and paintings and fresh-cut flowers. A great many flowers, in fact. 'Twas no wonder Miss Kilchrest hadn't been impressed with his offerings. She had no need of more flowers.

As he followed the housekeeper into the formal parlor, Isaac began to suspect that Miss Kilchrest was not in need of much of anything. The room was elegant, fancy even. His own home, in comparison, would seem run-down and plain to the point of being ugly. But that was one of the reasons he'd first began pursuing Miss Kilchrest. He had worked very hard for many years to make a success of his farm, despite the lingering shadow of The Great Hunger still clinging to the land. He wanted that bit of prosperity to be reflected in his home. He wanted his neighbors to receive a warm welcome there.

Who could do that better than a lady who'd grown up in refinement, learning from the cradle how to be sociable and genteel? The idea was a good one. He'd certainly spent enough months thinking on it.

Yet standing in the pristine parlor, his hat in his hands, Isaac felt very out of place. Elegance, he was discovering, was not always welcoming. Surely the version of refinement Miss Kilchrest would bring to his more modest home would be a bit less overwhelming.

The object of his matrimonial ambitions stepped inside a moment later. She wore the same smile she always did, content and calm.

"Welcome, Isaac." She motioned him to a white settee.

He brushed at his trousers, not entirely certain they didn't yet bear dust from the road. White was not the most practical color for furnishings.

Mr. Kilchrest came inside and crossed to where he still stood.

"I hear you took in a good profit on your crop this year."

Isaac nodded. Prices had been good.

"Good, good." Mr. Kilchrest took up a seat nearby and opened a newspaper. That was to be the end of their conversation, it seemed.

Isaac didn't know if such behavior was normal for Mr. Kilchrest, or if he simply didn't have anything to say to him. He knew many of Miss Kilchrest's suitors had been invited to call on her family over the months, but he'd never been among their number. Where were the others? He didn't think the invitations were generally kept to one man at a time.

"Is there to be no one else?" he asked.

Miss Kilchrest's smile tightened a bit. "Not this time."

None of the others could come? Or none of the others would *come?* He didn't know where the uncharitable thought came from. He dismissed it immediately.

Isaac sat on the edge of the settee, still clutching his hat. A person was afraid to breathe in a room like that one. Everything looked breakable and clean as new. If any of the other men felt half as uncomfortable as he did in that moment, 'twas little wonder they weren't coming around any longer.

He attempted to match Miss Kilchrest's small talk but never had been one for conversations that felt pointless. She spoke of fashions and the weather and stories she'd heard about people Isaac didn't know. He tried to discuss improvements to his land or difficulties he had about his home, but she only put on that everyday smile of hers and nodded without comment.

They'd not had enough opportunities to become acquainted. Isaac didn't think he'd do a very good job of it in her house. He simply couldn't feel at ease there.

Though he'd only been in the Kilchrests' home a quarter of an hour, Isaac was ready to be on his way. But he hadn't spent much time with Miss Kilchrest. He'd meant to further their connection, to make his case, to move closer to his goal of winning her regard.

"I'd be honored if I could walk ya home from church tomorrow," he said. An outdoor conversation would be far more enjoyable.

"Of course." *"Of course you can?"* Or, *"Of course you would be honored to walk with me"?*

He stood and inched his way toward the door. "I'll wait for ya outside the church, then."

She only smiled. He'd simply have to wait and see what happened the next morning.

He was well on his way in a moment's time. The finer houses gave way to smaller, plainer ones. For the first time all evening, Isaac felt like he could breathe.

His feet carried him, not to his friend's house where he'd be spending the night, but down the street where Alice's grandparent's lived. He wouldn't actually call on her. Alice had made quite plain that she didn't wish to see him. But he'd lost his footing at the Kilchrest home. He felt turned around and needed something familiar.

The sounds of laughter and music met him as he walked. He followed the noise to the side garden of a house two or three doors removed from where Alice spent her weekends. He wandered over to the low stone wall.

Quite a few people had gathered about, talking and playing music. There was chatting and dancing. Isaac smiled to see it. He'd attended many such gatherings as a child growing up in the countryside. His own neighbors gathered on occasion for traditional music and friendly chatter.

Just as he made to find the gate so he might ask to join them, his eyes fell on an achingly familiar face. Alice, her mouth turned up in a grin as broad as any he'd seen her wear, was dancing about the grassy area with the same man Isaac had seen her with several weeks earlier. Billy, she'd said his name was, and a "dear friend."

A dear friend.

A dear friend she was laughing with and dancing with. A dear friend she was smiling at. Isaac had enjoyed neither her laughter nor her smile in weeks. And he'd not ever danced with her.

Isaac spun about on the instant. The party held little appeal to him any longer. He'd wondered at Alice's absence, worried he'd offended her. All that time she'd simply found another whose company she preferred to his.

His steps echoed hard and fast around him as he trudged back to his friend's home. In all the months he'd watched Miss Kilchrest pay particular attention to any number of her suitors and not to him, he hadn't felt the deep, crushing disappointment he did in that moment.

Chapter Five

*B*illy Kettle did best when given tasks that were simple. Equally important to his success was a taskmaster who treated him with patience and understanding. Thus, when Alice learned he'd been retained to help serve at the Kilchrests' annual Christmastime party, she could not help a touch of anxiety. Mrs. Kilchrest didn't know Billy, didn't understand his struggles. Rumor had it the woman was a demanding employer.

Alice fretted over the situation throughout the week leading up to the party on Christmas Eve. She thought about it as she saw to her chores, as she lay on her cot in the tiny maid's room in the farmhouse where she worked. Isaac would have listened to her worries, would have sorted them out with her. But, she reminded herself, they weren't entirely talking to each other. Not that they'd sworn off each other's company. She simply couldn't face hearing him speak odes to Miss Kilchrest. So Alice avoided him. And he hadn't come by her grandparents' place, though he knew where they lived.

She'd simply have to find her own solution to the problem. By the time she arrived in Cavan late in the morning on Christmas Eve, she had settled on a course of action. She'd never warrant an invitation, and therefore couldn't keep a protective eye out for Billy that way. But she'd wager the Kilchrests could use an extra set of hands.

She spoke quickly with her cousin upon arriving in town then slipped over to the Kilchrests' home to offer her expertise. She knew better than to knock at the front door. A harried-looking housekeeper opened the back door, impatience written in every line of her face.

"I've no time for bothers just now," the woman warned.

"I'm not here to bother ya. I know ye've a party to put on tonight, and I came to see if ye're looking to hire more help for the day."

One of her eyebrows shot up even as her mouth pulled tighter. "Ya know how to work?"

Alice nodded. "I work at a large farm up the road toward Killeshandra during the week. I can cook, wash dishes, serve and clear tables—anything ye're in need of."

The housekeeper's eyes narrowed. "I'll pay ya a shilling for the day."

Alice managed not to roll her eyes. *An entire shilling?* The housekeeper gave new weight to the term "pinch purse." Still, Alice was taking the position so she could look after Billy, not to make her fortune.

"I'll take the work."

Without ceremony, Alice was ushered through the busy kitchen, up a flight of servants' stairs, and deposited in the formal drawing room.

"All the chairs and tables being brought in need polishing," the housekeeper said. "I trust I don't have to explain how that's done."

Alice shook her head. She didn't need the woman to hold her hand whilst she saw to basic household chores. In a moment's time she'd been provided with rags and polish and left to her work.

She'd not finished polishing a single chair before Billy came inside lugging a chair in each arm. He grinned when their eyes met.

"Are ya working here, Alice?" he whispered.

She nodded.

"I get to carry heavy things about tonight. Just like a regular footman, I'll be."

"Won't ya be a fancy servant, then?" Alice smiled at his eagerness. Just like a little boy anticipating a game of imagining things.

Billy set down his burden. "Da says I'm to wear m' fine Sunday clothes so I'll look respectable."

"Ye'll look fine, Billy. Right fine." She squeezed his arm.

His pout grew by the moment. "Fine clothes aren't very comfortable."

"No, they're not. *Necessary*, but not comfortable."

He nodded slowly and with great emphasis.

"You are not being paid to stand about talking."

Alice nearly jumped at the sudden voice, too refined to be any of the staff. She glanced toward the doorway. Mrs. Kilchrest stood there, looking at them with obvious disapproval.

"Yes'm." Alice gave a quick curtsey. To Billy's look of confusion, she added under her breath, "Best get back to work, Billy, and keep yer mind on yer chores."

Mrs. Kilchrest watched every step Billy took as he made his way from the room. Alice pretended not to notice, but set to her polishing again. Mrs. Kilchrest made a slow circle of the room, brushing a finger over chairs and tables, inspecting them for dust. Alice didn't voice her protest despite not having had a chance to polish anything in the room yet but the one chair.

No scolding was made. Either Mrs. Kilchrest realized things hadn't been attended to yet, or she was too distracted by the arrival of her daughter.

"Must we do this every year, Mother? It is such a great deal of bother." Miss Kilchrest leaned unladylike against the window frame, looking out over the street below with such an expression of dissatisfaction as one might see on a petulant child.

"It is expected of us, Sophia. And you will behave."

Miss Kilchrest gave a dainty shrug of her shoulder, pulling back on the white lace curtain for the briefest of moments, before letting it fall back into place.

"Do not give me that dismissive face, young lady. This is the most sought-after invitation of the season, and I will not have you ruin it."

Miss Kilchrest crossed to a gilded mirror, turning her head about as she spoke. "We could serve them cold tea and stale cakes, and the entire county would still come in droves."

Mrs. Kilchrest tipped her chin upward, eying her daughter with reproof. Alice watched the exchange out of the corner of her eye, making a convincing display of polishing another chair.

"One too many servings of your sharp tongue have driven away all your most promising suitors." Mrs. Kilchrest speared her daughter with a scolding look. "Where have the wealthy suitors gone? What of those with influence and standing? They've seen your temper one too many times and have flown like birds before the winter. And what have you left now? Farmers and tradesmen."

Alice bristled at the distasteful tone with which Mrs. Kilchrest spoke of those "farmers." Isaac was among their number, after all. He didn't deserve to be spoken of so dismissively.

Miss Kilchrest smiled vaguely at her mother as she flitted toward the door. "They'll be back, Mother. They always come back."

Mrs. Kilchrest watched her daughter leave. 'Twas not an adoring look she wore.

And this is the family Isaac hopes to be part of? Alice shook her head. *He could do vastly better for himself.*

"Those chairs will not polish themselves." Mrs. Kilchrest's words snapped like a flag in a gale.

Alice rubbed harder at the legs of the chair and muttered a quick, "Yes'm."

She spent the afternoon bringing a collection of mismatched chairs to polished perfection, her thoughts full of Isaac, drat the man. His empty-headed, single-minded pursuit of Sophia Kilchrest frustrated her to no end. That he'd not been by to see her fully broke her heart. She ought to be mad at him, ought to be leaving him to his stubbornness. But she could not, *could not,* leave him to certain misery in such an unhappy household.

How, then, could she help him see what a mistake he was making?

Isaac slipped a finger under his collar, stretching his neck to fit better in his very best shirt. Perhaps it wasn't the sermons that made sitting in church so deucedly uncomfortable. The staid and formal party he stepped into at the Kilchrests' was worlds different from the cheerful, laughing gathering he'd spied on the weekend before.

Of course, at this gathering he'd not have to watch Alice smiling at another man. That sight had haunted him all week. Enough, in fact, that he'd gone by her grandparents' house that afternoon, fully intending to ask her . . . something. He didn't even fully know what he would have said to her. In the end, it hadn't mattered. Alice wasn't there, and wouldn't be back all day.

SARAH M. EDEN

If he hadn't been expected at the Kilchrests' Christmas celebration, he'd have simply sat himself down at the gate of Alice's family's home and waited. Questions about her and Billy had plagued him all week. He'd struggled to concentrate on his chores. He'd nearly forgotten to put his finest suit and shirt in his bundle, despite bringing it along every weekend for church. He'd walked the entire road from Killeshandra without noticing whether winter had stripped the trees bare, nor the color of the water. He'd thought only of Alice.

"Isaac." Miss Kilchrest greeted him when he reached her side. In that moment, the smile she always wore rubbed him wrong. 'Twas nothing like the brilliant smile Alice had given her *dear friend*. Miss Kilchrest's smiles had never been like Alice's.

"Good evening." His eagerness to be going rushed the words from him. "Thank ya for the invitation." *Now let me slip out.*

"Of course."

Her tone never changed, now that he thought on it. She always sounded as if she only half-listened to what he said, and as if his compliments were her due. Either he'd never noticed that about her before, or he was simply in a sour mood and attributing motives to her that she didn't deserve. Either way, 'twould be best for everyone if he simply went about his business for the night.

"Isaac, have you met Mr. Byrne?" Miss Kilchrest indicated a man obviously very near Isaac's age. The similarities ended there, though. Mr. Byrne's clothes were not made of homespun, nor did his shoes show signs of heavy use.

There were not many, in fact, in attendance who looked quite as humble as Isaac did. And not one of those from his walk of life, he further noted, was introduced as Mister *Anything*. 'Twas first names for the farmers and the tradesmen and the less affluent. Did they feel as out of place as he did?

He searched his mind for a quick and tidy means of excusing himself for the evening. As he'd been particularly invited, he wasn't certain such a thing could be accomplished without giving offense.

"What business are you in, Isaac?" Mr. Byrne asked, sounding at least a little genuine in his curiosity.

"I've a farm up near Killeshandra." Isaac pulled himself up. He was proud of all he'd accomplished. "I've two-hundred acres of decent soil, good crops, a few animals to my name."

Mr. Byrne nodded, seemingly impressed. Isaac would not have guessed that. "And how many tenants do you have on that two-hundred acres?" He looked over at Miss Kilchrest. "A man can make a very good living if he divides his land up amongst enough families." He held his lapels, chest thrust out. "Rents can make a man wealthy."

"I've no tenants," Isaac said firmly, eying the man's signs of wealth with growing dislike. "I'll not be the reason dozens of poor souls are forced onto plots of land too small to support them. I'll be responsible for their deaths if we've another potato blight."

Mr. Byrne looked him up and down dismissively. "Is that old tired tune still being played?"

Isaac set his shoulders. "Not by the dead, it's not. But those of us lucky enough to have lived don't intend to forget it soon. Nor will we forget those who grew wealthy on the backs of the dying."

To her credit, Miss Kilchrest looked a little uncomfortable, though whether she found Mr. Byrne's insensitivity or Isaac's proud determination more upsetting, he didn't know.

"Now, if ye'll—"

His words stopped on the instant. Across the room, Alice stood at the sideboard, setting out plates of teacakes, wearing the frill-edged aprons all the other maids wore.

She doesn't work here.

Then again, he felt certain there were a great many more servants there that night than on his previous visit. The Kilchrests had taken on temporary help.

Had Alice taken the position out of necessity? What could have happened to put her in such financial hardship?

Without a parting word to his hostess or her infuriating friend, Isaac took a step in Alice's direction. He got no further than that. A footman, tall and broad, stepped directly in front of him, holding a salver of champagne glasses. Isaac had never been one for anything but a strong mug of ale from the local pub, or perhaps a pint of home brew. Yet he found his eyes drifting back to the bubbling drink. The glasses were shaking enough to be worrisome.

He looked up at the footman and recognized him right off. 'Twas Alice's Billy. Was he trying to keep Isaac away from her? He'd have a fight on his hands if that was the case.

Isaac stood as tall as he could stretch, still not coming close to the man's height, and set his shoulders. But a closer look stopped any challenging words he might have tossed at Billy.

The man stood, watching his tray of glasses, biting at his lip, brow deeply creased. His gaze flicked briefly at Isaac. "I can't make 'em stop shaking 'round," he whispered.

Something was odd in the way he spoke, even the way he stood and held himself. Isaac couldn't put his finger on just what was unusual, but the combination deflated his temper on the instant.

The glasses trembled all the more. Billy looked more than nervous as he eyed his tray of drinks; he seemed actually fearful.

"Do ya need to set those down?" Isaac asked quietly but urgently.

Even Billy's head shake was a touch clumsy, almost like a child who still hadn't mastered the moving of his own body. "The housekeeper said I was to carry it 'til all the drinks was gone. They're not gone."

They'll be gone quick enough if ya drop *them.* Isaac looked to Miss Kilchrest. Surely she'd see the difficulty and give Billy permission to set down his load. She watched Billy and his tray with misgivings but made no move to intervene.

Alice seemed to have noticed the difficulty. She abandoned her teacakes and crossed toward them.

Isaac whispered quickly to Billy. "Set the glasses down. Better that then letting them slip."

Billy's hands only grew shakier. His face turned equal parts pale and red. "She's wearing her mean eyes."

Isaac, himself, took a step back at the hardness in Miss Kilchrest's expression.

"You bumbling fool," she hissed at Billy. "Anything you break will come out of your wages."

'Twas the first time Isaac had ever heard Miss Kilchrest speak sharply to anyone. Though he'd had more than a few uncharitable thoughts where Billy Kettle was concerned, he found he didn't at all like Miss Kilchrest's reprimand.

Billy's face crumbled. "I don't have money. I can't pay for it."

"Ya won't have to." Alice had arrived in time to carefully take the tray from Billy's hands. She set it on an obliging table without the tray shaking in the slightest.

Miss Kilchrest set her hands on her hips and waited not a single moment after Alice turned back before correcting her. "He'll not be paid for work someone else is doing for him."

Alice didn't flinch, didn't hesitate. "He was not hired to serve yer guests drinks. Yer housekeeper was told in detail of his limitations. If ya have objections to how he performed this duty that was not his own, ye'd best take it up with that bothersome woman."

Miss Kilchrest's face pulled tight.

"How dare you speak to me that way?" She spoke through clenched jaw. "I do not pay servants to be insolent."

Alice managed to look down her nose at Miss Kilchrest, despite being shorter. "And the pitiful sum I'm being paid to be here tonight is not worth yer shrew's tongue. Good night to ya, Miss Kilchrest. Happy Christmas and all that."

Isaac knew a moment of pride hearing her speak with such strength of purpose. Alice was no wilting flower to shrivel at the slightest difficulty. A country lass, she was.

"Come, then, Billy. We'll take up the matter of yer wages with the magistrate if we must."

Billy's tall frame bent under what looked like embarrassment and disappointment. Alice took off her frilly apron and pressed it into Miss Kilchrest's hands before walking away with Billy, her hand resting on his back.

Isaac glanced back at Miss Kilchrest. Her gaze settled uncomfortably on Mr. Byrne. "I told mother not to hire that man. He's *simple*, you know. That kind always bumbles everything."

Isaac made a quick bow, excusing himself without a great deal of grace. He couldn't abide Miss Kilchrest's company a moment longer.

He's simple. *That kind always bumbles everything. That kind.* The words repeated in his thoughts as he walked away from the Kilchrests' party. Many of his neighbors were simple people, though not in the same way. They were the very best Ireland had to offer, the salt of the earth. Would Miss Kilchrest hiss at and insult them for their simplicity? Would she turn his home into a place where none of his neighbors or family would feel welcome?

Miss Kilchrest had added to Billy's pain. Alice had come immediately to his rescue.

Miss Kilchrest hadn't cared in the least about the flowers he'd given her a few weeks back. Alice had smiled sweetly at the simple wild bloom he'd picked for her at the lake.

He'd spent four months trying to be the person Miss Kilchrest would notice and care for. In those same four months, he'd never needed to be anything but himself with Alice.

His walk through Cavan Town drove home two indisputable truths.

Pursuing Miss Kilchrest had been a mistake from the beginning.

And he'd been in love with Alice Wheatley for months, but had been too much of a fool to realize it.

Chapter Six

lice hoped Miss Kilchrest's behavior had been enough to warn off Isaac. She'd been too upset, herself, to stay and talk sense into the man. That he'd come immediately to Billy's defense despite not understanding his circumstances only further endeared Isaac to her. He was a good man, no matter how misguided his matrimonial ambitions.

She packed her small satchel and pulled on her heavy woolen coat. 'Twas a cold Christmas morning, perfect for staying tucked in bed, curled up under the blankets. But 'twas also a Sunday, and Alice had no choice but to step out into the weather and make her trek back to the farm where she worked.

The hour was early, an approach she'd adopted weeks earlier after her falling-out with Isaac. Avoiding him was easier, kinder, on her too-tender heart. That morning there'd be no Billy to see her off. He'd been nearly in tears by the time she'd delivered him home. His da had thought it best to not wake him that morning, and not to find him work at the Kilchrests' again.

Alice slipped her satchel over her shoulder. She wound a thick scarf about her neck and tied her battered bonnet tight on her head. She couldn't hide in the warmth of her grandparents' house forever.

The air hung heavy and cold as she stepped out on to the streets of Cavan. A cold and lonely Christmas Day, indeed. If only men weren't so infernally blind and stubborn, she might have been spending her Christmas morning with Isaac at her side rather than missing him as she was.

Perhaps men weren't the only ones who clung to foolish notions.

'Twas something of a shame to mar the fresh, untouched layer of snow with her trudging footsteps. So few things in life worked out neat and tidy.

She passed the church where Isaac would be attending services.

And if I must be passed over for something, I suppose church on a Christmas morning isn't so bad a thing.

Alice turned her face into the light wind and continued on her way. The miles back toward Killeshandra would not be pleasant; that was quite sure and certain. Some other poor traveler was but a few streets ahead of her, braving the same elements.

She held her coat closer to her with her gloved hands. Perhaps if she thought hard on the blankets and the warm fire in the kitchen hearth in the farmhouse that waited at the end of that long road, she'd not feel the chill quite so deep and acute. If nothing else, the anticipation quickened her steps.

She quickly came even with her fellow traveler. He, apparently, hadn't sufficient imagination to push him onward.

Alice set her mind to offering him an encouraging smile and a Christmas greeting as she passed. A person ought to

43

receive at least that when alone on a morning such as that one. No sooner had she reached the stranger's side than he spoke.

"Have ya a friend to walk around Lough Oughter with ya?"

Her gaze immediately jumped to his face. "Isaac?"

He didn't look at her but kept his eyes trained ahead. "Might I make the journey back with ya?"

She didn't answer right off, but continued walking in confused silence. She'd not at all expected to see him on the road.

"Why is it ye're not in church this morning? I've never known ya to miss services. And on Christmas Day of all days." 'Twas more shocking the longer she thought on it.

He finally looked at her, but his expression was one of apprehension. "I didn't know when ye'd be passing by, and I didn't dare risk missing ya. I've been out here some time already."

"Out here? In this weather?" *Heavens, the man must have been near frozen.*

Alice opened her satchel as they continued walking, digging through her meager belongings until she found the woolen scarf her cousin had knitted her. She'd kept it tucked away should she need more bundling during the walk home. But one look at Isaac's red nose and bare neck made up her mind on that score.

He was still clearly unsure of himself. Did he think she disliked him? That she didn't want him about? He'd been thick-headed and stubborn, but love doesn't fly away for such reasons as that.

"Come, then," she instructed, stopping and motioning him closer.

She began wrapping the scarf about his neck.

"I can't take yer scarf, Alice. Suppose ya need it yer own self?"

She shook her head. "I've a warm one on already. Now ya just take this, and don't make a great fuss over it."

He held quite still as she finished wrapping and tying. Alice's heart pounded clear into her fingertips. Except for the occasional moment when he helped her over a muddy bit of road or bumped against her on accident, they'd never really touched. Yet wrapping her scarf about his neck, her hands brushed against him. She felt the tiny moment of contact clear to her very soul. She gazed up to find his eyes locked with her own.

They stood there at the very edge of Cavan Town directly on the road leading away, simply looking at one another. Each breath they took fogged the air between them.

"I've been a fool, Alice," Isaac whispered.

"Have ya now?" Her voice emerged even quieter than his.

His hand lightly touched her cheek, just inside the brim of her bonnet. Such a look of sad regret weighed down his handsome face. "I'm too stubborn by half, ya know. And when my mind's set to something I don't always heed the world about me. I miss a great many important things that way."

For the first time in some weeks, Alice's heart smiled along with her lips. "Ya *are* terrible stubborn, Isaac Dancy."

His eyes traced her smiling face, and some of the heaviness left his expression. His hand slid from her face to her shoulder, down to her arm and took hold of her hand. "I hope, Alice, ye're every bit as forgiving as I am dimwitted."

"I'm a woman." She shrugged. "We've had to be forgiving since time began."

"Speaking of which . . ." He set something in her free hand.

What in heaven's name? She examined the little cloth-wrapped bundle. "What is it?"

"Tis a present, it is. A Christmas gift."

"For me?" She'd not been expecting that.

"It's certainly not for Miss Kilchrest."

Alice shot him a look of warning at that. If the man truly wanted to get back in her good graces, he'd do well to leave a certain woman's name out of things.

Isaac looked immediately contrite, but with a hint of amusement in his eyes. Here was the banter she'd missed between them. Here was his silent, lighthearted laughter. She'd needed it these past weeks.

She untied the fabric and unwound the gift. After unlooping the fabric for a moment, she reached the center. 'Twas the most beautiful bit of jewelry she'd ever seen. Clearly it was a pin, but with a peg on the side. Alice pushed the peg in, and the round, blue and gold case opened.

"A watch." She'd always wanted a timepiece of her own, but never had she imagined one so beautiful.

"Ya need one, ya know," Isaac said. "Always pestering me to know the hour." He clicked his tongue and shook his head. "A man can only take so much aggravation."

"I don't know how to read it," she warned him.

His smile was kind and tender. "We've a long walk ahead of us. I'd be happy to show ya how."

Alice ran her finger over the delicate flowers on the deep blue watch case, inlaid with gold.

Beautiful.

"This must have come very dear." She knew he was not a wealthy man. He was not destitute, but he hardly had endless coffers at his disposal.

"It matches yer eyes, Alice. Matches quite perfectly. I couldn't pass it by."

Matches yer eyes. That he even knew the color of her eyes came as both a surprise and a comfort. Perhaps she'd not been so overlooked all those months. "Ya had to have purchased this before the party last night." Before Miss Kilchrest made her nature quite clear.

Isaac nodded. "I decided on a lot of things before last night, though the evening firmed up my resolve on most of them."

How she hoped one of those decisions was to toss aside Miss Kilchrest in favor of her.

She pinned the watch to the front of her coat, careful to clasp it securely. "Will it do, do ya think?"

"Lovely." But he wasn't looking at the watch. "I don't know how I didn't see it before."

"Blinded by ambition, ya were."

He nodded solemnly. "And by my own stupidity."

"Aye. That, as well." She set a hand on his chest for balance as she stretched on her toes and placed a single, brief kiss on his cheek. "I thank ya for the fine Christmas present. I'll cherish it always."

"Will ya let me cherish *you*, Alice?" One of his arms wrapped around her, keeping her nearby. "Will ya at least let me prove to ya that I can, that I *will*? All these months, I've grown to care more for ya than any person I know. I tell ya my thoughts and worries. I trust ya with my concerns. I miss ya when ye're away and worry over ya when ye're not close by. All these months, and I never realized—"

"Ya talk too much, Isaac Dancy." She took hold of the scarf about his neck and pulled him within an inch of herself. "It's not words I'm needing just now."

His smile tipped a bit roguishly. "I'm most happy to oblige."

And he was. And did. His lips met hers in a caress so gentle at first, she hardly knew he'd begun kissing her. But his efforts quickly grew more urgent. Alice slid her arms around his neck and held fast to him.

Here was the affection she'd longed for from him, the reassurance that he cared for her just as she cared for him. 'Twas home.

Flakes of snow drifted softly and slowly down around them as they sealed quite a few unspoken promises with a fine bit of kissing on a peaceful Christmas morning on the road to Cavan Town.

ABOUT SARAH M. EDEN

©Annalisa Rosenvall

Sarah M. Eden read her first Jane Austen novel in elementary school and has been addicted to historical romance ever since. An avid researcher, she loves delving deep into the details of history. She was a Whitney Award Finalist for her novels *Seeking Persephone* (2008) and *Courting Miss Lancaster* (2010).

Visit her at www.sarahmeden.com

It Happened Twelfth Night

by Heidi Ashworth

Other Works by Heidi Ashworth

Miss Delacourt Has Her Day

Miss Delacourt Speaks Her Mind

Lady Crenshaw's Christmas

Lord Haversham Takes Command

Prologue

England, 1812

Luisa waited behind the tree with bated breath. Percy, a black handkerchief about his eyes and arms outstretched, was close enough to touch. Did she, however, wish to be found? To be discovered by the grazing of his fingers against her gown amidst shrieks of his friend's laughter would be delicious. Yet to win the day and carry forth the trophy (this year it was a basket of delightfully pink blooms) had been one of her heart's desires for almost every one of her eighteen years.

Percy's father and mother, Sir Walter and Lady Brooksby, loved a good celebration and eagerly availed themselves of every opportunity to welcome throngs of people to the abbey. This June day was the 74th birth anniversary of old King George and, though he was not likely to have been the least aware of it, it was a long standing tradition to invite the entire village to a celebration at the abbey on His Majesty's behalf. The itinerary was the same every year: lawn games were followed by the unveiling of tables groaning with delectable foodstuffs both sweet and savory, each dish interspersed with pitcher after pitcher of tart lemonade. The pure white batiste cloths adorning the tables, so long they swept the green blades of grass, were so beautiful they made Luisa's heart ache.

In point of fact, in her eyes, everything Sir Walter and his Lady set out to create was executed to perfection, including their eldest son, Percy. Those golden tresses! Those smoky eyes! That chiseled chin! Luisa was persuaded there was never another like him in all of England.

But now it seemed she was to be caught after all. The idea was every bit as intoxicating as she had hoped, especially since he seemed to know at once whose waist was suddenly between his warm palms as he spun her around to face him. Pulling the cloth over his head, she looked up at him, a question in her eyes. His slow answering grin caused a fluttering in her stomach, a sensation with which she had been most familiar of late. She couldn't be certain when Percy-her-friend had become Percy-her-beau, but there was no mistaking the gleam in his eye as he tugged her by the hand and led her to the relative privacy of the summerhouse.

Leaning against a shadowed wall of the round stone structure, Luisa tried to catch her breath, but the way Percy was looking into her eyes was, for her lungs, a bit of a dilemma. For Luisa herself, it was nothing of consequence; who needed whole draughts of air when one could be gazed at in such a searching way? As for herself, all she was able to find, to see, to dwell on, was the perfect pink of his lips as they descended upon her own. Her eyes fluttered shut, and all sound was reduced to a rushing in her ears; all thought tuned to the rhythm of his heart hammering in unison with hers.

"I love you, Luisa Darlington, and when I return from this unforgivably interminable trip abroad, I shall look for you, right here, directly upon my return."

Luisa opened her eyes to find his gaze locked on hers. Unaccountably, she began to giggle. "Won't the summerhouse be shut up for the winter? Shan't I wait for you in the abbey instead?"

"No, right here! While we are parted, I shall think of you every minute of every day just as you are, your hair divinely tousled and your lips swollen with desire. *Vous avez l'air parfait comme vous êtes.*"

"You know I don't comprehend a word of French," Luisa murmured, secretly hoping he would be just as content to discover her by the blazing fire in the library on that long-to-come December day.

He must have seen doubt cloud her eye, for he took her by the shoulders, and with a little shake, said in a voice full of urgency, "Swear it! Luisa, you must!"

"Yes! Of course! Did I not say so?" she asked with a buoyant smile calculated to dispel all misgiving. A barely audible moan of longing escaped his lips before he once more pressed them to hers with great affect.

Taking her again by the hand, he said, "It is settled, then. You shall be here when I return, and only then will I feel truly happy."

How Percy would convince his parents that she, daughter of the keeper at the abbey gate, was a suitable bride for their son was a question that nibbled at the edge of her mind, but she put it aside. His father was a baronet, not an earl or marquis. "It is an accord," she replied with a squeeze of his hand and with a gentle tug, Luisa led him back to the gaiety of the party, her heart swollen with love and her mind full of the knowledge that true happiness had already found her.

Chapter One

Louisa knew herself to be lost. Yet, how could she be? Though not an inhabitant, she was nearly as familiar with this house as her own. She and Percy had spent countless hours racing through the halls, playing Hunt the Slipper in the conservatory (Lady Brooksby did not regard playing such games in the abbey with much favor) and eating jam tarts straight from Cook's oven. Long, rambling walks had commenced from the gothic front doors and concluded by stumbling with fatigue through the full-length windows of Sir Walters's library. Though Percy's mother and father didn't exactly wish for Luisa to be forever underfoot, the strength of her friendship with their son led them to treat her as a bit of a fixture, something to be accepted and abided, if not fully appreciated. Their attitude towards her was of no consequence to Luisa; Percy had loved her, and that was enough.

However, she now felt more than a bit out of place. Not only did she not recognize the passageway upon which she had stumbled, but Percy was nowhere to be found. The decline in her social standing in the past six months since Percy had gone abroad had made her quite melancholy, and his neglect to call upon her since his return had driven her nearly to madness. This in spite of the bitterly cold afternoon, she had trudged from Darlington Cottage, home of her ancestors since time immemorial, through the abbey parkland to the summerhouse where she waited until her feet froze, and she was finally forced to seek asylum in the kitchen, only to learn that Percy had gone to a party. She had left him a note, but there had been no reply.

Christmas came and went without so much as a quaff of wassail shared between them. Therefore, it was with extraordinary joy and anticipation that she accepted the invitation to attend the annual Twelfth Night party at the abbey.

Now that she was here, returned to the scene of so many happy memories, not a soul would speak to her. As for Percy, he had barely acknowledged her presence. Could the news of her best friend's scandalous flight to Gretna with her dancing master have tarnished even Percy's regard for her? It was monstrously unfair that local society, that of sleepy little Wymondham, had painted Luisa with the same brush as the silly Sally Constable, but the inhabitants of villages had little to do but determine who should sit below the salt and who should go in to dinner on the arm of Wymondham's most eligible bachelor. It would seem that Percy's ears were tuned to the wagging of catty tongues, turning his dog-like affection to whichever cat was closest.

At dinner she had done her best to behave exactly as if she were part of any number of conversations occurring around her at table, but once the dessert course had been consumed and the ladies were sent to the parlor to await the gentlemen, she felt it no use and gave up all pretense at social inclusion. Choosing the darkest corner in which to pine, she pinned her hopes on having a chance to speak to Percy privately, just the two of them, as it always used to be. Presently the cold shoulders and disapproving glares of the other ladies proved too much, so she fled out the door, her eyes obscured with tears, and ran until she could no longer discern evidence of merriment from any quarter.

Realizing she must have unknowingly passed through the baize door to the servant's quarters, an action nearly as beyond the pale as eloping with one's dancing master, she began to panic. It was in this morbid state that, through a haze of tears, she ascertained the approach of a dark, masculine shape from the far end of the hall. Believing it to be the butler, her friend of long standing, or one of the footman to whom she had handed off her cloak and gloves any number of times over the years, she ran forward with a cry of relief.

As the shadow approached, however, it loomed larger and larger in the dim light and took on an odd and eerie structure. What had seemed the indistinct form of a man now appeared to be a bear with, unaccountably, a large bird riding his head. She shrank against the wall, her tears vanishing as swiftly as they had come, and prayed she would not be seen by whatever this apparition might be.

Despite closing her eyes tightly and sending aloft a prayer on wings of hope, her wish, like so many others of late, went unconsidered. When she once more opened her eyes, she barely repressed a shriek of terror as the apparition slowed and the great bird, an enormous black crow with dark and shining eyes, turned to gaze down at her.

She could not have been more astonished when a melodious voice of a pleasing timbre issued forth from the shadows gathered beneath the crow's perch, but her heart hammered so that she was powerless to decipher a single word. Whether he spoke English, German or Italian, she could not have said, but she recognized the courtesy in his voice, and owned that it felt pleasant to be spoken to, whatever the language.

"Pray forgive me, sir," she said at the top of a deep sigh, "I do not perfectly understand, but I would be grateful for some assistance. Which is the way back to the party?"

In answer, he offered her his arm, but she was loath to add one iota of scandal to her already heavily blotted copybook. To descend on the elite of Wymondham under the protection of whatever kind of creature this must be would only add fuel to an already raging fire.

"No thank you, sir. I am most aware of your kindness, but I wish to abide a few moments more to catch my breath."

The birdman inclined his head and pointed straight across, towards a door she could now see was indeed of baize green and designed to delineate the barrier between the portion of the house meant for the occupants and that of the servants. She murmured her gratitude, and, with mingled trepidation and fascination, was unable to tear her gaze from him as he passed her by in the narrow corridor, so close that his voluminous cape brushed the tips of her petal-pink dancing slippers. Just before he swept through the door, he looked back, and the light from the wall sconce picked up what could only be his eyes. They were like two emeralds swimming in a box of deepest black velvet. The overall affect only added to the otherworldliness of the man. It was with great difficulty that Luisa suppressed a cry of alarm.

The last thing Luisa wanted to do was to follow the bear-like man through the door. However, neither did she wish to remain in the forbidden passage. With fear and trembling in her heart, Luisa inched open the door to survey her options. The strange man was nowhere to be seen. Coaxing the door to stand ever so slightly more ajar, she risked a long look down the opposite hall that led to the grand salon, where bursts of laughter and general merriment could be heard. She had to time her emergence just right so none who might pass would know of her *faux pas*. Idly she wondered who the man could have been that he felt so comfortable in both parts of the house. Only a servant would wander about with such confidence, but he was dressed like no servant she had ever seen.

Taking a deep breath, she was just about to push the door wide enough to allow her passage but was stopped short by the sounds of a muffled conversation bearing down on her.

With a snap, she allowed the door to swing to and pressed herself against the adjacent wall. The voices drew closer until it became sickeningly clear that they belonged to Percy and Miss Cassandra Gardner.

"Now, where to meet?" Percy asked in an urgent whisper.

"The summerhouse?" Cassandra suggested.

"No, the summerhouse is far too cold! We wouldn't want those silky eyelashes to break like so many icicles, now would we?"

Luisa felt her heart turn to ice and burn with rage all at once. How was the freezing summerhouse good enough for her, but not for Miss Gardner? Weren't Luisa's eyelashes just as worthy of Percy's protection?

"The stables, then," Cassandra murmured. "But pray, not until after the entertainments. I am persuaded that all will be disappointed should you not appear in the Mummers Play!"

"Why should I choose to play the mummer when I could be making these delightfully plump lips my own?" Percy demanded.

Luisa's gasp went unheard, as it burst forth in unison with Cassandra's own. "Percy!" she said, followed by what sounded like a stamp of her foot. "You go a bit too far. Please return me to the party. If I am not mistaken, the pistachio ices are about to be served, and I do so adore Italian ices."

Through the wall, Luisa heard Percy heave a sigh. She imagined his smile of chagrin as he conceded to Cassandra's wishes. There came a rustling of skirts as they wordlessly returned from whence they had come, the very part of the house Luisa must now return to if she were to sample one of the ices under discussion. She waited a few moments more, so as not to let on that she had been privy to what could have only been a private conversation, Cassandra having been betrothed to Donald Adamson this age. It wasn't enough for Percy to have every girl in the village following him around like so many sheep; he must need enslave girls who were spoken for as well?

It was all Luisa could do to refrain from fetching her cloak and walking home alone in the cold, dark air. However, her mother, never a particular comrade of Lady Brooksby's, and therefore warming her widow's weeds by the fire of her own cottage, would scold Luisa for abandoning the shelter of the abbey at night without so much as a chaperone or a lantern to light her way. The fact that snow had begun to fall shortly before she had arrived meant she would need to remain until the end and beg a ride home. Stay at the party she must, so, gritting her teeth, Luisa found her way to the warm, brightly lit salon and secured herself a shadowy corner in which to pass the remainder of the night's revelries.

"It took ye long enough," came a voice from just behind her right shoulder.

With a start, she whirled around to find herself once again staring directly into a pair of impossibly green eyes set below two well-shaped, jet-black eyebrows. Farther up, a row of matching curls danced across a broad brow that merged into a thatch of the blackest, thickest head of hair through which Luisa had ever yearned to run her fingers. It seemed a chore to look elsewhere as the flash of a set of decidedly white teeth bracketed by a pair of devilish dimples claimed her attention, a circumstance that caused her no regret. The fact that his nose was neither too long nor too snub, and his skin without blemish, was all of a piece. In the face of all this masculine glory, Luisa was at a loss to remember his remark entirely.

"I beg your pardon?" she managed to stammer.

Thrusting a glass into her hand, he said, "Here, have some orgeat. Something tells me ye've had a bit too much of the so-called 'punch' being ladled out in yon corner to a scandalous number of unsuspecting young ladies."

Luisa could feel color rise in her cheeks, wishing that even a thimble's worth of alcohol could account for her recent childish behavior. She had barely formulated what she hoped was a much more sophisticated reply when, with a swoop of his well-formed hands, he pulled his cloak from behind his shoulders and produced a hideous bird-shaped hat from its resting place on the ground beside him.

"Oh!" was all Luisa managed to say before he, with a paltry bow, pushed his way past her and everyone else he encountered in the course of his journey to the front of the room. Two other men, one wearing a jester's hat and the other fingering a mustache so thick and luxurious it could only be counterfeit, were already waiting by the fire, their entire beings appearing to throb with anticipation. Once the birdman joined them, they conversed in low tones, scanning the crowd and generally seeming to be at a loss.

Finally the man with the mustache stepped forward and addressed the crowd consisting of twenty or more of Percy's closest friends and admirers. "Ladies and gentlemen, please," he stated, raising his hands and beseeching them with a severe look. "We are ready to begin our Mummers Play, but seem to be missing a key ingredient. Has anyone seen our good host?"

Luisa could have owned that she had indeed seen Percy, and only moments hence, but deemed it unwise to say so.

Cassandra stood with her Donald so it would seem that Percy was meeting yet another girl, perhaps this one in the summerhouse, providing she was in possession of more robust eyelashes than Miss Gardner. The crowd burst into babbled conversation teeming with speculation; however, no one possessed any knowledge as to Percy's whereabouts. Glancing at Cassandra from the corner of her eye, Luisa thought she looked a bit flustered, but Cassandra merely grasped Donald's arm more tightly and fluttered her too-delicate lashes.

Another whispered conversation was conducted by the three men at the front of the room, whereupon the mustachioed one again raised his hands and called for a volunteer. "We are missing an important player for our traditional Mummers Play. Who would like to be the hero? We need a strong gentleman to volunteer!"

The crowd once again erupted into babbling, but it was clear there was not one gentleman willing to participate. In point of fact, all of the players were utter strangers. Needless to say, mumming was beneath the dignity of upper class Wymondham society.

Without further ado, the birdman stalked into the crowd, his musty old cape swirling behind him, and the crow on his head glowering at all he passed, whereupon he came to a halt directly in front of Luisa. Taking her by the hand, he drew her, swift and sure, to the front of the room.

Luisa, finding it necessary to walk at a spanking pace to keep up with his long strides, had little breath to object. Once she was ensconced in front of the fire and turned to face the *crème de la crème* of her village, most of them known to her all of her life, but none of whom she might currently deem her friend, she felt incapable of speech. The crowd murmured in feeble protest, and she felt a deep sense of doom as she contemplated the additional lowering of her standing in society as a result of this night's work.

Suddenly there was a heavy hand on her shoulder and a puff of air in her ear as the birdman whispered, "Ye are not to worry as ye need say nothing. Just take the sword and flail it about a bit."

On instinct, Luisa took the wooden sword from him just as realization dawned. "You mean to say that I am to be the hero?"

"Yes. But that's all right," he said with what Luisa was coming to realize was an Irish accent. "Only you shall be the one kilt. Just be sure to watch your skirts when you go down," he said as his face split into a wicked grin.

There was no time to speak and little to think before the twin of her sword came crashing towards her. With an admirable parry she could credit only to indulging her little brother, William, in an occasional game of Knights and Soldiers, followed by a decent thrust whose quarry danced away from her with ease, she was in the thick of the Mummers Play. There was no turning back.

Barely aware of the narration given by the jester, she concentrated on keeping her opponent's wooden sword from making mice-feet of her new gown, a sheath of pale rose enveloped in a cloud of creamy gauze and adorned by the sweetest little puffed sleeves she had ever worked, until the killing thrust came, and she had no choice but to allow herself to crumple to the floor in what she prayed was a ladylike death.

The silence of the audience as the birdman hovered over her was more than a little unnerving. As she lay on her back in an imaginary pool of blood, she wished she knew whether or not her skirts were adequately obscuring her limbs from view. She wished she dared risk a peek, but surmised doing so would not be wise, as the dead generally remained still with eyes closed. Fervently she wished she had chosen to stay home this night, but it was more than a little late for that.

Restraining a sigh, she turned her attention to the narration of the jester.

"And thence came upon this terrible sight a doctor of great renown. It was his gift to restore life to the lifeless, heart to the disheartened, strength to those lacking strength!"

Luisa heard the rustling of the birdman's cape as he moved over her in some way she could not fathom. The rustling went on for what seemed a needlessly long time until, of a sudden, she developed an itch to the side of her nose that would not be quieted through pure force of will. Hoping all eyes were on the birdman, she risked a twitch of her nose as a means to find relief and immediately the audience roared with laughter. It seemed unbearably unfair that everyone but she could enjoy the proceedings, so she very slowly opened the eye farthest from the crowd only to find herself once again staring into those most remarkable green eyes that danced with far more fun than the narration warranted.

The audience again roared with laughter as she fully opened both eyes just as a feather descended upon her, and, finally, she understood exactly what had caused her discomfort.

"The great doctor brought life once again to the brave knight," cried the jester, "through the offices of a common feather as the continuous waving of his magical potion over his, er, *her* dead body had no demonstrable effect!"

"Ye're alive, now," hissed the birdman as he took her by the elbow with one hand, by the opposite shoulder with the other, and brought her speedily to her feet. He refused to let go until she found her footing, a circumstance for which she was grateful, as she felt a bit dizzy after her sudden flight through the air. She scanned the crowd for their reaction to her performance but found that she was distracted by the warmth of his arm around her as the spicy scents of shaving soap and an odor she commonly thought of as *l'eau de horse,* mingled in a not unpleasant aroma.

The crowd began a healthy round of applause; Luisa realized the play must be over. Intending to move out of the circle of the birdman's arm, she pulled away, but he held her back, saying to the crowd, "Let's have another round of applause for our compassionate heroine known to ye all as . . ." Then, bending his head to her lips, he asked, "What is it ye are known as, *cailin?*"

Flustered by the strands of her hair caught in the stubble of his cheek, she pulled them free, stammering, "Oh, ah . . . Darlington. Miss Luisa Darlington."

"Luisa Darlington, ladies and gentlemen! Let's show our appreciation for her bein' just the darling' that she is!"

Luisa would have supposed she'd imagined the audience's lackluster response, but there was nothing imaginary about the way the birdman's black brows pulled together in consternation in the face of their rudeness. It was a warming sight in contrast with the frowns adorning the faces in the crowd. Instinctively she drew back into the shelter of his arm, where she allowed herself to wallow in the warm and comforting smell of his recently starched cravat. His arm tightened around her shoulders in response, making her feel safe, truly safe, for the first time since her father had been killed in Bussaco under Wellington's command over two years previous.

Luisa wanted nothing more than to bury her face, along with her shame, into his collar and allow the circle of his arm to enclose her in the shelter of his enormous cape for the rest of the night, but she knew that would never do. This man was a stranger, and, like it or not, those who were even now condemning her for events entirely out of her control were those amongst whom she must live, most probably, for the remainder of her life. With a murmur of thanks, she gently pushed his fingers from her shoulder and walked through the wide berth afforded her by the crowd.

She shivered, suddenly as cold as one of the ices no one had thought to offer to her, especially where his large hand had been clasped round her shoulder. Somehow the fact that her heart seemed frozen to a numbness did not affect the functioning of her brain. She managed to make her way to her place at the back of the room without incident. However, once she arrived, she had no idea what to do with herself. Everyone seemed to be having a marvelous time, with the exception of Cassandra Gardner who appeared to be in a snit about something, and her betrothed, Donald, who gazed at her, his mouth agape, and his eyes large and round as two buttons.

"You can't mean that, Cassy!" he expostulated with great feeling.

"It's *Cassandra* or *Miss Gardner* to you, Mr. Adamson," she replied in a tone so haughty that Luisa was taken aback. Cassy was a pinch irritable now and again, but nothing in her character would lead her to haughtiness.

"She's a fair bit o'trouble," came a voice, this time from her left shoulder.

Turning, she found herself looking once again into the birdman's brilliant eyes. Quelling a desire to lean in and breathe more of his comforting aroma, she instead vented some spleen on the absent Percy. "She isn't usually, but our errant hero awaits her, and she must give her betrothed a reason to wish her at Jericho for the present."

She thought she detected a shadow move across the birdman's face as he turned his attention to a bowl of pistachio ice. "Here, I thought ye might like one," he said, handing her the treat just as Cassy stalked off in the direction of the library, the doors of which led directly out to the stables.

Luisa felt the tears start in her eyes, but whether they were for the betrayal of Percy or for the kindness of Mr. Birdman, she couldn't say. "Thank you," she said in what she hoped was a cheerful voice. "I most particularly love sweets." She took a bite of the cold, green ice, so unlike the emerald fire of his eyes, and hastily looked away. Fixing her gaze in the direction of the floor, she noted that he shifted from one foot to the other as if he felt as uneasy as she.

"So," he finally ventured, "I had heard our Sir Percival had a *cailin* waiting for him at home, but I didn't think he would fall for someone as heartless as that one. How long after his departure did she become entangled with another?"

Luisa, choking a bit on a tiny spoonful of ice, allowed her eyes to open wide with surprise. "Percy told you he had a sweetheart? Did he ever mention her name?"

"O'course. He spoke of her incessantly. I thought it was Teresa or Bautista or something Spanish-like. I suppose I had it wrong, though I would never ha' guessed him to be inclined towards one with the charms of your Miss Gardner."

Luisa could have sworn the same but kept her own counsel on the subject. "Yet it would seem he finds ebony curls and fine gray eyes to be most particularly charming." She burned to repeat Percy's earlier remark with regards to Cassy's plump lips but swallowed it down with another demure spoonful of ice.

He shrugged his shoulder, causing one of his black curls, at the moment happily free of the evil hat, to fall across his brow. "He never mentioned the color of her hair and eyes, only that she... how shall I put it?" He pressed his lips together and glanced at the ceiling with a sweep of his sinfully long lashes, then back down at her with a smile. "That she was 'a pretty girl and an honest one.'"

Luisa hoped she looked far less flushed than she felt. "But Miss Gardner is more than pretty, is she not?"

He looked to where Cassy's fiancé stood staring after her. "I daresay Mr. Adamson finds her far less so than he did an hour since. As for honest…" He raised his brows and let them fall.

Deciding the conversation had centered on Cassy long enough, Luisa tried a new tack. "You speak as if you have spent much time with Percy, yet I have lived in the village all my life and never met you before tonight."

"Aye, I hadn't met him prior to his coming to Ireland, did I? He and his parents were doing a bit of a grand tour, and buying a horse was on the schedule."

"Oh, I see," Luisa said. "So, you're a dealer of horses, Mr . . .?"

"Flynn," he said with a bow of his head, "and, no, I don't sell horses. I groom them."

Luisa opened her mouth to say something, anything at all, but was at a loss. How could a stable boy be standing with her, here, amongst the cream of village society? Were Sir Walter and Lady Brooksby aware that a servant was sipping from their best crystal, whilst commenting on the character of their guests? She thought of the ease with which he'd strode the hallway beyond the baize door, the same ease with which he'd strode to the front of this very room with Luisa's hand in his and a nasty black crow on his head. Whatever his calling in life, she owned that he was a remarkably confident man.

Mr. Flynn cocked his head and asked, "Am I not dressed properly for the occasion?"

Luisa laughed outright. "I daresay that old cape is exactly what a mummer should wear. But you are not simply a mummer, or you would have left this house the moment the play was over," she observed with a quick glance around the room which was conspicuously devoid of the three other players.

"I own it to be the oddest thing," Mr. Flynn admitted, slipping the ugly cape from his shoulders to reveal a perfectly cut evening suit paired with a burgundy waistcoat adorned with tiny pink rosebuds and a quantity of bright green leaves. "Some way or t'other, Percy and I have become friends. Being often in the sole company of his parents and their acquaintances whilst abroad, he had little to choose from."

It was Luisa's turn to cock her head and regard him at length. She found no fault in his attire or appearance, and his attitude had the polish of a prince. "I would never have guessed, but I suppose I am as unlikely a guest as a groom, so who am I to say?"

"Never say ye are the daughter of the butler!" he accused in mock horror.

His eyes were so merry that she could not help but laugh again. "No, but close enough as to make no difference. I live in the gatehouse with my mother and brother, as did my father before me, and his father before him."

Mr. Flynn raised his brows again—fine ornaments to a face full of expression. "And ye all turned out fine as a new penny!"

"My mother is clever with a needle and makes the most of Lady Brooksby's cast-offs," Luisa said, her eyes fixed on the melted remains of her pistachio ice. "Now that Father is gone, Willy must man the gate. You have doubtless met up with him a time or two on your way through."

"A fine lad, indeed! Your father no doubt smiles down on him from heaven."

Luisa looked up with a grateful smile and was stuck by the wistfulness in Mr. Flynn's face. "Do you think so? Really? I miss Father so much, and Willy . . . he is a big boy now, but I still hear him weeping at night when he thinks I am asleep."

She thought Mr. Flynn would laugh at her and make fun, but he stared directly into her eyes, and, without so much as a smile, said, "Yes. Really. And may the road rise up to meet ye, Luisa Darlington." And with that, he turned on his heel and strode away.

Chapter Two

*L*uisa watched Mr. Flynn disappear from view as the last of her pistachio ice melted into a sticky puddle at the bottom of her dish. With nothing left to do, she took in her current surroundings, which consisted of the faces of friends and neighbors, and felt profoundly alone. How was she to endure another fifty years in Darlington Cottage at the bottom of the drive of Percy's home, the house in which he would live as baronet, with some other lady as his wife and the children she bore him? It did not bear thinking on. Nor did the thought of another winter like this one, and she was less than a fortnight into it.

With a sigh, she bid adieu to the dreams of a glorious holiday party with Percy, as well as to her hopes for a return to her previous social standing, the one she had enjoyed prior to the elopement of Sally Constable. Suddenly she was struck with a thought so clear it stole the breath from her lungs: Percy had never meant to marry her! She was the gatekeeper's daughter at the grand estate of the richest couple in the village. She had never been anything but Percy's plaything. All of those moments she had spent dreaming of their life together at the abbey were the same ones he planned on something else altogether.

How foolish she had been.

For the second time that evening, she knew she would be undone by tears and wished for a private place to give vent to her emotions. Fixing her gaze to the door through which she had entered less than an hour previously, a voice in her head bade her stop. What would Mr. Flynn have to say about her if she ran—again? He was the one who put a sword in her hand, however flimsy, and called her back from the dead, however fictitiously. More importantly, he had spoken to her when no one else would, had comforted her when she was friendless, and had brought her an avidly desired treat when none other had thought of her at all. She had the absurd idea that he would be disappointed in her if she hid herself away, and for what? To weep over the feckless Percy?

True, Percy's friendship had been of long standing, and it had given her much comfort when her father died. He had made her so happy, and yet here she stood, her basket of summer bounty turned to ashes in the space of a single heartbeat. Trembling, she again contemplated the long winter ahead. However, unlike the girl who had been admitted through the front doors of Wymondham Abbey a few hours previously, she knew that this line of thinking would never do. Percy was not worth so much as a stray thought, let alone an entire winter of her life.

It was time she began a new life, one that did not include Percy. She started for the inner bowels of the house, those which lived and breathed behind the forbidden baize door. She headed there, no longer caring what anyone thought of her. She was nothing but a servant, herself, after all. What difference did it make, really, should she be seen searching for her hat and gloves in the cloakroom? It wasn't as if she could fall one mite lower in the esteem of those assembled.

Through the door she went, a sense of exhilaration flooding her veins. No longer would she be so very careful of what she said to whom, what books she borrowed from the lending library in the village, or whether or not her bonnet or gown was the first crack of fashion. For the first time, she realized that her friendship with Percy had led to her entertaining pretensions of being a lady, something she could never be. She was Luisa Darlington, and though she was not to be lady of the manor, she could be the best daughter, the best sister, the best grower of her own pink blooms and, she vowed with determination, the best consumer of chocolate bonbons Wymondham had ever seen.

The thought brought forth a bubble of laughter, the first in an age, but it caught in her throat at the sight of Mr. Flynn in the cloakroom, hanging his cape and musty crow hat on a peg. Her chin seemed to lift of its own free will, and she felt her spine straighten as well. She would not allow anyone, least of all this man, to think she mourned the loss of such a one as Percy Brooksby.

"Good evening, Mr. Flynn. I have just come for my cloak, as I am wanted at home."

Without hesitation he reclaimed his cape from its hook and swirled it around his shoulders. "Ye can't go alone, not on a night like this. I'll see you home in a proper conveyance, something with wheels that won't stick in the snow. It was piling up like spawning fish an hour past."

Luisa was pleased to the point of being unwilling to examine the cause for his consideration. She silently owned that it would be pleasant to be driven home in the shelter of his towering height, warmth and unlooked-for kindness. "I suppose my mother would not object." After finding her cloak, bonnet, gloves and scarf, she pushed her feet into her outdoor boots.

Taking her party slippers from her hands, Mr. Flynn tied the ribbons into a neat knot and hooked them over his arm before holding it out to her. "I am glad to know your mother would not mind, but do ye?"

"No. I . . . no, of course not, why should I?" she said, startled by his words. She could not fathom why he would ask such a thing.

"Ah, well, ye know how it is, I being naught but a stable groom, and a strange one at that," he said with a wry smile, leading her through the kitchen and to the back door.

"Well, there is that," Luisa admitted. However, she truthfully could not bring herself to think of him as a mere servant. She knew that he was, but there was something about him—the tilt of his head, the angle of his arm, the light in his eye—that bespoke nothing short of nobility. As she took his arm and tucked her hand far deeper into the crook of his elbow than the old Luisa would ever have dared, she gave him a reassuring smile. "Mama knows I am a good judge of character, and something tells me that you mean me no harm."

His face split into a huge smile full of very white teeth, and the dimple to the left of his mouth made a welcome appearance. "Well, then, let us make haste, and while we are at it, may the dust of your carriage blind the eyes of your foe!"

Luisa's laughter was natural and gurgled from her throat with ease as she allowed him to lead her through to the kitchen and the back door. "What is that, some kind of poetry?"

"Aye, I suppose. It's the Irish in me; that's what it is, sayings I have heard and known since I was a babe in my cradle. They fill my head at the least opportune moments and are out o'my mouth before I have time to think."

"Oh? What is inopportune about this moment?" Luisa asked.

But she was never to learn his answer, for he had hauled open the door to reveal a curtain of swiftly falling snow. Luisa felt her heart sink. How was she to escape Percy and his perfidy now? Hoping her dismay did not show on her face, she turned to Mr. Flynn and asked, "What am I to do?"

"The same as all of the Brooksbys' guests this night, I warrant. They can hardly turn them out into this. God is good, but never dance in a small boat," he said, shaking his head. Pushing the door hard against a blast of wind, which sent eddies of snow across the flagstone floor, he added, "Nor can they turn ye out, no matter that ye live at the end of the drive. It's nearly a mile. Ye'd not make it, nor have I a wish to face your mother when she learns I allowed ye out in this."

Luisa shivered, feeling it to be a most appropriate response.

"Well," he drawled, "the kitchen fire will no doubt burn high with a bit o'coaxing, and there are plenty of the guests' cloaks and capes and I don't know what else to make ye a nice, soft pillow and mattress."

"You don't suppose the owners will mind, do you?" Luisa asked with some anxiety.

"Mind? They, as will be sleeping in soft beds while you have naught on which to lay your head but the flagstone floor?" he insisted. "The proper question to ask is, will *ye* mind?"

"Well, yes, I suppose I would. In fact, it won't do. I'll be fine with just my own," Luisa insisted, yet touched to the core that this man, whom she had only just met, would make her wants and needs his duty to fulfill. "But what of you?"

"Oh, I'll find me something somewhere; never ye fear." He then took her by the elbow and steered her to the bench by the fire. "As they are fond of saying in my country, 'firelight will not let you read fine stories, but it's warm, and you won't see the dust on the floor.'"

She did as he suggested, taking off her boots and hat, and stealing as many sidelong glances of him as she thought would go unnoticed. He certainly was the best-groomed groom she had ever met, though she had to own that she hadn't met many. However, he was also possessed of a natural confidence that seemed more in common with the noble classes than that of an obsequious servant.

As he held aloft his large cloak in front of the fire, raising it up and then lowering it to warm it evenly, she couldn't help but notice the way his muscles rippled under the perfect cut of his evening coat. That, too, seemed a paradox. She knew very well that clothes cut to fit the owner were terribly expensive, as were the elegant fabrics from which his ankle-buttoned pantaloons, coat and waistcoat were constructed, not to mention his neckcloth, a veritable confection of lace. Though they had no groom of their own at Darlington Cottage, and she had no practical knowledge of such things, she had a strong suspicion that a year's salary could not have paid for his ensemble. Yet each piece fit far too well to have been borrowed unless he had a brother of equally excessive height who had recently come into funds.

It was all far too much to work out, what with the warmth of the fire having made her drowsy and a bit bemused.

"Go lie down before ye fall over," Mr. Flynn insisted, and as she could think of no reason to refuse, she did. Once she had laid her cloak on the floor as close to the fire as she dared, and had worked her scarf into a serviceable pillow, her eyes closed of their own accord.

A few moments later, she was unexpectedly enveloped in a layer of warmth as Mr. Flynn tucked another cloak around her feet and shoulders. With a sense of deep amazement, she realized it was the one he had been warming by the fire. Tears of gratitude came to her eyes when the aroma she had enjoyed earlier in the evening found its way to her nose. How very kind he was to gift her with his own cloak for the night! She wanted to open her eyes and thank him but pretended to be asleep, instead. She was a bit unsure of herself and so very drowsy.

However, a few moments later she was fully aroused by the sound of wood scraping against stone and, startled, she opened her eyes to witness Mr. Flynn decamping with the bench upon which she had earlier been sitting. "The boot boy won't thank me for filching his bed," he whispered, "but I can't have him spending the night in your chamber, now can I?" And with that he lifted the bench in his arms and took it with him from the room, leaving Luisa to lay awake for some time wondering what she could have done to deserve such kindness from a stranger.

Sleep did claim her at last but a few hours later she awoke to a low-burning fire and the sounds of an argument in the passageway. One of the voices was Percy's; she was sure of it. After pushing aside the heavy cloak, she went to the door and pressed her ear against the cold wood.

"I just wish to speak with her," Percy said, his voice thick with drink. "I want to 'pologize for ignoring her all evening."

"Ye can tender your apologies in the morning," came the firm response, one Luisa recognized as Mr. Flynn's.

"But I love her, and she loves me!" Percy expostulated.

There followed a profound silence; Luisa felt a stab of pain in her heart, the source of which she couldn't begin to fathom. It couldn't be sorrow for Percy; she wanted him no longer. Finally came Mr. Flynn's deadly calm reply. "If that were true, ye would have found her long since and seen to it that she was well looked after."

"I had my duty as a proper hos'," Percy insisted, his pickled tongue clearly reluctant to cooperate. "Had the devil of a time getting everyone bedded down; you can't even imagine, Flynn!"

"Ye say ye love her, yet ye leave her comfort for last?" Mr. Flynn demanded. "She is, as ye have told me often, a fine girl. She deserves better. And you! Fiend seize me, it doesn't matter. Och, man, if ye came to the wedding, ye would stay for the christening. Now go!"

"I can't," Percy said, whimpering. "Mother made me give up my room to that over-sized lout, old what's his name. The one as big as houses. I can hardly crawl in with *him*, now can I?"

"Nor can ye lie next to me on this bench, so off with ye," Mr. Flynn said with a patience Luisa wondered at.

"But I must see Luisa first. She'll know what to do. She always does. A right fine girl that Luisa is!"

"No, ye shan't," Mr. Flynn said in a tone not to be argued with. "I won't let ye. If I had my way, ye would never see her again."

Someone must have thrown a punch, for this pronouncement was followed by sounds of a scuffle, and from what Luisa could ascertain, the boot boy's bench was heavily involved. Feeling it far beyond fair that Mr. Flynn's gentlemanly behavior should be met with such a lack of appreciation, she meant to put a stop to it and opened the door. She should not have worried; Mr. Flynn had Percy trussed up in his arms like a Christmas goose with only a jet-black curl fallen against his brow to show for his efforts.

Both looked towards the door with alarm, but it was Mr. Flynn's face she sought first. He looked briefly into her eyes long enough for her to know that he had guessed it was she who had been Percy's summer sweetheart. Then his eyes slid from her gaze in tandem with his arms as they slipped from their grasp about Percy, and, with a deep sigh, he took a step back.

Percy seemed hardly to notice. "Luisa," he whined, "I must speak with you. And as for you, Flynn, you were meant to be my friend!"

"As you were meant to be mine," Luisa said in a firm voice.

"Yes! The best kind of friend a woman can know. I loved you. Love you still," Percy said, his hands stretching towards her across the bench that kept them apart.

"Is that what you said to Cassandra Gardner when you met her in the stables earlier tonight?" she asked in a voice growing stronger.

While she waited for Percy to respond, she flicked a glance at Mr. Flynn, standing with his arms crossed and looking even more sinister than he had when he was but a shadow with a bird's head. Something about his expression bespoke disappointment, even sorrow, but whether it was for herself or Percy, she couldn't guess.

"Wha . . . what was that you said about Miss Gardner?" Percy countered, lifting his chin a fraction. "I mean to say, what is it you know about her?"

"For one, that she has promised a fine man to be his wife, and it is not you," Luisa replied in a voice strangely devoid of rage. It struck her that it was of no consequence to her to whom Percy was wed and that she hoped only for Cassy to escape an entrapment that would splice Percy to her side.

"I told you, Cassy is just a friend. I don't love her, not the way I love you," Percy insisted.

Nothing. Percy's words had no impact on her at all whatsoever. It wasn't until Mr. Flynn emitted a low hiss and turned away, pushing his hand through the ebony locks that tumbled across his brow, that Luisa felt a pricking of her heart. It would seem she cared more for the feelings of Mr. Flynn than her childhood friend; however, it would hardly do to say so. Instead she said in a voice that did not waver: "Percy Brooksby, I wish to never see you again." Before pushing the door shut she took one last look at his face and was gratified by his expression of total amazement. However, it was the look of relief washing over Mr. Flynn's face that gratified her most. She marveled that it would matter so much what an almost perfect stranger thought of her, what he might think about her . . . even what he might feel about her.

The cold from the stone floor against the soles of her feet put a stop to her thoughts and she bounded back to the warmth and safety of Mr. Flynn's large woolen cloak that smelled of soap, starch and safety. Sleep, however, was not to come again that night. Knowing he was there, just outside her door, passing the dark hours on that hard, narrow bench . . . Knowing that he chose to suffer for her benefit made her feel both cherished and ungrateful. How could she be so selfish as to sleep? How could she stop thinking about him long enough to still her mind and emotions, not to mention the over-rapid pounding of her heart?

With the morning sun came a sense of calm she hadn't felt since before the day of King George's birthday fete, in fact, since before her father's death. Percy would marry someone else, and Luisa would not live a life of luxury and privilege. She would return to her home and tend to her mother and brother. She would plant roses and read novels and eat chocolate sweetmeats. She would perhaps be invited to sup at the vicarage once a year or however often the vicar's wife took pity on her in her fallen state. It all sounded perfectly ghastly, but somehow she felt it would be all right.

But first she had to leave the house. She knew Cook would soon be in to build up the fire for the morning chocolate and Luisa would rather not speak to her if it could be avoided. Luisa would have liked to see Mr. Flynn to thank him for all he had done, but she needed time to collect her thoughts; a carefully worded letter would be best. Quickly she donned her cloak, gloves and boots and opened the back door to a glittering world of white. It was breathtakingly beautiful, but the snow was too deep for more than a short trudge to the privy.

"Why walk when ye can go by sleigh?" She whirled to find Mr. Flynn rapidly closing the space between them, and before she could decide what was best to be done, he was by her side. "Thanks be, the sun is shining, but the snow is still too deep to take ye safely home on your own."

"It's only a small journey, and my mother will be glad to know I'm all right," she began, but he hushed her.

"Nay! There's a lovely little sleigh in the stables, and we will have left before anyone else is even awake to know it's gone. You know how late these ladies and gentlemen sleep. Meanwhile, you will be on your way with a hot brick at your feet and a rug on your lap. But first ye must have something to eat!"

Once again the thought of possibly encountering Cook, an old friend from her days of larder raids with Percy, caused Luisa's stomach to clench in anticipation of looks of pity and sighs of commiseration. Then again, perhaps she was simply hungry. "A roll and a bit of milk is all I need, though perhaps you require a bigger breakfast. I can wait. You have been so kind to me; the least I can do is to be patient."

"Breakfast for one tastes best when eaten by two," Mr. Flynn said as he disappeared into the larder. He emerged with a basket of eggs and potatoes, a board of bread and butter and a rasher of bacon under his arm. "Cook will doubtless have plenty to do serving hot chocolate to all those fine misses upstairs and who knows what else for the fine gentlemen, so you must leave it to me."

Setting a chair by the fire, he bade Luisa sit and handed her the tongs, whereupon he cut several thick slices of bread and passed them to her to toast over the flames. He then filled a black skillet with lard and cut up the potatoes. Before long Luisa's nose was tingling with the smells of a delicious English breakfast. He even found time to make her a bit of hot chocolate, all while she turned the toast over the fire.

By the time they were seated at the table and eating,

Luisa felt the last of her reserve melt away. As she watched him tuck into his food with more than the polite amount of enthusiasm, she began to wonder about his life in Ireland. "Is this what a good Irish breakfast is made of?" she asked.

"The potatoes, yes. We eat potatoes at almost every meal back in Cork. But we would have tea rather than chocolate or coffee, and sausage rather than bacon. And fish—lots and lots o'fish! Oh! And if I had had the time," he said around a hearty mouthful, "I would have made ye a batch of m'mother's scones. They melt in your mouth faster than the butter that's on them." He liberally slathered a piece of toasted bread. "But your toast is just as delicious," he added with a smile and a sly wink.

Luisa laughed and buttered her own slice. "I surely should have made breakfast for you rather than the other way around. I have been hoping for a chance to do something to show you how grateful I am that you have looked after me so well."

"Gratitude is not only the greatest of virtues but the parent of all the others," he replied, reaching out to cover her hand with his for a moment. Luisa felt the moment to be both scandalously long and far too short. Her hand felt cold when he drew his away.

"Was it your mother who taught you to cook?" Luisa asked.

"Oh, aye. My parents raised us to fend for ourselves. We were made to learn it all, don't you see?"

"You can't have had much time for cooking once you went into service as a groom," Luisa insisted.

Mr. Flynn dropped his gaze from her face to his plate and made a great deal of fuss over which piece of potato to spear with his knife. "I'm not precisely in service."

"Oh," Luisa said with some surprise. "Then you aren't here at the abbey to act as groom to His Lordship?"

He swallowed a mouthful of egg and shook his head. "I am here more as Percy's reluctant companion than anything else, though I oft' feel more like his nursemaid. I am the groom only in my father's household, leastways when I'm home. We were all made to work; it's his way."

Luisa wondered again about Mr. Flynn's background. A man who had horses to groom, but hadn't the money to pay someone to do so was a puzzle indeed, but perhaps that was how it was done in Ireland. "I am the one who benefits, as it means I shall have the escort of an experienced groom for my journey home," she said with a warm smile.

"Aye, that!" he said, with what felt like a sense of relief. "Ye are a brave soul to trust such a poor groom as I!"

"Me? Brave?" Luisa exclaimed. "The first time you saw me, I was hiding in the passageway like a quivering blancmange, I beg you to recall."

"I know that ye are brave," he said, shaking his head in denial of her words. "How much it must have cost you to come here when everyone has been so against ye."

It was Luisa's turn to swallow hard. "You know about that, do you? I suppose Percy spoke of it to you." She felt her body turn cold and then hot with shame.

"He didn't have to; I saw it for myself last night. But, yes, he did, and I confess, I couldn't understand it." He gave another shake of his head. "One minute you are the Sun, the Moon and the Stars to him, and the next he has a letter from someone telling him of your friend's unfortunate marriage. Suddenly you were beyond the pale. It was then I decided I had had enough of Percy Brooksby."

"Then why are you yet here? You could have been home with your family for Twelfth Night."

He opened his mouth to answer, but he paused, looking, for the first time since she'd met him, a bit unsure of himself. Leaning back in his chair, he asked, "Would it sound like a load of slippery untruths if I told ye I had a mind to meet this paragon of his?"

Luisa felt her cheeks blush; she looked down at her plate. "No. That is, yes! Oh, I don't know!" She raised her gaze to see he was laughing, if only with his eyes. She laughed too, then asked, "All right then, Mr. Flynn, what do you make of her, pray tell?"

Mr. Flynn cleared his throat and returned to his breakfast. He took so long to respond that Luisa wished she might sink through the floor. Finally he said, "Well, it's clear to me that ye have not an ounce of spite in ye, else ye would have had Miss Gardner between your claws such as I have seen with any number o' girls of my acquaintance. She deserves no less. Yet ye seem to bear her no ill feelings."

"I confess, I did at first, but then I realized she's just as much a victim of Percy's whims as I."

He nodded. "It's naught but the truth. Your seeing that so clearly, it's that which makes ye wise. Ye are also humble, else ye would have thought naught of borrowing a few fine cloaks for your bed. Then there's the way ye let Percy off so lightly. Had I been ye, I would have given him the tongue lashing of his life. That tells me that ye are kind and forgiving."

"It is *you* who are kind. So very kind!" Luisa dared to look into his face and was taken aback by the tenderness in his eyes.

Again he cleared his throat and, in a lower voice, said, "Ye are pure and chaste. From all that Percy said of ye, I knew it could not be otherwise. And ye are honest." He hastened to add the last as if he was as anxious to change the subject as she was for him to do so. "There is no pretense about ye. Ah! And ye are grateful!" Placing his hand again on hers, he asked, "How could I forget that?"

Abashed, Luisa could not bring herself to look at anything but his hand covering hers against the rough plank table, but soon an undeniable force pulled her line of vision to meet his own. They sat, searching each other's faces for answers to queries she had never before considered, until finally he said, "How so many virtues could be in one *cailin*, one who is so impossibly beautiful . . . There are no Irish proverbs that speak to such a miracle as that!"

Luisa thought of her hair—such a commonplace brown, and her skin—marred by a spatter of freckles across her nose and cheeks. Her eyes were large but of an indeterminate color, neither blue nor green nor brown nor gray, and her nose was far from what one would find gracing the face of a Diamond of the First Water, as it had a bit of a tilt at the end. That he found her beautiful was a miracle indeed!

She was saved from formulating a reply, as Cook bustled into the room. "Who would have thought we would be in such a taking this morning?" she cried. "I have never had the pleasure of waiting upon such a lot of whining, demanding, ungrateful children!" Reaching for a large pot, she groused on as if there were no one there to hear her. "Now, if they had been the master's London set, well, that would have been different. I would have expected them to sleep late and wish to wake with a roll in their mouths before their eyes had fully opened, but not those as live in this here village, I declare!"

Luisa was relieved that Cook had other things to think of besides Percy's perfidy, and she was happy to have a reason to jump up from the table to help. Mr. Flynn also lent a hand between his tasks of heating bricks for their journey and hitching the horses to the sleigh. When all was ready, and Cook was carrying up trays of hot chocolate and cold butter and rolls to the guests, Luisa waited, somewhat reluctantly, by the door for Mr. Flynn to fetch her. It stung to know that she was not likely to speak with Mr. Flynn again, but it also thrilled her that, first, she had an entire sleigh ride with him ahead of her. She intended to savor every moment and store them up, like jewels in a case, against the stormy weather ahead.

Finally the door to the outside opened, and Mr. Flynn was there. She was startled but pleased when he lifted her into his arms to carry her through the snow to the waiting sleigh. After placing her carefully in her seat, he drew a warmed rug onto her lap and adjusted the heated brick at her feet. As he climbed in beside her, she smelled again the wonderful scent of his wool cloak and thought of how this would be the last time she would be close enough to him to notice. This was the last time she would speak to him, the last time she would see him.

Turning in her seat so she could fill her gaze with him for the length of the journey, she asked, "What is your home like? Do you look forward to returning?"

Giving the horses their head, he loosened his grip on the reins and turned to face her, as well. "Ireland is the fairest place in all the world, and I would live nowhere else."

"And your house—is it as large as my gatehouse? If there are stables, surely it must be at least as large. And you live there as your father's groom?"

"Aye, well, I might have misled ye a bit about that," he said, his green eyes ever more brilliant against an infinite background of white. "I do groom for my father, but only because he insists that his sons work at something, and I have an accord with the horses. My brother Sean is a genius with the numbers, so he helps with the accounts. My brother Seamus rides the land and helps with the sheep."

"You have sheep?" Luisa asked, more than a little surprised.

"Oh, aye, a few. Everyone around us, as well. Ireland is littered with sheep," he said, with a shrug.

"But sheep require the care of many people, as do horses. You must have a large household and a larger house to keep them," Luisa suggested.

"Yes, I suppose it's large. Some say it's the largest in County Cork, but I wouldn't go so far as to boast that."

"So," Luisa said, "you live in a large house with a stables and horses, on land large enough to sustain a few sheep and an income that requires your brother's help to keep track of. Mr. Flynn," she asked tartly, "who are you?"

"Nobody," he said, with another shrug. "Leastways, not anyone who is someone here in England. Back home I am known as the Master's eldest, but it would be uncanny strange if anyone here were to have heard aught of a simple Irish lord."

Luisa restrained a gasp of dismay. Mr. Flynn was no "mister" at all—he was heir to a lord. Her heart sank, and with it her barely formed hopes that Mr. Flynn would choose to stay in England and be, at the very least, her dear friend. Turning to face the road again, she asked stiffly, "How could your family let you go? They must be anxious to have you back."

"And myself returned to them, as well," he said as he slowly reclaimed the reins and gave the horses a flick to speed them on their way.

The rest of the journey was silent, strained and excessively cold. Luisa was glad of it, as the tears froze along her lower lashes before they could slip down her cheeks and betray her. She felt as if it were her heart that had frozen then fallen to the stone floor of the abbey kitchen to break into a thousand jagged little pieces. The pain was far sharper than Percy's rejection, far deeper than the rejection of the entire village put together.

How could she feel so much for a person she had met barely twelve hours previous? That he cared for her a little, she was sure of, but how was it possible? And so unfair; he was the heir to a title, and she the daughter of a gatekeeper.

The horses stopped on their own after they reached the large, black, wrought-iron gate. There was nothing to be done but move her feet, climb out of the sleigh and begin her new life, one without hopes or dreams to keep her warm, and with spring so long in coming. Someday soon Percy would marry. Her brother would open the gate to his bride, and

Luisa the Spinster would watch life go by through the window. And Mr. Flynn—he would be gone, far away, in Ireland. It was an unendurable thought, and she felt sobs clamoring in her chest. Mortified, she gave in to the temptation to flee, but as she leaned forward to rise, she felt a large hand on her arm and Mr. Flynn drew her gently back to her seat.

"Ye don't have to get out," he said, as if it were a summer day full of sun and possibilities and, above all, time.

Brushing ice-cold tears from her cheeks, she turned to face him. "I don't understand."

"Don't ye, *mo chroi*?" he said, his words escaping his lips as softly as the puff of steam rising on the air.

"No, I don't. Not French or Gaelic or anything at all!" she cried. "You are looking at me as if I should, but it seems I am wrong, unforgivably wrong, about most everything."

Taking her hand, he laid it against his cheek, trapping it in place, making it utterly impossible to finger the dimple she had been longing to touch all day. "It's the Gaelic for 'my heart.' It's what a man calls the *cailin* who has stolen his."

Luisa stared at him in disbelief, but her own heart told her he was speaking truth. Not daring to trust the wild leap of hope that rose in her chest, she said, "But your family is waiting for you. You must go back." She pulled her hand from his face and let it fall to her lap. "You are the son of a lord," she said, her words catching in her throat, "and I am nobody's daughter."

Taking her hand again, along with its fellow, he pressed them between his own. "There is time and enough. I will make time! And when I return, you will come home with me as my bride."

"But you mustn't! You can't marry me," Luisa heard herself say when all the while her heart was shouting, *Yes!* "What would your family say?"

"They would say what a lovely *cailin* ye are and welcome to the family."

Luisa stared at him as if he had taken leave of his senses. "Mr. Flynn, even if that were true, we have only just met. Why, I don't even know your given name!"

"But I know all of yours, and they are beauties, every one."

"Whatever can you mean?" Luisa asked, mild irritation at his puzzling reply rising to the surface of a mass of competing emotions.

"My beauty. My grateful one. My kind and forgiving one, humble and patient one. What other names would ye have me call ye?"

Tears, happy ones, began to form in her eyes and roll down her cheeks. Her lips would insist on turning up into a smile. "I have always loved my given name. It's Luisa."

"Yes, I remember," he said, lifting a finger to gently touch a tear cradled in the corner of her mouth. "Mine is *Iosua* but you would know it as Joshua."

"Joshua," Luisa breathed. With a cry of joy, she leaned towards him and laid her head against his chest. More quickly than she thought possible, he had both of his arms around her, and she was warm and safe and exactly where she belonged. "Thank you, Joshua, for saving me—from Percy, from this village, from myself. For that, if nothing else, I could love you all the days of my life." Pulling her head from her sweet and warm cocoon, she looked up at him so as to read the expression in his eyes. "But what about you? You deserve a true lady, someone who comes with land and money or at least a title."

In answer, he pulled her close until her face was inches from his own. Then he kissed her with lips stiff and cold, but which were soon warm and pliable and eager as she could wish. "Ye are a perfect lady," he murmured, brushing his lips against her forehead. "One imbued with the only riches that matter." He pulled back to search her face and must have approved of what he saw, for he drew her even closer so that she could feel the thundering of his heart against her own, and then kissed her until she thought perhaps she would melt away into nothingness.

Finally, one last time she whispered, "Are you sure? Are you very, very sure that you love me? I have nothing to give you but myself. Oh, and Mother and Willy."

"I'll take ye all. I was not born for aught else but to protect ye, to care for ye," he said, his words coming faster and faster while his voice grew thicker with each. "To love ye as I have loved no man, woman or child on this, God's green earth." Taking her face between his hands, he asked, "Can ye leave your home to come to a wild and beautiful new place that will make your heart sing and your husband delirious with joy?"

"Oh, Joshua, how could I not?" With a smile, she shrugged out of his grasp, picked up the reins and called out to the hills of snow, "To Ireland!"

ABOUT HEIDI ASHWORTH

Heidi Ashworth is an anglophile who loves to read and write books that take place in England. She also enjoys hanging out with her family, blogging, DIY home improvement projects and spending time in her garden, one composed mostly of roses, including a Double Delight, the variety on the cover of her first book. She wrote her first "novel" when she was a very determined ten-year-old, though her debut novel, *Miss Delacourt Speaks Her Mind*, wasn't written until she was married and raising children. Its success upon publication in December 2008 spurred her to write a sequel, *Miss Delacourt Has Her Day*, which was published in February 2011 and was a finalist in the Whitney Awards. Both of her books are available in hardcover, paperback and Kindle via Montlake Romance.

Heidi's Website: www.heidiashworth.com
Heidi's Blog: www.heidiashworth.blogspot.com

An Unexpected Proposal

by Annette Lyon

Other Works by Annette Lyon

Band of Sisters

Coming Home

A Portrait for Toni

At the Water's Edge

Chocolate Never Faileth

The Newport Ladies Book Club Series

*There, Their, They're: A No-Tears Grammar Guide from the
Word Nerd*

Chapter One

Logan Canyon Wood Camp, Utah—1880

Caroline tucked a stray piece of hair behind her ear and set to filling the bread basket with slices of rye and wheat bread, all the while wishing she could stay in the kitchen the entire evening instead of serving the workers. She hated the evening meal; it was the worst part of the workday at Wood Camp, and had been ever since Butch Larsen showed up to cut and haul trees two weeks ago. Today she'd first hinted at, and then begged Mrs. Hansen, the foreman's wife, to let her stay in the kitchen to prepare the serving platters and get a start on cleanup, with Mrs. Hansen doing the actual serving.

"Why in the world would you want to spend your evening in here?" Mrs. Hansen said, shooing Caroline into the main room to serve the sweaty, tired men seated on benches around long tables. "It's hot and stuffy."

"But—" Caroline cut herself off, unsure how to proceed. She adjusted her hold on the bread basket, which was nearly overfilled. She glanced over her shoulder at the door toward the main room and winced.

"Well, now, get on," Mrs. Hansen said with another shooing motion, and then wiped her brow with the back of her wrist. When Caroline hesitated a second time, Mrs. Hansen placed one bony hand on her equally bony hip and tilted her head. "Tell me truly, child, what's the problem?"

Caroline closed her eyes and confessed. "It's the new Larsen boy. He makes me uncomfortable." She shuddered at the memory of how he'd encouraged her to lean forward so he could get a proper view of her bosom—even though it was modestly covered, with a high neckline of navy calico with pale pink flowers. She never mentioned the time he—she would swear it on a stack of Bibles—had patted her behind— her behind!

It was one thing to flirt with the men; she'd done that plenty of times. But Butch Larsen took the whole thing too far. She'd come to the point of staying mute in the serving room and avoiding any eyes but her old chum James's.

Not that ignoring everyone but James had helped much; Butch still tried to get her attention. He made off-color comments, laughed, and then went right back to his mashed potatoes as if nothing had happened. At times she wondered if she'd imagined the whole thing, but each time, his grin and the way he nudged his seatmates with his elbow told the truth.

Now Caroline searched for a way to explain that wouldn't denigrate a camp employee. "Mr. Larsen is not . . . now I hate to speak ill of anyone or spread gossip, but, well, he hasn't been entirely . . . appropriate in his behavior toward me."

There. She'd said the words she'd been holding back for a nearly fortnight, ever since Butch started getting fresh with her. Her old childhood chum James—a boy who'd grown up on the neighboring farm—arrived at the camp two weeks before Butch, the day after Caroline herself came to help the Hansens in the cookhouse and with other odd jobs like mending the men's work clothes. Unlike Butch, James worked on road construction duty, so the two men didn't interact except for during meals, and even then they rarely spoke.

The roads up the canyon were always rutted and filled with holes, especially in the spring and fall, due to the rain and the snow and subsequent freezing and thawing, making the ruts and holes even bigger. It was the job of the road team to keep the way passable for horse-and-mule teams pulling wagons filled with newly felled trees destined for the Mormon temple, the recently arrived telephone company's poles, construction scaffolding, and other uses in the city of Logan in northern Utah.

As Caroline waited for a verdict about the evening's service, she bit the inside of her lip. Mrs. Hansen pressed her lips into a thin line as she eyed at Caroline critically. "Very well. I'll do the serving . . . today," she said, with extra stress on today. "But then I expect you to do all of the cleanup afterward. Every pot, pan, plate, and spoon. All of the sweeping and mopping and wiping down of countertops and tables. Hear me?"

"Yes, ma'am," Caroline said with a bob at the knee, too grateful for a reprieve from Butch's unwelcome advances to care that she'd be working an extra hour or two after supper by herself.

Mrs. Hansen took the bread basket from Caroline and marched into the main room. A distinct moan of disappointment went up, and Caroline had half a mind to peek out the doorway to see who all was reacting that way— surely more than Butch. Did James wish to see her? Possibly. Most nights after her duties were finished, the two of them took evening strolls along the canyon paths and roads together, chatting about old times at school and church, or whatever else struck their fancy. It was pretty much the only time she looked forward to during this job of hers that had taken her so far up the canyon.

She'd been at the Wood Camp barely over a month, and already she was sick of it. She wouldn't have come at all if it hadn't been for the fact that her family needed the extra funds. They'd lost most of their spud crop to disease. Worse, her little sister Bertha suffered from a rare and chronic form of tuberculosis, requiring frequent physician visits and medication that seemed to do nothing, or make things worse, as often as it helped.

Bertha's condition is what finally sent Caroline up the canyon for employment. Mr. Hansen had heard about Bertha; as a child, he had battled the same disease for the better part of a decade. It had left him weak as a young man, unable to do manual labor, so he'd turned to tailoring to make a living before emigrating from Denmark. He'd offered the job to Caroline as a way to help pay for little Bertha's care.

He'd taken to teaching Caroline how to mend the workmen's torn shirts and trousers, and she could now mend better than even her mother had taught her. She looked on the lessons as a gift, as each time she fixed someone's worn-out or torn clothing, she was paid directly by the worker, which added to her stash for Bertha and the rest of the family. And maybe, if Providence shined upon her, for herself and her trousseau.

Her position at camp would last a few more weeks, and then she'd head home for the remainder of the winter, during which time the Wood Camp would have a skeleton crew, and her services wouldn't be needed. If they found they required help in the cookhouse again in the spring, she'd return then.

Would Butch—or James—be here in the spring? She could hope not on the first count, and hope yes on the other.

The men would take time yet to finish eating, but eventually they'd leave the building in search of evening pursuits, whether singing, reading scriptures, or resting.

With the food already prepared, Caroline set to heating a pot of water on the stove to wash dishes in. First it would be the plates, cups, and silverware, and later the pans, bowls and other big dishes. With two pots of water settled to heat on the stove, she found two saucers and put butter in them for when they ran out. They always ran did, as the men generously slathered the stuff on their bread. She refilled the pewter pitchers with well water then prepared servings of peach cobbler for dessert before checking on the heat of the wash water, all while Mrs. Hansen bustled to and from the main room, serving the tired workers.

As Caroline wiped her hands on her apron, she couldn't help but think that even though the kitchen work kept her hopping, it was so much nicer than being in the main room. Butch was always the worst part of the experience, whether it was for breakfast, dinner, or supper. He managed to make things particularly uncomfortable for her at supper, when he seemed to lose some his inhibitions after a long day's work. She had to wonder if he indulged in spirits after the work day was over, even if consuming alcohol was against Wood Camp rules. She didn't know what alcohol smelled like, but even if she did, she wouldn't have dared say anything to Mrs. Hansen about Butch imbibing; he scared her too much for that. She'd already stepped beyond her bounds today admitting that he made her uncomfortable.

When she did have to serve the men, James was the one saving grace, whether she was handing out bread or serving up ladles of soup. With his unruly mop of curly hair, he always sent her encouraging smiles—and gritted his teeth whenever Butch tried to step over his bounds. Butch was subtle enough the few men were aware of his knavery, and no one would have dared confront him about them, not when he was from a respected family—and weighed almost twice what the other men did, his the extra weight being all muscle. More than once, James looked ready to pummel Butch, but Caroline always shook her head at James, begging him to never utter a word. She didn't want him to risk his job by insulting Butch—who, they soon learned, was the great-nephew to Mrs. Hansen, or fourth cousin, or some other distant relation. No, insulting the blood of the foreman or his wife wouldn't do.

No one did, not to Butch, and not to the Hansens. Not even to Caroline.

She kept her distress to herself as well.

Chapter Two

The men had retired from the cookhouse, as had Mrs. Hansen, leaving Caroline alone to finish the work of cleaning up the messes from the meal. She hummed to herself, caring nothing for the extra work or for being alone; after the dread of facing Butch again, the work and the time were nothing. She worked quickly and efficiently, changing songs as she went on to the next task. The only part of working late that she regretted was missing out on the chance for a walk with James. She hadn't been out front at all—a time they usually confirmed their plans surreptitiously. First it was eye contact, then a subtle nod from James as he casually rested fingers on the table with fingers extended, representing how many hours from supper he'd come to fetch her from the foreman house. She always managed a wink as an affirmative answer.

Tonight she saved for her final chore the trip outside to dump the dirty dish water. She hated the cold and the snow—and now, the darkness of winter. She wrapped a shawl around her shoulders, put on mittens, and then hefted the big tub of dirty water, which was now lukewarm and cloudy, with bits of carrot and parsley floating at the top. As she lugged the tub with both hands and headed for the back door of the cookhouse, she decided to find a way to get a message to James to apologize for not being available for a walk.

The tree and bushes she usually dumped the water by stood where the ground sloped away from the cookhouse so nothing would drain back to the building. Cache Valley winters were always cold, but this was worse than usual. Often the dumped-out supper dishwater was frozen solid by morning.

As Caroline walked to the tree, careful not to spill anything onto her dress, she pondered how best to get a message to James. A note on his bed? No, that might get stolen by another worker. Or, worse, she'd be seen going into the men's bunkhouse—a fool's errand, as she would have no idea where he slept. Besides, she'd end up with a reputation of a loose woman—something her mother had specifically cautioned her against before she came, what with being the only young, single woman at the camp.

That realization eliminated the notion of tucking a note into one of his shirt pockets as well, which was a silly idea, as there was no knowing which shirt he would wear on the job tomorrow—possibly even the one he had on right now.

She reached the tree and was about to lower the tub of water to the ground and let the water spill out, when a shadow stepped out from behind the tree and a deep voice said, "Missed seeing your figure at dinner, I did."

Caroline yelped, and the entire tub of water spilled everywhere—down her apron, to the hem of her dress, across the ground into a puddle, and onto the boots that belonged to none other than Butch Larsen.

As she stared at him—unkempt hair, three days' worth of stubble—she took one step backward, followed by a second. She spun on her heel and tried to run away, but Butch grabbed her arm by the elbow, making her cry out in pain as he twisted it—and her, to face him.

"You're hurting me. Please let go," she said, her voice quiet but shaking.

Butch squeezed her arm harder; she winced, knowing she'd have a bruise tomorrow. With a pleased smirk, he said, "I don't think I will be letting you go. In fact, you've been teasing me so much these past weeks that I think I'll not only hang on a bit longer, but take a little something for my troubles. A fragile lily like yourself can't flaunt her petals like ye've been doing and not expect a man to pluck the flower for himself."

With his other hand, he reached behind her head and grabbed her chignon, yanking her head back. She gasped as he drew close, eyeing her mouth. His fetid breath made her nostrils flare with disgust. But she couldn't get away, and this man was ready to kiss her against her will—or do who knew what else to her.

"Let go of me!"

"Oh, come now," Butch said, his stale breath hovering above her face. "I've seen how you tease the men. It's time you give me a little attention . . ."

Scream! But she couldn't. *He's the foreman's family. You can't scream.*

Butch paused briefly before releasing her elbow and hair. She breathed out with relief, but it was short-lived—he reached around her waist and pulled her close, grasping her right breast with one hand as he leaned low for a kiss. The shock and disgust overrode all else; she cried out—loudly.

"Let me go, you brute!"

Butch's eyes widened with surprise, apparently at the idea of his prey fighting back, but Caroline was far from done. His pause gave her courage and the slightest bit of time. She lifted the heel of her boot and jammed it hard onto his toes. She jammed her elbow backward into his nose. She barely registered a disturbing—and somewhat satisfying—crunch—before she ran, taking no chances as Butch yelped and hopped away, releasing her in his pain. As she ran, he doubled over and moaned. The foreman's house was too far away for an escape, so she headed straight for the cookhouse, where she locked the back door then rushed to the front door and locked it as well.

She went to the back door again, ear pressed to the surface as she listened, unsure when it would be safe to emerge. Several men's voices came from the other side of the door—half a dozen or more, based on the noise, including Mr. Hansen.

"What's the meaning of all the hollering?" the foreman demanded. "And why is this tub lying here? The snow will warp the wood, and it'll be useless by morning."

Let the tub get warped in the snow. Caroline didn't care. She could pay for the tub from her wages if need be, but she wouldn't go back out. Not as long as Butch was out there.

Mr. Hansen continued, his voice rising. "And what's the matter with you, Larsen? Why's your spud of a nose bleeding all over the place? Huh?"

His nose was bleeding. A fraction of a satisfied smile curved Caroline's mouth; she'd shown him what kind of strength a "fragile lily" really had.

A woman spoke next; it had to be Mrs. Hansen. "I heard Caroline yelling at him to let her go. By the looks of the spilled tub there, I'd say Mr. Larsen here was trying to have his way with her."

"I was doing no such thing," Butch insisted. "She misunderstood my offer for gentlemanly help. Flew into a mad craze. She's a crazy, I tell ya."

Caroline wanted to yell at him over that accusation, but Mr. Hansen came to her defense. He grunted as if he didn't believe a word Butch said.

"Son, you're walking on thin ice. This ain't no place for fraternizing with the help. Before you signed on, you agreed to abide by camp rules. If you can't do that, you'll have to—"

"You can't fire me," Butch interjected. "I'm family." But his voice was muted, as if he held a hand over his nose.

Knowing that reinforcements had arrived, that Butch wouldn't be breaking into the cookhouse, Caroline extinguished the two lamps in the main room then crept to the side of the building near a window and peered out. Bless Mrs. Hansen for figuring it all out even if she had doubted Caroline earlier.

Mr. Hansen grabbed Butch's arm in his own old, but beefy, one and began carting him back to the main house with the help of three other men. "You may be family, but you're a disgrace to the parents who raised you. And you're not to set foot at my camp again. You leave first thing in the morning, and I'll personally stand guard over you all night if I have to make sure you don't cause any more trouble."

Butch seemed to whimper—actually whimper!—while unsuccessfully resisting those who restrained him. Mr. Hansen grunted and said, "Here, take some snow and pack it around your nose. It'll help with the swelling."

As they walked back to the house in the darkness, the burst of energy that had carried Caroline seemed to drain away all at once. Her knees felt ready to unhinge completely, and her whole body starting trembling. She stumbled to a bench at a table, where she dropped her head to her arms and let herself cry.

She'd been sitting on the bench for a few minutes, letting her terrified, exhausted, confused emotions stream out, when a knock came on the front door of the cookhouse. Caroline's heart thumped so hard that she sucked in her breath and sat bolt upright, unmoving.

"Caroline? Are you in there? It's me, James. I couldn't find you, and after what I heard about Butch, I've been looking all over for you." He knocked again a few times then tried the door handle. "Please, if you're in there, open the door."

Relief coursed through her; James was here. She'd be safe with him. She extricated herself from the bench and all but flew to the door. Her hand shook as she tried to turn the heavy iron key to let James in. Finally the lock released, and he pushed the door open. She held her breath until she was certain the figure really was someone she could trust.

"There you are." That was James's voice; she'd know it anywhere. She threw her arms around his neck and sobbed into his shoulder at the horror or what might have been—and at the relief of what hadn't been.

Chapter Three

They stood by the doorway for several moments while her sobs gradually calmed. She lifted her head and wiped at his worn work shirt. "I've gotten you all wet."

"I don't care," James said. "Here, let's close the door and sit down."

She hadn't noticed the swirls of snowflakes twisting about in small circles about their feet. With a nod, she stepped backward, away from James's touch so he could close the door. The heavy door shut with a thud.

"Lock it?" she said, hating that her voice sounded so mouse-like. She'd never thought of herself as a weak woman in need of rescuing. She may have fought Butch off—ultimately with success, especially when others had heard the commotion—but with the confrontation over, she couldn't so much as turn a key in a lock. Once was almost more than she could do, just to let James in. Butch may be under watch now, but she still wanted the extra security of a locked door.

James nodded and turned the key. By the light of the nearly full moon, Caroline made her way to a bench and dropped to it. When he stepped away from the door, he peered through the windows as if checking for anyone lurking outside. Apparently pleased with what he had—or hadn't—seen, he came to the table and sat beside Caroline. They sat side by side, backs to the table.

Not until James sat only inches away, the silver light from outside spilling across his chest, did she fully realize that she was alone with a man, and with no chaperone in sight. And after all the warnings and talks with her mother before her mother had agreed to let Caroline take up employment at the Wood Camp.

If she could see me now, she'd fall down dead from shock.

Yet somehow, Caroline didn't care. James wouldn't hurt her, not like Butch had threatened to. James was here to keep her safe. He wouldn't impose upon her in any way.

Even if the men spread stories did, she hadn't the heart to care at the moment; her reputation could go hang. For right now, she needed to be safe—needed to know that no one would hurt her. James had always looked out for her ever since they were ten years old and he'd chased off two boys who'd harassed her during lunch hour at school.

James took her trembling left hand between his two rough but gentle ones. "I am so sorry you had to go through that." Caroline nodded mutely, unable to speak. "Butch finally confessed after Mrs. Hansen raked him over the coals, defending your morals." He chuckled. "I don't envy the man."

Caroline breathed a sigh of relief, but she couldn't relax entirely. "I can't stay here. Not after this."

"But you can," James said. "Mr. Hansen bellowed all kinds of things, about keeping Butch locked up overnight and Mr. Hansen's sending him back to town in the morning—likely farther than that, if the foreman has his druthers. Butch can't hurt you now."

"Good," Caroline said in whisper, her body letting out some of the tension from before. She looked down at their joined hands, and her heart rate sped up, not unlike when Butch had confronted her, but this time the feeling wasn't one of fear. No, instead she felt warm and eager.

And *then* she grew anxious. What was her heart doing, hammering like that, betraying the friendship she held so dear?

We're both adults. Childlike friendship doesn't have a place in our lives anymore. He'll be looking for a wife soon. And I'll be finding a husband.

The thought felt far more bitter than sweet. She was young yet, and had plenty of opportunities for many beaus and proposals. She planned to turn down the first few with aplomb, breaking hearts while keeping herself free to enjoy her youth before settling down to married life. She would certainly need several beaus before she truly knew what it meant to fall in love; she'd settle for nothing less.

James scooted a few inches closer on the bench; Caroline's heart hammered against her ribcage. Certainly he could hear the thumping in her chest. And then a thought came to her: perhaps James could be her first real beau. Certainly their relationship couldn't remain as school chums much longer. Yet could she ever see him as something more than a dear friend?

Perhaps, if it means having my first kiss. She'd certainly grieve the loss of their friendship later, after they'd had their share of innocent fun. *Might as well enjoy the change if it must happen.*

"Three men in addition to Mr. Hansen are watching him," James said, bringing her back to the present.

That was right; she'd just been near attacked. James's warmth—in his voice as well as his touch—had melted away her concerns. For a brief moment, she'd forgotten the terror that she'd fought against so recently.

"A lot of us are pretty riled up that he'd try something like that. I heard Mr. Hansen saying that Butch had to leave for home at first light. If it weren't winter, he'd probably have kicked him out tonight."

"I'm glad." Caroline finally raised her head and looked into his eyes. The glow from the full moon glinted through the windows, lighting up his hair from the back and leaving most of his face in shadow. His eyes looked dreamy, his jawline more chiseled than she remembered. He almost fit her ideal image here, in this moment. Yes, James would do for a first beau quite nicely. She was glad he hadn't brought a lantern with her, and that she'd extinguished the ones inside. The semi-darkness provided the perfect ambience for a romantic moment.

James brushed a lock of hair from her eyes and smiled. "I've always thought you were beautiful, but you're even more so by moonlight."

"I was thinking the same thing about you," she said, then shook her head and laughed. "But not beautiful. *Handsome.*"

He chuckled then lowered his head the slightest bit, so little that she wondered if she'd imagined it. She decided to risk her pride by leaning forward herself, closing the gap between them by a few more inches. If possible, her heart sped up even further, and her breathing became erratic. Was she about to experience what she thought she was? Surely the anticipation of her first kiss was the reason for the thrill shooting to her toes, even if it would be with her old chum.

She glanced up, looking into his eyes, which didn't hold their usual playful spark, but instead held something deep and serious behind them. She swallowed as she flicked a glance down to his lips and back to his eyes.

At that, he smiled with one side of his mouth, closed the gap, and pressed his lips to hers. This time, the eruption wasn't contained in her heart; Caroline's entire body seemed to come alive with tremors of excitement coursing through her limbs as his mouth moved over hers. She shivered with delight, not having known that a simple thing like a kiss could feel like this. He threaded his fingers into her hair and rested a hand behind her neck; she leaned closer, eager for more, and wrapped both arms about his neck as the kiss deepened.

Far later than she'd ever anticipated—yet all too soon—James's lips broke away from hers. She gasped slightly as the kiss ended, suddenly aware of every nerve ending in her body and wanting to feel this way always.

James leaned in again, but this time, he just pecked her lips. She wanted to pull him back and kiss him again, hard and long, but restrained herself.

This—her first real kiss—was a moment she would treasure and remember all her life, but she also knew that James wasn't for her, and that the romantic moment had happened purely out of the intense emotions they had both experienced immediately prior. That, and the bewitching moonlight.

Surely he knew that. James, sweet, sweet James, certainly knew that they weren't a match. Wouldn't he? He'd heard her talk for years about her ambitions for a handsome, mysterious—and, preferably, wealthy—future husband, someone who could take her away from tiny Cache Valley and show her big cities and exciting adventures. James knew he didn't fit that mold. Of course he did.

Yet as they held each other's hand afterward, she had her doubts. James seemed a bit too content. No, not content—pure joy seemed to radiate from him.

The realization that this moment hadn't been something purely spontaneous, the end result of a crisis, sent her reeling. She no longer worried about Butch—he'd be under guard all night, she was certain—so she decided it was time to leave. Every moment she stayed with James tonight would only solidify any silly idea that she cared for him in the way he—clearly—cared for her.

I never knew . . . I didn't. Did I?

She stood suddenly, pulling her hands from him. "Thank you for coming to check on me. I'm most indebted to your kindness."

Silly girl. Why are you talking like some formal school marm?

Her tone clearly confused James; his brow furrowed, and he looked at his hands as if trying to puzzle out why they were no longer holding hers. She'd never spoken to him like this. But they'd never experienced or done anything like this. James tilted his head ever so slightly to one side, as if puzzling out on an arithmetic problem during their school days.

Don't think of school now, she ordered herself. They'd been in the advanced class for math; they'd stayed after school with the teacher for help on the more complicated problems. *Had he set his sights on me even then?* Who was this man? She felt as if she didn't know James at all. *Yet his was so strong . . . maybe he does care for me in that way . . .*

"Of course I came," James said, answering her words from a moment before. His voice sounded wavering. "You owe me no debt. It's what friends do."

Friends. Thank the heavens he'd used that word. She sighed and breathed a bit easier.

"Yes. Yes, it is what *friends* do," she agreed, feeling the tight mask on her face melting away. She could smile and be herself again. "Good night, James. Thank you for coming when you did; I didn't even know I needed you, but you came."

He reached out and touched the tips of the fingers on one hand. A jolt of lightning went up her arm, and she had to hide the fact that her breath had suddenly grown uneven.

Would he kiss her again? She equally hoped for and dreaded another kiss.

"I'll always be here for you, Caroline," he said. Then, letting go of her fingers, he headed for the front door of the cookhouse. He twisted the key, pulled the door open, and, before stepping out into the night, added, "Good night."

Chapter Four

For the next several days, Caroline continued to plead with Mrs. Hansen to let her stay in the kitchen again.

"But Mr. Larsen is gone," she countered the first time. "Surely no other workmen have behaved as he did."

Eventually the foreman's wife gave in, and as time went on, she seemed plenty content to let Caroline stay late and do all of the supper cleanup herself.

Tonight, as Caroline set aside a clean frying pan that had browned beef for the workmen, she wondered if it was the panicked look on her face that had convinced the foreman's wife. She may have assumed that Caroline was still shaken over what had happened the night before.

That is true, but not in the way she may think. Caroline was shaken about what had happened with James, not with Butch—but Mrs. Hansen didn't know about the latter incident.

Truth was, Caroline could not bear to face James, let alone speak to him. Not after they'd kissed and she'd realized that he had feelings for her. That look of joy and love in his eyes still haunted her. She'd crushed his heart.

She scrubbed a knife, and with her worries tumbling inside, nearly cut herself with the blade. She rinsed the knife and set it aside, feeling the trembling shakes that seemed to follow any thought of James and the kiss they'd shared.

After finishing the last of the supper dishes, Caroline dried her hands on her semi-damp apron then dabbed a dry dish cloth across her perspiring forehead, sighing. It had been a long day. A long week. Every hour, especially one where James might show up, dragged by, and she seemed to age a week with each day. Maybe part of it was due to winter—the shorter days, the cold, the snow—it all made her more tired than when she worked similar hours and did similar chores in the summer and spring.

Maybe she could go home early. The camp crew was already dwindling, and soon the winter skeleton crew would be all that was left—only two to four men besides the Hansens, men who would drive sleighs over the snow-packed canyon road and into town. She'd talk to the foreman tonight; no need for an extra set of hands in the kitchen when the camp had dwindled in size by half since her arrival.

As she had every night for a week, she wrapped a shawl about herself, put on her mittens then carried the tub of dirty water out to the tree in the darkness. Before retiring to bed, she whispered a prayer of thanks that Butch wasn't around to surprise her here ever again. She'd never dare step into the winter night had he still been at camp.

The tub felt heavier today as she thought of going home. She'd miss the camp, what with the jokes and silliness—at least, she'd miss what had been pleasant about it aside from Butch Larsen. Most of all, she'd miss the time she'd spent with James, walking together along the canyon road, picking flowers, talking about nothing and everything. But that part was over anyway.

After reaching the pine tree, she tilted the tub, supporting it with one leg, and dumped the water at the base of the tree. Tracks made by past dish water had frozen into thick ice that looked both beautiful and dangerous at the same time. With lantern light spilling from the cookhouse behind her, she watched the water splash onto the ground and run over ice. Every movement she'd made since beginning the dishes was mechanical; it was how she could keep herself from thinking too much about James. She'd seen those flickers in his eye that meant he hoped for something more between them, a flicker she absolutely had to extinguish before he totally ruined their friendship, assuming it wasn't already ruined.

What was the man doing, kissing her like that? How could she ever have an intelligent talk around him again when all she could do was think about the way he'd kissed her by the light of the moon? Why did he have to turn their friendship on its head?

"Caroline. I hoped I'd see you." James's voice jumped out of the darkness. She clutched the top of her dress, as if that might help still the racing of her heart that came from the shock. Her other hand unceremoniously dropped the wash tub, which clattered to the ground loudly. She'd started at the sound, heart beating so hard, so erratically, she could hear it rushing in ears. She reached out for the support of the tree, but it was too far away. She clasped her hands in front of her and wondered where to look.

Not at his eyes. I can't do that.

"James. I didn't see you there. Good evening." She decided to be grateful that Butch was gone, and that she felt completely safe, physically speaking, with her old friend. But something in the tone of his voice put her senses on alert, like a bear sow protecting her cubs.

James stepped out of the darkness made by the trees and into the soft golden glow spilling from the cookhouse door. Shadows played across his features. Had he always had such a defined jawline? Such strong shoulders and arms? Perhaps he'd gained that shape, gradually, from working the roads in the canyon, and she simply hadn't noticed the change until now. At the sight, she had to force her gaze away.

She'd noticed some of these things when they'd sat together the other night; she wouldn't let herself think on them now. And she would never again look at James that way—as a *man*. He might try to ruin their friendship, but she wouldn't be party to it. No more than she already had been, at any rate.

Their friendship could yet be repaired after their kiss. And then they'd find other people to marry. Yes, she'd lose him one day when he fell for a silly girl and married, but with any luck, her future husband would like James and his wife enough that the four of them could go on carriage rides and visit one another for meals—perhaps even share holidays. She purposely ignored her dreams about seeing the world and escaping the valley.

Only after all those thoughts crossed her mind did she realize that he hadn't replied, that they'd been standing in silence for near half a minute.

"Do you—do you need something?" she asked. *Please need something from the cookhouse. Don't be swooning again.* She cursed the full moon above them for providing just the right romantic setting. The yellow-white moon made the snow sparkle. It could have come to life from a poem, and under normal circumstances, Caroline would have enjoyed the sight. *And don't mention the other night. Please, oh, please.*

"I do need something," James said, stepping forward. He held out his arm. Caroline braced herself, hoping he wouldn't touch her. But he held out a simple work shirt.

"Got a tear in one sleeve. Hoped maybe you could repair it for me."

Caroline suddenly found it easier to breathe. A tear that needed mending—that was all? Perhaps she'd avoided him all week for no reason. Finally able to smile, she reached for the shirt, not closing the distance between them, though, and inspected the fabric. The tear was clean and straight, right along the grain of the fabric. "I can fix this pretty easily. You'll have it back tomorrow after the midday meal. Will that work for you?"

"Yes, thank you," he said, but his voice seemed to say so much more.

She cleared her throat, slipped the shirt over the crook of her elbow and smiled. "Good night, James." She reached for the dish tub, intending to step past him and head to the cookhouse, where she'd put away the tub, wipe down the counters, then go to her room in the Hansens' house, where she'd get herself ready for bed.

She managed to take not three steps before James reached out and took her by the arm. Gently, not like Butch had. But all the same, her heart hammered against her ribs. She was acutely aware of the cold seeping through her boots, of her hem resting atop the snow—it would be sopping wet if she didn't get inside soon—and of her flaming cheeks, which had to be bright red, they felt so hot.

Unhand me, she wanted to say, but she didn't utter a word. Nor did she shake off his arm. A small part of her warmed at his touch; she could feel the heat of his hand through her shawl and sleeve—which sent her into further exasperations. She would *not* turn into a silly school girl. This was James, for heaven's sake. *James.* She turned her head to look at him, her brows raised in question. He nodded toward the tub, hinting that she needed to go.

"Caroline . . . Miss Campbell . . ."

Oh, no—not my formal name. If only Mrs. Hansen would come out of the cookhouse and call to her, saying that she'd forgotten to scrub a pot. Anything. But Mrs. Hansen had gone to the main house more than an hour hence.

Her eyes moved uneasily across the snow and up a tree trunk. They paused briefly at James's shoulder then lifted, slowly, to meet his gaze. She swallowed, her nerves making her unable to form a coherent thought.

I must know what to say to him. I must.

James reached forward and took the tub from her hands, then set it on the ground before grasping her hands in his. He gently rotated her to face him. His chin lowered, making one of his brown curls fall onto his forehead. She had an unruly urge to brush it away. She could brush it to the side and kiss the spot on his forehead where it had been.

Argh! The moon was playing tricks on her, too.

"Caroline," James said forcefully. "We have known each other for a very long time."

"Yes. Yes, we have." She wanted to pull away before the moon glittering on the snow made them both nonsensical, leading them to make a big mistake.

"I—I love you, Caroline," James said fervently. "I've always loved you. At first it was because you were a grand playmate. Then it developed into the infatuation of a young boy." He smiled his crooked grin, and, even knowing what was coming, she couldn't help but smile a bit in return. How could she not respond to that crooked smile and the compliment behind it?

But she couldn't encourage him. So she shook her head. "James, please . . ." Her voice trailed off as she tried to pull her hands away.

"Just hear me out. I have to say this."

She lowered her gaze to the ground, to their snow-covered boots, to the dish tub lying askew. A light snowfall began, dusting everything around them. The perfect setting for romance—except that her toes were nearly frozen, and she wasn't supposed to be wooed by her childhood chum, kiss or no kiss.

Except for the maddening fact that she could still feel his kiss on her lips.

James would not be swayed, and there was no way to escape this mess unless she made a ruckus and yell—not an option with someone as kind as James. After all their years of friendship, she had to let him speak, however miserable the prospect made her.

"But boyhood infatuation has changed, blossomed, right here as we've been together. I cannot imagine my life without you. I love you, Caroline. Truly. I'm *in love* with you. Will you—"

His voice caught, and took a steadying breath. His thumb stroked the top of her hand. It only made her heart beat faster.

Then, right there in the middle of the snow, he dropped to one knee. Caroline tried to urge him back to his feet. "Get up. Please. You're going to soak your trousers and catch your death of cold—"

"Then you care about me? About my well-being?"

"Of course I do. You're a dear." Only after she'd spoken the words did she realize what he meant—did she love him? "But not in the way you—"

"Will you do the honor of accepting my hand in marriage?" The words came out in a rush, as if they had been rehearsed a thousand times.

And there it was. She'd dreamed of her first proposal— the first of many, she'd dreamed—but the young man asking for her hand wasn't supposed to be James. How could she reject his offer and expect him to be her friend after?

But she couldn't very well accept him, either. She didn't love him that way. Marriages of convenience and necessity happened often—several of her neighbors had them, and by all accounts, they were "successful." But she wanted nothing to do with being bound to someone out of either convenience or necessity. She wanted passion, love.

She shook her head. "James, I'm—" Now it was her voice that caught. She was already mourning the loss of what they'd had and would lose—what they'd lost after their kiss and what would be lost to them forever after tonight. "I can't. I'm so, so sorry."

With that, she abandoned the dish tub and the cookhouse. She ran blindly through the snow to the foreman's house, where she flew inside and slammed the door, caring nothing about stopping to stomp the snow off her boots on the porch before entering. No, she had to find some semblance of asylum, even if it meant dripping melted snow all over the tiny house.

Mr. Hansen sat in a rocker by the fire, a pipe tucked into the corner of his mouth. "You look like you've seen a ghost."

"I'm . . . I'm not feeling well. I should go lie down." Caroline headed toward the back room, where her bed was, but as she crossed the space, Mr. Hansen apparently had other ideas.

"I'm thinking you look touched by cupid, I do—but upset over the direction of his arrow." He chuckled, his chest shaking as she whirled around, hand on the door to the room as she gaped at him with disbelief. He stroked his beard, removed the pipe, and smirked at her.

"I—I—" Why could she not form a complete sentence?

Mr. Hansen shook his head and clucked like an old gossipy woman. "You young things, always making everything worse for yourself than it needs to be. Just say yes to the boy. You'll both be much happier—trust me on that account."

He knew? He didn't even ask *which* boy. Presumptuous man. Anger boiled inside her. How *dare* he give her advice on love and marriage? This gray-haired, wrinkled man, who'd been married not one, but *four* times. A biting retort hovered on her lips, but she opted to not disrespect her employer and instead managed through clenched teeth, "I plan to head for home in the morning, as I believe my services are no longer needed. If you could arrange transport, I would be grateful. Good night, Mr. Hansen."

Chapter Five

ortunately, Mr. Hansen took Caroline's declaration seriously, arranging for her to be driven home on the next load of wood headed to town the following day. She packed up her few possessions and climbed onto the back of the wagon with the stack of fallen trees, refusing a spot on the bench up front. She may have made the mistake of spending time alone with a man without a chaperone, but she wouldn't do it again—particularly in public.

The ride home felt twice as long as the ride to camp, and maybe it was somewhat longer, what with the added snow. She purposely kept her eyes fixed on her lap until she figured they'd certainly traveled enough miles to be beyond the road crew. Only then did she raise her eyes to look at the canyon and its snow-covered trees. And there was James, filling a hole in the ground, shovel in hand. He glanced up, did a double-take, and then his gaze locked on Caroline's. She swallowed against the knot in her throat. They were far enough apart that speaking wasn't an option, but she could see a new tension pinching his eyes, a gentle downturn of his mouth.

I did that. I made him sad.

He raised a hand and waved. Caroline couldn't sit there without responding; she hesitantly lifted a mitten-covered hand in return. It felt like lead.

With a lurch, the wagon turned from the Wood Camp road onto the main canyon road, throwing her to one side of the wagon as it veered hard left. By the time she'd righted herself, her vision had blurred with tears. She blinked hard and wiped them away, but James was no longer in sight.

◦◦◦

Caroline should have been glad to be home, but not even seeing Bertha's improvement raised her spirits. Her mother was a breath away from calling the physician for Caroline. "You're so melancholy all the time," she said. "What if you caught something at Wood Camp?"

"I caught nothing, Mother," Caroline said. "I'm just tired. " But inside she added, *I caught nothing but a guilty conscience.*

So it was with pleasure and relief that Caroline saw her best friend Sarah arriving one day with word of an upcoming dance at the city dance hall, in just three days, and it would go well past midnight. For the first time in far too long, Caroline felt excited. She would spend the evening twirling about the floor with as many young men as she could. She would laugh and flirt and fly across the floor until her sides *and* her feet ached.

The day of the dance, Caroline went to Sarah's house, gown in tow, and the two young women got ready together. They curled their hair with tongs. Sarah wove a pale pink ribbon throughout Caroline's dark hair, creating a stunning effect.

"Too bad we don't have fresh flowers this time of year," Sarah said, tilting her head as she studied Caroline's hair.

"You would look devastating with a sprig of baby's breath tucked behind your ear."

An hour later, they entered the dance hall and discarded their wraps in a side room. Caroline watched the milling crowd, heard the small band at one end, and a thrill fluttered in her chest. Women twirled in a reel, wearing colorful dresses and hairstyles. Clusters of attendees hovered at the edges.

Sarah clutched her arm. "Isn't this better than the boring old Wood Camp?"

"It is," Caroline admitted, her voice breathy with excitement. The Wood Camp had held a few evening reels, but it was only ever the men clapping and dancing alone by the fire—assuming they were fortunate enough to have a fiddler. Of course, she could never participate in such an activity, not as the only female. Even if Mrs. Hansen had agreed to dance, it wouldn't have been proper—two women with nearly twenty men? And after Butch arrived, she'd shunned all the men . . . except for James.

But here, oh, it was much different: plenty of men and women both, and the chance to dance with lots of different partners.

Yes. Different partners. Lots and lots of partners. That's what she needed—a bit of fun to distract herself from the awful moment behind the cookhouse with James—and of the final moment she'd see him on the wintery road as she left. Her stomach turned on itself at the memory of his voice, his pleading eyes, as he knelt in the snow and asked for her hand. How he'd begun the moment with confidence and a glint of happiness—love?—in his eye, but she'd left him, run away, and hadn't spoken to him since. She felt like a coward, like she'd shoved a dagger into his heart.

But it wasn't my fault, she argued. *He should have known I never meant anything to come of it. All we had was a harmless flirtation—a harmless kiss—and before that, a pleasant friendship. I never meant more than that. He ruined all of it.*

But even she couldn't quite agree with herself. James was a good man, just not . . . well, not what she imagined her future husband would be like. James was an open book, easily read and comprehended the first time through. She wanted someone with a little mystery, someone with a little unpredictability in them. Excitement. No life of drudgery and boredom for her.

As sweet and kind as James was, her future lay with someone else.

Another flash of memory, of a different evening came to her mind, when he'd found her crying in the cookhouse after the incident with Butch. The way he'd spoken to comfort her, his strong embrace, his kiss . . .

She inhaled sharply. *Stop it. That kiss meant nothing. It was a moment of weakness for us both; he took it too seriously.* But the swirl of butterflies in her middle wouldn't agree.

"Here," Sarah said, nudging a cup of punch toward her. Caroline had been lost in her own thoughts long enough that she hadn't noticed Sarah's absence. She welcomed the interruption as well as the cause for it.

"Thank you." She took the cup and sipped the pale pink drink.

"It's already sweltering in here," Sarah said, waving her hand before her face to cool off. "Strange that it's winter, but hot enough in here to fry bacon." She laughed and drank her punch, downing it in a less-than-feminine manner.

Caroline smiled and forced herself to sip from her cup in spite of her thirst. Even the mention of bacon made her ache; she'd forever think of James complimenting her on her perfect, crisp bacon at the Wood Camp. Her eyes watering, she tilted her head to the ceiling and blinked, willing the tears not to fall.

I said no for a reason. I won't marry just for security, just to avoid being an old maid.

Her thoughts were interrupted by a deep voice. "Miss Simpson? May I have the next dance? A mazurka is about to start." It was Lawrence Campbell, a young man she'd known for years. But she hadn't realized he'd grown so tall, nor that his voice had lowered so much. Surely he hadn't changed so much since she'd left for the Wood Camp? Or had she just not noticed young men like Lawrence before she left?

Tall, with thick blond hair, broad shoulders, and a cleft in his chin. He was *handsome*. Lawrence. Who would have thought? Better yet, the mazurka brought couples into an almost closed dance position. She'd even get to touch his waist briefly. It was almost—but not quite—as scandalous as the waltz.

Only after she'd taken in Lawrence was she aware that the music and dancing had stopped temporarily—the reel had ended, and new couples were taking the floor for the mazurka. A bald man with a pink face was calling for partners to take the floor.

"We'll be starting in just *one more minute*," he said, almost like a threat, as he held up one finger high and showing it off to the room, first to his left and then to his right.

"Miss Simpson?" Lawrence said again. This time he glanced over his shoulder at the bald man and then the floor, which was filling quickly. The fiddler and other players were ready to begin a new piece.

At the sound of Lawrence's deep voice, a rush went through Caroline. This was her chance to show that she was moving on, available, and ready to enjoy her time as a young woman before settling down. Not that she intended to "settle" for anything. How she'd find a way out of secluded Cache Valley, she'd never know. At least the railroad spur had come to town. She could save money—somehow, maybe doing sewing and mending and odd jobs—and buy a ticket to . . . where?

Caroline shook her head, refusing to think of either the past or the future. The present was all that mattered. Lawrence was waiting for an answer. She quickly gathered her senses and flashed a wide smile.

"I'd be honored, Mr. Campbell." She thrust her half-full glass toward Sarah. With a prayer shot heavenward that she didn't look as ready to cry as she really felt, she said, "Yes, of course." She took his arm, and he led her to the floor.

The dance with Lawrence passed in a delightful blur, her feet keeping time, her skirts swishing across the floor. Every time they faced each other, he smiled at her, and she smiled back. At first, each touch of his hand, covered with callouses from physical labor, reminded her of James, of the blisters he'd gotten fixing the Wood Camp road, the ones she'd cleaned and bound after his first week when his hands weren't used to the new work.

The dance ended, and as the room applauded the band, she was able to stop thinking about James. Again. She had to find a way to keep him from her mind once and for all. It was only guilt for hurting his feelings that she kept thinking of him. Nothing more.

Lawrence bowed formally, which made her laugh. She curtseyed, and then he took her arm and brought her back to Sarah, who still stood where Caroline had left her, looking every inch green with envy.

"I don't suppose those feet have a polka in them?" Sarah asked him with a musical lilt in her voice. She cocked her head coyly, waiting for an answer—and knowing that a polka was next.

Lawrence looked between the girls, and Caroline saved him. "I'm sure he'd be happy to escort you onto the floor." She shot him a grin, assuring him that she wouldn't be jealous. And she wouldn't be. She had every intention of dancing with as many eligible men as she could tonight.

Lawrence had no sooner walked off with Sarah than Matthew Cook appeared, asking her to join him for the polka, and just in time. And so it went. Dance after dance, Caroline twirled across the floor. Every time she was certain that she couldn't take another step, that her feet ached too much, and that she was too out of breath, another handsome man snagged her arm, and she was off again—and loving every moment of it. At times, she wondered what dances couples enjoyed in big cities like New York, rather than the old-fashioned ones played every time here in Cache Valley.

As a quadrille began, she released her partner's arm as part of the pattern on the floor, and found herself turning in a circle, holding a familiar calloused, gentle hand. Her eyes flew up to James's, and she had to squelch a little gasp.

No reaction. None. Don't you dare.

The moment passed quickly as the pattern changed and she returned to her partner, Michael Bradford. During the rest of the dance—especially when she and James touched—avoiding a hot flush creeping up her cheeks took effort.

When had James gotten back in town? Of course, it made perfect sense; the roads didn't need to be constantly fixed when they were covered with snow and loads and loads of wagons weren't being taken down the canyon. He probably could have left camp weeks before she had, but he'd stayed . . . why? For her?

Somehow she managed to nod at him, smiling ever-so slightly then look forward in the direction they were moving. She hoped that outwardly, she looked calm and composed, because inside she was nothing but a disturbed hornet's nest, buzzing in circles around and around. She was sure that if the music didn't end soon—and it surely had several minutes to go—that her heart would leap out of her chest. Or she'd collapse on the floor—from exhaustion or emotion, she wasn't sure which. How had she not seen him at the dance before now? Had he just arrived, or had she been so involved with her partners that she hadn't noticed him on the floor?

Without warning, the band's two horns squeaked to an abrupt halt, the three strings sharp, and the piano halted, all before the rest of the room had any idea what was going on. Caroline and Michael both cringed at the screeching sounds and turned as one toward the band, as did the entire room, to find the source of the disturbance.

A man wearing a winter coat, snow still on his shoulders, stood where the bald man had earlier. He pulled off his knit cap and raised his hands, motioning them downward to quiet the room. Soon the hall was silent save for the dancers' breath, which was gradually returning to normal.

"There's been a snow slide up the canyon," he said, puffing as if he'd run a mile being chased by a bear. His cheeks were bright pink; he'd been out in the cold for some time. The throng murmured in surprise and worry. Based on the man's movements, facial expression, and tone, something was wrong. Deeply, deeply wrong. Something clenched in Caroline's chest as she waited for the noise to die down and for him to go on.

He took a deep breath, evening it out so he could speak loudly and reach the entire room. "A team went up to Wood Camp to get to work before spring. They got caught in the slide. Appears we've got at least two men buried in the snow. We need as many able men as possible to come right away to help in the rescue." A roar of dismay went up as several men headed toward their coats and hats, when the man stopped them.

"Wait!" He yelled this, his voice somehow reaching above the chaos. Everyone turned. "It's a dangerous job we've got. We'll be digging through a snow slide, and who knows but what we'll trigger another slide and lose some men who came to rescue those already buried. Consider carefully before you volunteer. For those going, meet me out front in twenty minutes in full winter gear and with shovels, lanterns, and any other supplies you may have, including food. This may take days." He looked over the crowd. His mouth trembled, as if he fought back emotion. "That's all," he managed, but it was quiet, and Caroline could barely hear him even though she stood only feet from the band.

An odd, numbing shock washed over her as she watched people rush around her and the band members hurriedly putting away their instruments. Men said goodbye to their crying wives. The dance had clearly come to an abrupt end. Shaken, Caroline determined to find Sarah and her parents so they could go home.

Turning one direction and then the next, she scanned the crowded room for Sarah or her parents, but her eyes instead caught familiar curly brown hair—James moving toward the door, with a purpose in his step.

No! Caroline cried inside. James could *not* go with the rescue party, risking his life. What if he were to . . . She ran across the floor, reducing the distance between them, hoping to reach James before he made such a terrible, dangerous decision. His mother saw him too, as she ran up from behind, reaching him first. She stopped him, taking him by the shoulders and turning him around.

"You can't," she said. "You're my only son."

"I have to. So many other men have wives and children at home. I . . . don't." He gently but forcefully removed her hands from his shoulders. He kissed her cheek, and she reluctantly moved to the side, nodding as if she understood. She stood right in front of Caroline. If he were to raise his eyes even a fraction, he'd see her.

His mother lowered her hands and clasped them to her chin. "Please, James . . . please promise me you'll be careful."

"I'll be careful. I promise." As he spoke, James turned his head looked directly at Caroline, as if he'd known exactly where she'd been standing. Maybe he did. His eyes look pained—not unlike the night she'd turned him away . . .

She willed the memory to leave her mind, but it clung to her as their eyes locked for a few seconds—an eternity that lasted for the briefest breath.

James still gazed at Caroline as his mother cried into her hands. "I have to go. Maybe I can help one man return to the one he loves."

He was speaking directly to Caroline, no question. His words were for her and her alone. If she hadn't spurned him, he wouldn't feel the need to leave, endangering his life. He was being stubborn and . . . and yes, courageous. What if he was doing this solely because he didn't have a loved one waiting for him besides his mother?

What if I had accepted his offer? Would he have stayed behind for the sake of his fiancée—for a loved one at home who needed him?

Before she could gather her wits about her, he turned and was gone. His mother wept even harder. Caroline wanted to do the same, drop to the floor, even, and sob openly. Or run after James and tell him he couldn't go. Never. He couldn't.

Because . . . well, because he can't. That's why.

Chapter Six

All thoughts of finding Sarah and her parents had fled. Caroline stood by the door, heedless of the chill as she watched several sleighs heading out, away, shrinking from sight. She stayed there until the last was a speck on the horizon. Her chest felt oddly heavy and hollow all at once, as if her heart rode on one of the sleighs, and lead had filled its place. As if she'd never feel quite whole again unless her heart returned, safe and sound.

I love him. I really, really love him. The words echoed in her mind, and for the first time, she didn't fight them or qualify them. James didn't resemble the man of her fantasies—never would—but suddenly that didn't matter. Only his well-being did. He held her heart, and if he were hurt or killed by a snow slide, she'd never recover.

It's my fault he left. It will be my fault if something dreadful happens to him. Oh, what a fool I've been!

Who cared of adventures and dashing men and trailing beaus on a string? Living here in the valley would never be drudgery if it was with James. She knew that now. But would she ever have the chance to make it so?

"Caroline, come. You'll catch your death of cold." Sarah's voice pierced the haze, and her warm touch made Caroline blink and turn to face her. Her friend's brow crinkled with concern. "You look unwell—ready to faint. Come. We must get you home." She put her arm around Caroline's waist.

"I'm fine," she tried to protest, although she wasn't fine. She wasn't well. Indeed, she felt so weak that had Sarah not come when she did, Caroline may have dropped right to the floor as Sarah had predicted.

"Come," Sarah said again, this time gently leading Caroline away from the door and to a bench along one wall. Her father arrived a moment later and spread her wrap across her shoulders, which he must have retrieved from the coat room.

"Thank you," Caroline managed, holding it together in front and wishing it would warm the cavity inside her that seemed filled with ice.

Sarah's mother fussed over Caroline, bringing her a drink, stroking her hair, wiping her brow with a damp cloth. Part of Caroline wanted to scream and demand she be left alone in her misery, but she didn't have the strength, and she knew Sarah's mother only meant well, so she submitted to the woman's well-intended ministrations.

Somehow she got home and ready for bed, but every movement felt forced, empty. She couldn't. Her parents stayed up later than she did, talking in a flurry over the disaster in the canyon. Lit candle in hand, Caroline climbed the stairs to her bedroom, secretly grateful that they weren't talking to her about the accident, that they were too caught up in their own emotions to notice that she moved about like a ghost.

In her room, which she shared with Bertha, Caroline didn't go to bed at first. She told herself it was because she didn't want to disturb her sister, who seemed to be sleeping peacefully, something that didn't often happen. In reality, Caroline knew she wouldn't be able to sleep, and the idea of lying awake, staring at the cracks in the ceiling for hours on end, made her shudder. She set the candle on the windowsill, sat on the small bench beside the window, and gazed out at the wintery night. The moon itself felt cold and hard with its silvery light, not like the warm glow she remembered from the night James had proposed.

James. She closed her eyes, and for the first time since the dance had broken up, tears fell. Caroline leaned against the window pane as she cried, almost glad for the biting cold on her forehead. It seemed wrong that she was safe and warm in her home, while so many men were out in the brutal cold, going up the canyon to either save the men in the slide or retrieve their bodies. To come home . . . or get caught in a new slide triggered by their movements.

She tried to calm her emotions by breathing through her mouth. All that did was fog up the window, making it hard to see out of. She brought up her forearm and wiped her breath away with her forearm. She couldn't see the canyon road from here, but a clear view outside gave her an odd sense of comfort, as if it brought her the slightest bit closer to James, who was out there, somewhere.

Oh, please keep him safe. Please. At least long enough to tell him I was wrong. That I love him.

But she could see part of a crossroad and Main Street below. There was a good chance that any rescue party would pass by that way. *It could take days before anyone returns,* she reminded herself. Yet she gazed on.

As a little girl, she'd knelt on the floor against this bench, clasping her hands and whispering prayers. She'd had such faith. Caroline looked at the floor, half expecting to see a six-year-old version of herself in a little blue nightgown, praying for whatever weighed on her heart. Caroline remembered praying—intently—for something, even crying. But today, she couldn't fathom what could have caused such pain in her little heart.

I never knew pain until this night.

Caroline kept vigil at the window, not leaving her spot once, keeping her eyes trained on the sliver of Main Street, all night. She pulled her knees to her chest, leaned against the wall beside the window, and rested, as much as she could, all the while thinking of her hopes and dreams and what she could say to James if she ever saw him alive again.

༺❦༻

She didn't think she'd fallen asleep until someone nudged her arm and she awoke with a start.

"Were you here all night?" he mother said, concern lacing her voice. She whispered, surely to avoid waking Bertha, who still slumbered in the bed she and Caroline shared.

Caroline merely nodded, heartsick and weary, unable to explain what was wrong with her. She felt as if speaking of her love for James would somehow diminish it, at least for now. She wouldn't speak of it to anyone unless it was James himself.

Which means I may not ever tell a living soul.

"Come, rest in bed," her mother urged. "You look so tired."

Caroline gave a sharp shake of her head. "No. I can't leave the window. Not until I know . . ."

When her voice trailed off, her mother's eyes lit up with understanding. Her gaze went to the window, and she took a step closer. "Are you looking for the rescue party then?"

In part, yes. All Caroline could do was nod.

Her mother leaned close and kissed Caroline's temple then whispered in her ear. "He will come back, right as rain. You'll see."

With that, her mother stood, straightened Bertha's blanket, and walked out of the room. Caroline turned to stare at her mother's retreating figure. How did she know? Had she always known, when Caroline herself didn't, not until last night? Oh, how blind she'd been! How could she have not understood?

Her mother didn't bother her further. She brought food and drink at times throughout the day, but didn't so much as ask whether Caroline planned to clean the chicken coop or churn the butter or help around the house in any other way. Caroline ate a bite of food here and there, but had no appetite; everything tasted bland, like paper. She spent the next night at the window as well.

The following morning, her mother woke her again, but this time with an eager shake of her shoulder. "Caroline! Caroline, wake up. Mrs. Holmes next door says her husband returned with one group last night—and that James was in the company."

"He's . . . alive?" She hardly dared say the word.

Her mother nodded, eyes watering. "The other companies are still in the canyon, but so far, the only men they've lost were the two originally caught in the slide—bless the poor King and Osterholdt families."

"He's alive." Caroline said the words a second time, trying to hear them and believe them. "Is he home?"

"I believe so, yes," her mother said.

Caroline jumped up from her place on the bench. Her muscles ached from being cramped in the same position for so long, but she cared nothing for that; James was alive, and he was home, at the neighboring farm!

Still in her nightgown, she shoved her stocking-covered feet into her boots, flung a knitted shawl about her shoulders, and raced out of the room, down the stairs, and out of the house. Her hair had been in a long braid, the same braid down her back that she'd put it into when she'd gotten ready for bed after the dance. Hair stuck out from it at odd angles, but she didn't care. All that mattered was James.

She raced past the barn, around the corn field, and eventually through the hole in the fence between farms that she and James had used as children to travel between the two lots. Heart pounding, she put all her strength into her legs, flying through a spud field and an orchard before reaching the back of the family house. She rapped hard half a dozen times if once, then stood back to wait, breathless.

That's when she caught a glimpse of herself in the side window—night clothes, boots, part of her legs showing above the boots, hair standing on end, dark circles under her eyes. What would James think of her showing up in such a disgraceful condition? What would his mother and father think? She glanced back toward her family's farm; should she hurry home and avoid the humiliation of being seen like this?

But no. She tilted her head up to the bedroom window where James had always slept. He was up there right now, probably sleeping hard after a night, a day, and a night of straight work. It was early in the day, but his mother was already working in the kitchen; Caroline could see the glow of candle or a lamp or two through a window.

The door opened suddenly with a click and a squeak, drawing her attention back to the door. "Caroline? Is that you?"

The voice wasn't female, and it wasn't old. It was . . . dare she hope . . .

"James?" Her voice came out as barely a squeak.

He opened the door all the way then pushed the screen door open on its creaking hinges. "Caroline, it *is* you. What in tarnation are you doing here, like this?"

He wasn't happy to see her; he was embarrassed. She shuffled her feet and swallowed, her throat having suddenly grown thick and dry. "I—I—never mind. I'll be on my way. I'm glad to see you home safely." Likely the greatest understatement she'd ever heard, and it had come from her own lips. Feeling her face flush hot, she whirled around, wishing she could escape gracefully instead of tromping away through two feet of snow.

"Don't go."

She stopped but didn't turn around. She closed her eyes, not trusting herself to speak without revealing her true emotions. James would never want her now that she'd disgraced herself like this. Would he?

"Caroline, come here. You don't look well."

Slowly, fearing her heart would fail her, she pivoted to face him again, knowing that she looked atrocious and had come here in a manner that no young woman hoping to have a beau—or fiancé—would ever dream of. Yet when she met his gaze, she saw the same thing that had been there before when he'd kissed her. After he'd kissed her. Outside the cookhouse when he'd knelt in the snow and took her by the hand.

He still loves me.

"Please come inside," James urged. "You must be freezing."

She shook her head. Not that she wasn't cold—she was; she could hardly feel her toes, and the winter chill had bitten her nose and the tips of her ears something fierce. But she didn't feel cold, not inside. The icy hollow in her chest was melting, the light that had left her life when James drove off into the night had returned. Hope. That's what it was. And love.

But he was a proud man. He might love her—she could tell by the look in his eye, and if a man loved her when she looked and acted opposite of what a ladylike young woman should, then he'd always love her. How to close the gap?

She licked her lips, knowing what she had to do. It wouldn't be easy. It would take a healthy dose of humble pie. But she would do it.

Caroline stepped closer to the house and held out her hand. Eyebrow rising with curiosity, James stepped beyond the screen door, which shut behind him with a metallic clang. "What is it?"

She held his warm, calloused hand in both of hers, hardly able to believe that it was still warm—alive!—and here, in her hand. How did she get to be so lucky?

Before her courage failed her, she dropped into the snow on one knee.

James gasped. "What's wrong? Have you caught cold?" He must have thought she'd fallen from weakness, not that she'd intentionally knelt on one knee.

Instead of answering his question, Caroline licked her lips again and forced words from her mouth. "James, would you do me the honor of making me your wife?"

Nothing but silence for at least the span of five heartbeats. She prayed that no one else had seen what she'd just done; she'd be the laughing stock of the city if anyone knew that she had proposed marriage to a man.

He hadn't answered. Maybe he didn't want her after all. When she could stand the silence no longer, she looked up, face hot, arms trembling from the building emotions inside her. James's brow had drawn together into a look of confusion.

"I don't understand. I thought—"

"I was wrong," Caroline interrupted. "I *do* love you. I didn't know it. Not until I thought I might have lost you forever." Her voice caught, and she took two steadying breaths before going on. "I cannot imagine living my life without you. I love you James. I do. And I want to be your wife. If you'll still have me. I'll—I'll understand if you don't, after the way I treated you."

James urged Caroline to her feet. He took both of her hands in both of his and gazed into her eyes. Forget melting; her insides simmered and boiled over. "I've never wanted anyone else."

He leaned in. Caroline met him halfway, knowing what was coming. Her stomach flipped three times before their lips touched. Their last kiss had woken something inside her, but it paled in comparison. This time she knew he loved her, and she knew she loved him in return. And that made each touch, each movement of his lips on hers, mean ten times more than the other kiss ever could have. He released her hands to wrap his arms around her. She reached around his neck, gently pulled his face closer to hers as the kiss deepened into something she hadn't known could exist.

She could have contentedly stayed in his arms forever but finally managed to pull away from his lips—those lips that fit hers like a puzzle piece—and say, "Is that a yes?" She thought that the kiss had given her his answer, but she needed to hear the words. "Will you marry me, James?"

He stroked her hair; she closed her eyes and reveled in his touch, not thinking of her disheveled hair. A shiny tear appeared in his eye, tumbled over, and tracked down his cheek. She reached up with a finger and wiped it; he closed his eyes at the touch. She cupped his face in her hand and took in the face of this amazing man who'd waited for her heart, not knowing if his feelings would ever be requited.

"Yes," James said. "I'll marry you, Caroline Campbell. Nothing would give me more joy." She pulled back enough for them both to peer at her snow-covered boots. "And I'll try very hard to never tease you about the manner in which you asked for my hand."

She laughed, full and warm, the first time in days, if not weeks. "I won't mind teasing at my expense if it means having *you*."

James stepped over to a bush beside the house, where he broke off a thin twig. He returned to Caroline, who watched in confusion as he first held it between his palms and blew on the twig to warm it then formed it into a circle, tied the ends with a knot then broke off the rest of the twig. "I'll get a better ring for you soon, but until then, here's something little so everyone will know you're taken."

He slipped the makeshift ring onto her left hand then kissed it. She'd keep the ring forever, tucked inside a jewelry box, or perhaps on a chain. She never wanted to forget this moment.

She hoped the thrills jumping inside her body when he touched her would never die. He kissed her hand, then her wrist, and her forearm then shifted to her ear, her jawline, her chin, and finally, her lips.

ABOUT ANNETTE LYON

Annette Lyon is a Whitney Award winner, the recipient of Utah's Best of State medal for fiction and the author of nine novels, a cookbook, and a grammar guide as well as over a hundred articles. She's a senior editor at Precision Editing Group and a cum laude graduate from BYU with a degree in English. When she's not writing, editing, knitting, or eating chocolate, she can be found mothering and avoiding the spots on the kitchen floor. Find her online at http://blog.annettelyon.com and on Twitter: @AnnetteLyon

Visit Annette Lyon's Website: www.annettelyon.com

Caroles on the Green

by Joyce DiPastena

Other Works by Joyce DiPastena

Loyalty's Web

Illuminations of the Heart

Dangerous Favor

Candlelight Courting

The Ring

"Father, must we feast like this every night? I shall be quite fat by Epiphany."

Lord Stephen answered his daughter with barely a glance. He swirled the mulled wine in his goblet and mumbled around a mouth full of roast capon. "Ask Isabel. We will do what your sister thinks best."

Isabel sat between her father and younger sister at the high table on the dais of the great hall of Weldon Castle. She smiled at Agnes, but beneath a white tablecloth stained with grease and sauces from their meal, she tapped her toe impatiently in response to her sister's question.

"Had you eaten more than three bites of tonight's feast," Isabel said to Agnes, "I might feel myself reproved by your complaint. I have spent a month planning these festivities and a good fortnight laboring over the menus for our guests. You were too busy flittering about like a bird to help me, and now you peck at your food like one. A willow reed would have to double its width to compete with your slender figure."

"I would not flitter so if you would give me something more amusing to do than embroider more shirts for Father," Agnes said with a pout on her pretty fifteen-year-old lips.

"Like what?" Isabel asked, though she already knew how Agnes would answer.

"Like do sums. I am ever so much more clever with numbers than you are, but you will not let me near the household accounts, even when you have added the columns so many times that your eyes grow red and it gives you a headache."

"Sweetness, your husband will have clerks to add sums for you, as we did before Edmund Clark retired to the abbey."

Agnes twisted a lock of golden hair about her finger as she did when she was vexed. "That was four years ago, and every time Father wishes to engage a new clerk, you say that Edmund mismanaged the spice accounts, and you will not let us be cheated again by dishonest or incompetent servants. So you add and add and add, double and triple checking, when I would be sure of the correct sums on the very first try."

"I let Edmund teach you to read," Isabel said. "I assure you, reading is vastly more enjoyable than adding numbers. Come, Agnes, let us not quarrel about this now. Father has agreed to let us dance some caroles after dinner. You will like that."

Isabel had flirted before with the idea of dancing the lively circle songs, which were frowned on by the Church, but she had respected their father's hesitance until this year. Once she had made up her mind to find a husband for Agnes, she had firmly factored dancing into the Christmas celebrations, winning their father's consent by promising to keep the dancing circumspect and private—as though she would be caught doing anything as undignified as dancing on the village green like her father's serfs, even were the green not covered with snow. Carole dancing would be the perfect opportunity to watch Agnes interact with prospective suitors.

The soft strains of recorder, rebec, and viol floated down from the musicians' gallery, weaving their melodies in and out of the steady patter of conversation rumbling through the hall. Isabel nibbled on a mushroom pasty, savoring the smooth richness of the cheese that flowed over her tongue as she studied by turns the knights who ate at the sideboards below the dais. She had made certain to sprinkle a fair sampling of handsome young men among the graying men and women of her father's generation. Perforce many of them had brought their sisters, but Isabel held little fear of any of them posing a serious threat to Agnes's delicate beauty. She had invited a few knights on her own behalf as well: Sir Theo of the shy smiles, who had sent her that pretty posy of periwinkles and white violets at the end of last summer; Sir Eustace of the smoldering eye and flattering tongue, who had made her feel desirable again after the debacle of her courtship with—

"You do not mind that I asked Sir Lucian to join us, do you?" Agnes asked, apparently following Isabel's gaze to the broad-shouldered knight wearing an acorn-shaped cap atop his dark blond curls. The exotic embroidery worked around its brim bespoke of an Oriental influence favored by many knights returned from the last Crusade. He would have been the most handsome knight at the feast had it not been for his slightly off-kilter nose. A stir of guilt squirmed in Isabel, but she tamped it firmly down.

It was your own fault, Lucian de Warrene.

"I only invited him because Ronwen begged me to," Agnes said, nudging Isabel's gaze away from Lucian to the flaxen-haired woman who sat on Lord Stephen's left. "And because you told me you were at quits with him. Are you truly? Because I would never, ever have agreed to it otherwise." Agnes drew Isabel's hand beneath the tablecloth and squeezed it fiercely, whispering, "It frightened me, Bel, to see you weep so. Did I do wrong?"

Isabel felt her smile become more strained as she met her sister's anxious eyes, but she kept the corners of her lips relentlessly turned up. "Nonsense, dearest. They were tears of relief that I came to my senses before it was too late. Sir Lucian and I should never have suited each other in the least."

She made no effort to lower her voice to match her sister's. Lord Stephen thumped down his goblet and turned to his eldest daughter with rare sternness. "You may do as you will with Sir Lucian, Isabel, but you have given me your word—"

"Yes, yes, Father, I know. I told you I would choose a husband by Epiphany, and I will."

Lord Stephen grunted and returned to his roast capon.

Isabel saw her cousin Ronwen smirk. This marriage mischief had been her doing. Lord Stephen had been perfectly content to let Isabel walk in her mother's slippers after the Lady Felicia's death four years ago, directing the affairs of their family, until Ronwen had come to live with them. Lord Stephen had made a few half-hearted suggestions for marriage partners for his eldest daughter through the years, but he accepted Isabel's rejection of each, allowing her to reach the age of nineteen still unwed. Isabel suspected he had actually been pleased when a promising courtship by their neighbor's son, Sir Lucian de Warrene, had unraveled, for she knew her father was far too indolent to go through the trouble of finding himself a new wife when he had a perfectly capable daughter to maintain the tranquil flow of his life.

Isabel and Lucian had grown up together as little more than casual friends, but had reunited with a fresh perception of each other after Lucian returned from the Crusade with his father. The formerly rawboned squire had become a bronzed, muscular young knight who carried himself with a compelling self-assurance. Ronwen, sent to join her uncle's daughters by a disinterested brother when her parents died, had strutted and simpered and fluttered her flaxen lashes in vain, trying to win Lucian's attentions away from Isabel. But time had accomplished what Ronwen's flirtations had not. Provoked beyond bearing by Lucian's high-handed manners, Isabel had at last declared him intolerable and banished him from the castle and her sorely tried affections.

It had not surprised Isabel that Ronwen had swooped in to pick up the shattered pieces of Lucian's heart. It had appalled her, however, to discover Ronwen to be so insecure in the knight's budding devotion as to feel as if the only way to secure him safely and permanently was to see Isabel married to another man.

"You really mean to do it, Bel?" Agnes whispered, clearly wishing not to draw Lord Stephen's attention again. "Marry one of these men?"

"Any one but that one," Isabel murmured, nodding her head in Lucian's direction. This time she kept her voice soft as well.

"I thought you would talk Father out of it again."

"I tried. But Ronwen told him he was selfish to make me a spinster merely for the sake of his own comfort. She was right, of course, about Father being selfish, but when she added that men would think he had sired a termagant whom he could not marry off, her words stung his pride as well as his conscience. Just because he is lazy does not mean that he wishes to admit it. He cares for the world's opinion enough that he will no longer listen to me, especially when he thinks he has another daughter to take my place when I am gone."

"Does he not?"

"Of course not, sweetness. You are much too beautiful to let Father turn you into a drudge. Why do you suppose I am determined to see you betrothed before I wed? But I cannot leave Father miserable, so I must find him a wife as well."

"You have always been extremely efficient, Bel, even if you struggle at sums. Will you please choose me a man who is stupid with numbers, so perhaps he will let me help with his accounts?"

Isabel laughed, winning a suspicious look from Lord Stephen and, to the dismay of her suddenly tripping heart, a quick glance from Lucian's cornflower blue eyes.

A servant appeared with a tray of apple tarts baked in small, individual shells for each guest. Isabel turned her gaze away from the side tables and reached out to take one.

"If it please you, my lady," the servant said, "Marjory Cook prepared you one with extra apples. She marked it there, with that little cross on the top."

Isabel plucked the indicated tart from the platter and set it on her trencher. "Pray, thank Marjory Cook for me."

The servant bowed and offered a tart to Agnes. Although she took one and cut it open with her little dining knife, Isabel knew she meant to do no more than spread the filling around a bit. Isabel's own mouth watered for the treat. She had given explicit instructions that it be baked with minced apples, rather than ground, and that the filling be firmed with crushed almonds. With her knife, she cut a small hole in the upper crust, as was her habit, and employed her spoon in fishing out the raisins. Isabel could rule everyone in the castle except Marjory Cook. Neither blandishments nor threats had ever convinced Marjory to leave raisins out of Isabel's apple tart. "They simply belong there, my lady," Marjory always said.

Agnes reached her own spoon over, scooped up a few raisins from Isabel's growing discard pile and slid them into her mouth. "Mmm."

Isabel's tongue recoiled from the tiny wrinkled fruit, but she was pleased to see that they tempted her sister into delving for the raisins in her own tart.

"Do you think they will suit better than you?" Agnes asked after she'd nibbled the raisins in silence for a few minutes.

"Who, sweetness?"

"Ronwen and Sir Lucian."

Isabel resisted the impulse to glance down at the sideboards again. Instead, she stole another look past Lord Stephen at their cousin. Ronwen had plaited her flaxen hair with red holly berries. Isabel could not deny that the sixteen-year-old girl was lovely, though her insistence on wearing pale shades, such as the honey-colored gown she had donned for tonight, washed some of the bloom out of her cheeks. Isabel had sense enough to select rich greens and reds for herself, knowing they set off her black braids to their best advantage. Men called Isabel elegant and graceful, and since her father's ultimatum—"Choose, or I'll choose for you!"— she had not wanted for eager suitors of her own.

She saw Ronwen smile like a satisfied cat and tilt her head coyly while gazing steadfastly at someone sitting below the dais. Isabel need not look to know who the recipient of her cousin's coquettish approval might be.

"I am sure they will suit each other splendidly," Isabel said to her sister's query.

She plunged her spoon more vigorously into her tart, seeking a raisin that threatened to swim away then heard a tiny clink. Alarm flickered through her. Oh, she hoped a careless scullery maid had not spilled some broken pottery into the filling. Why, one of their guests might break a tooth! She must be sure before she sprang to her feet and shouted an embarrassing warning. She swished her spoon beneath the suspicious lump and lifted it free of the tart.

It took only two heartbeats to recognize the lump. It was no pottery shard. Quickly, she lowered the spoon nearly to her lap, bunched a wad of tablecloth into her free hand, and wiped the object clean of the rich apple-gold filling. A ring with a yellow topaz carved in the shape of a heart winked up at her, set in a band clearly cut small for a woman's finger.

She heard the hiss of Agnes's breath. "Is that from one of your suitors?"

Isabel detested the little flutter in her breast that drove her eyes first to Lucian. He had removed his cap and was showing it to the gray-bearded man on his left, no doubt explaining how he had come by the style in the East. Ignoring an emotion she refused to name—he had always said that if he had the means, he would drape her in rubies, anyway—she quickly surveyed the rest of the company. Sir Theo smiled up at her shyly. Sir Eustace grinned his rakish grin. Without doubt, one of them had sent the ring and waited to see what she would do.

A movement from the corner of her eye tricked her into turning her head. Sir Lucian redonned his hat, then smiled warmly at Ronwen.

Isabel drew a sharp breath and slid the ring onto her finger.

"Isabel, what are you doing?"

"Father bade me choose, but I have not been able to make up my mind. I shall let this ring choose for me."

The Carole

Sir Theo was the first to reach Isabel when the sideboards had been cleared from the floor and the first carole was announced. Isabel had been careful to don the ring behind the drapery of the tablecloth so that none, not even the man who sent it, would see it on her finger before she wished him to. She knew that by accepting the gift, she had as good as plighted her troth to the giver. Some women might be avaricious enough to encourage men to shower them with expensive trinkets, but Isabel was not one of them. She had seen such behavior raise expectations in men's minds, which often led to slanderous rumors, even if one remained as virtuous as a nun. No, once Isabel stopped hiding her hand in the flowing folds of her crimson skirt, there would be no turning away the man who claimed the prize on her finger.

"Shall you dance with me, my lady?" Sir Theo asked.

She wondered if the blush on his fair cheeks betokened his usual bashfulness or a hopeful anticipation that she had found and accepted his ring and all that it implied. His sandy hair fell over his eyes as he bowed, and then he shook his head like a shaggy hound to clear his sight when he straightened.

I shall clip his hair into order when I am his wife, she thought—assuming, of course, that he had sent her the ring.

She swept him one of her graceful curtsies. "'Twill be my honor, Sir Theo."

She knew her words might carry a double meaning. Tension jittered through her in spite of her determination to surrender meekly to fate's decision. One man is very like another, she had told Agnes with a philosophical shrug when Agnes had protested Isabel's uncharacteristic rashness. Certainly none of them could be as obnoxious as Lucian de Warrene.

It could not possibly matter if none of them kissed as well as Lucian either.

She banished the thought and drew her right hand out of her skirt's folds. Her wide sleeve with its gold embroidered cuff belled out from her elbow, sweeping just short of the rushes on the floor. She disdained the extreme of fashion Ronwen followed, with sleeves so long they must be knotted to avoid treading on them. She extended her hand so that Sir Theo might kiss it and hence see the ring. She had placed it on her third finger . . . time enough to change hands once she had confirmed its owner . . . but he startled her by reaching his left hand across to catch her left fingers instead. He blushed, as though realizing some mistake, and shifted her hand into his right as he pulled her to the head of the circle.

She had forgotten that he was left-handed, and having never danced a carole before, he apparently expected the circle to turn to his left. Isabel had watched the serfs dance enough times on the village green to know his mistake. The other couples had seemed to instinctively reach the same conclusion as the serfs. The men had set their chosen partners to their left, but Isabel was the chatelaine of the castle, so if she chose to dance to the right of her partner, everyone else must follow. Several minutes of disorder ensued while all the men rearranged themselves around the women.

She glanced at Sir Theo. Perhaps he merely wished to wait for a moment of privacy to speak of the ring.

"We are to dance sinister, eh?"

Isabel stiffened at the voice. Amidst all the shuffling, she had not seen Lucian maneuver into position on her right. Or perhaps it was mere coincidence. Had they been dancing the other direction, he would have been on the opposite side of Ronwen. She certainly looked unhappy to see him take Isabel's free hand in his. Lucian lifted her fingers lightly and gazed for a moment at the pale yellow stone. Did he remember that she preferred the deeper hues of emeralds and rubies to set off her dark coloring?

"They begin the circle to the right in the East," he said, as he slipped her fingers into the strong grip that she remembered so well.

She felt herself recoiling ever so slightly from Sir Theo's weak clasp on her other side and silently chastised herself. She would teach him that he need not be so diffident, once he knew that she wished to marry him.

"I do not see that it matters which direction we circle, so long as we all move in unison." She tossed Lucian one of her haughty looks but felt a little hitch in her breath. He had recovered quite splendidly from their last encounter, when he had sported two black eyes and a swollen nose. The latter cast slightly sideways, a departure from the arrogantly straight nose she remembered in his youth and in the proud young crusader who had returned from the East. Judging from the dagger looks Ronwen threw at her, the flaw in his otherwise absurdly handsome face had not dampened her cousin's welcome of Lucian's courtship one whit. Then why

157

did he not gaze at Ronwen, instead of holding Isabel's eyes with a weighing look, which she refused to break first?

The hollow *thump thump thump* of a drum finally broke the spell for them both. As the music started, Isabel saw confusion flooding the circle. They surely wondered which way Sir Theo would decide to step first. She would have leaned over to him, but felt the subtle pressure of Lucian's hand guiding her into a gentle bounce on the balls of her feet in rhythm to the beat of the drums. She fought back waves of memories at his touch even as she watched Sir Theo's face flame when he realized himself the center of attention. All the watching eyes seemed to freeze him into place.

Isabel's bounce grew more impatient until at last she tugged on Sir Theo's hand, trying to signal him to begin. Sir Theo gave a visible start, and, apparently thinking she wished him to move her direction, lurched so suddenly to his right that he crashed into Isabel's shoulder and sent her stumbling into Lucian.

Lucian's fingers fluttered around hers, as though instinct commanded he release her hand and steady her with his strong arm around her waist. Or so rose the unbidden vision to her mind, a vision which the crack of his chin against the top of her head obliterated. She heard the clack of his teeth as his chin snapped up. The blow reverberated through her skull and left her leaning against his chest, momentarily stunned. The decorative band of embroidery running around the breast of his deep blue tunic swam before her watering eyes.

His hand tightened on hers, and he nudged her upright with his shoulder—but not before he lowered his head and murmured into her ear on a soft note of mockery. "The same old Isabel."

"My apologies, Sir Lucian," she said coldly, ignoring the way the top of her head throbbed. "I am not normally so clumsy." She hoped she had left him with a bruise on his chin. She turned pointedly towards Sir Theo and saw his eyes fill with mortification when several in the circle snickered at his blunder. She pressed his limp fingers. "Do not mind them, Sir Theo. They will soon appreciate how thoughtful you were to think of their comfort before your own when you decided we should begin to the right."

He gave her a wobbly smile of gratitude, but at the back of his eyes she saw the horror of another error strike him once more into inaction. Isabel drew a deep breath, bracing herself for a fresh quip from the man on her right, then shifted herself, deliberately this time, into Lucian. She prodded him firmly sideways as she pulled Sir Theo to follow. Lucian took her hint and helped draw the circle into a rightward motion. He squeezed her hand. She slid him a sideways glance, ready to parry whatever impudent remark he let fall. The wistful little smile on his lips caught her by surprise.

"The same old Isabel," he repeated softly, this time without the jeer. "You will lead him through marriage with honeyed words that soothe his pride, as you lead him through this dance. I will give you this much, Bel, you were headstrong and stubborn, but you were never unkind."

She focused her gaze straight ahead. "I am not leading him through anything," she insisted, refusing to be stirred by the unexpected warmth in his voice.

"I saw you pull on his hand so that he would follow us to the right. You led me blissfully about by the nose as well before I caught on to your tricks."

She squirmed a little at the word "nose," but responded with a scornful huff. "No one ever led you anywhere, least of all I. You were a domineering bully."

"It is not bullying to offer a common-sense warning to a woman who cannot see past her own reckless conceit. I never doubted your courage and intelligence, Bel, but you never could admit that, however rarely, someone else might know better than you."

"I did not need you to take care of me. I have governed my father's household as capably as any man."

"As I've no doubt you will govern Sir Theo when you are his wife."

"What makes you think I mean to wed him?"

"I can feel his ring pressed against my palm. You were never partial to pale colors, so I doubt you purchased such a stone for yourself. Nor were you one to lead a man on with false hopes. You would not have accepted Sir Theo's hand for the carole if you did not believe . . ."

She slid him a glance as he paused and caught him smiling down into Ronwen's cross face. Isabel felt a bristling sensation along the back of her neck. "If I did not believe?" she queried, wishing unaccountably to shake his attention away from her cousin.

"—that he had sent you the ring and wished to marry you," he finished as a man distracted, as he no doubt was by the sudden pelt of Ronwen's questions. "Yes, my dear, this is how we danced it in the East. No, I meant that we circled to the right. Of course we did not simply go round and round in a circle. Yes, we sang as we danced. No, I have not danced to this song before, but—Yes, I think I could find a pattern for it, if I—"

The watchful corner of Isabel's mind that ever carried a protective awareness of her sister recognized the tones of Agnes's voice where she moved in the circle between Sir Gavin and Sir Eustace.

"Oh, show us, Sir Lucian! Pray show us!"

Isabel had studied carefully the way the serfs danced on the green and had made up her own steps for this tune, which she would have inconspicuously whispered into Sir Theo's ear for him to repeat to the others had Lucian's unexpected appearance at her side not so disrupted her thoughts that she had forgotten her plan.

The other dancers joined Agnes in chorus. The movement of the circle stalled while they awaited Lucian's instructions. Lucian hesitated, then released Ronwen's hand. To Isabel's shock, he did not release hers.

"Forgive me, Lady Ronwen, but in the East, the man always dances with the woman on his left. If you will indulge me, Lady Isabel?"

Isabel chided herself for not realizing what she had done. She knew her father's serfs danced the same. When she had urged the direction of the circle to the right, she had turned herself into Lucian's partner rather than Sir Theo's.

She could scarcely snatch her hand out of Lucian's now. She allowed him to draw her to the center of the circle. They stood a moment, waiting for the strains of the music to return to the beginning of the melody. In all the years they had known each other, Isabel had never heard him sing. His resonant bass quickened her heart and stole her breath.

"The holly and the ivy . . ." He led her two skips and a step to the right, releasing her hand to clap on *when* . . . "they are both full grown . . ." Two skips and a step to the left, with a clap on the beat after *grown*, then he laid their hands palm to open palm at shoulder height and guided her into a skipping spin to the right. "Of all the trees that are in the wood . . ." Left palm to left palm, they skipped to the left . . . "the holly bears the crown."

Isabel would never have admitted it aloud, but silently she confessed the steps as good as those she had composed. She joined her voice to his as they repeated the pattern for the refrain.

"Oh the rising of the sun, and the running of the deer, the playing of the merry organ, sweet singing of the choir."

The men and women who watched them burst into approving cheers. Lucian bowed with so buoyant a grin that Isabel trilled a mirroring laugh as she sank into a curtsy.

"And now we must all try it," Agnes cried.

Isabel turned with Lucian back towards the circle just as Ronwen moved to the left and Sir Theo to the right, no doubt each determined to reclaim their original partners in the newly designated order. But in their impulsive haste, their hands tangled with each other's before Isabel or Lucian could join them. Ronwen glared at Sir Theo, and Sir Theo went red. Apparently more anxious to mollify his new beloved rather than Isabel's prospective betrothed, Lucian drew Isabel into the gap created on Ronwen's left and took Ronwen's free hand in his. Isabel, still on his left, would remain his partner for the spins, but when the circle moved together, he would hold Ronwen's hand, too.

Her cousin pouted at having to share his attention, but he disarmed her with one of the crooked, rueful smiles that had healed all except the final quarrel between him and Isabel.

Ronwen gave a simper that jangled in Isabel's ears, and she fluttered Lucian a conditional forgiveness with her lashes.

"I shall make you repent for this later, sir," she promised, a purr in her voice.

The music struck up again before Lucian could answer. Everyone now skipped and stepped and clapped and spun about the circle, Lucian singing each verse and the rest of them, following Isabel's earlier example, joining him on the refrain.

Each new song required a new combination of steps. Lucian returned Isabel to Sir Theo for the second carole. He tried to work out the next pattern with Ronwen for the others to imitate, but despite her bright pleasure, she seemed incapable of understanding the steps. She went left when she should have gone right, skipped when she should have spun, and trod on Lucian's feet so many times that Isabel found herself doubled over with the rest of the company, giggling at the grimaces on Lucian's face each time he tried not to wince.

"You must show us with Isabel," Agnes said, to which everyone in the circle save Ronwen and Sir Theo chorused, "Aye, aye!"

Isabel could not deny that she relished taking Lucian's hand again, though she dared not voice it in front of Ronwen. It had nothing to do with Lucian anyway, but only the delight she had discovered in dancing. She seemed to instinctively understand what he wished her to do, when to turn this way and when to turn that. When they rejoined the circle, she danced between Lucian and Sir Eustace. She registered only vaguely the hot glances Sir Eustace occasionally tossed her way. She was too caught up in the merriment of skipping around the circle and echoing with the others Lucian's beautiful bass voice to be much aware of anything but her own gladness.

By the fourth song, suggestions had begun to spill eagerly from Isabel's lips.

"What if we did a double skip here? Let us try here a step, a skip, a step and another skip. I think we should clap thrice on this beat. Oh, Lucian, what if you held both my hands just here and spun me around like this?"

She dimly saw the exasperated look on Lucian's face before he whirled her around at arms' length in the center of the circle. She flung back her head and laughed, feeling almost wanton with her ribbon-wrapped braids swirling in the air behind her. Joy bubbled in her like a heady wine. She had never imagined that dancing could be so intoxicating. Another spin and she might take flight. Her head continued to reel when Lucian pulled her to a stop, leaving her so dizzy that she had to grip his forearms to prevent herself from falling.

Oh! How hard his muscles felt beneath her hands. His strong grip cupped her elbows, holding her upright until her giddiness ebbed. As he steadied her now from the aftereffects of her demand to be whirled, she felt in his clasp the power and promise of a man who would hold a woman forever safe from her own headstrong folly, if that woman could only swallow her pride enough to confess that she desired such a man.

When his face ceased to swim, there was no one else in the hall but he, gazing down at her in a way that weakened her knees all afresh, for just so had his blue eyes grown dark before he had kissed her that day beneath the great oak tree.

"Oh, Isabel, that was splendid!" Agnes said. "Sir Eustace, hold my hands and spin me the same. Oh, fie on you, sir. Then Sir Gavin, I know, will oblige me."

The world collapsed back around Isabel at Agnes's cry. Lucian drew his hands away, leaving her suddenly deflated and cold in the midst of a hall that blazed bright with the Yule fire and a circle of knights laughingly whirling their own partners as they had seen Lucian whirl her. Ronwen was tugging on Lucian's sleeve, smiling up at him with her most beguiling smile. She slipped in front of Isabel and slid her hands into Lucian's, a clear signal that she expected him to spin her next.

"Oh, I hope my husband will dance with me thus at our wedding."

The coy innuendo in Ronwen's words slapped Isabel across the face. Had her cousin and Lucian progressed so far in their courtship? Isabel turned away from them. Fool, to think she could swallow her pride. Pride was all she had to cling to.

Sir Theo had backed slightly outside the circle, his sandy hair fallen forward into his eyes. Isabel wondered if he hoped that by thus obscuring his vision, no one could see him either. She sensed his alarm in his quickly tensing body when she stopped before him with a curtsy.

"Pray, my lady, do not ask me to spin you. I should be certain to let your hands slip, and I could not bear to be the cause of injury to you."

More likely, he feared he might die of embarrassment if he dropped her. Isabel suppressed a sigh. It would not quite be an equal exchange for Isabel's indolent father, but she would have no trouble ruling a man like Sir Theo. Unlike Lucian, Sir Theo would let her do as she pleased and be gratified when she found some small trait in him to praise. It had not seemed so ill a trade before she had danced the caroles.

"I shall not ask you to spin me," Isabel said quietly to Sir Theo, her heart beating a dull counterpoint to the sounds of music and laughter that floated around them. "But I think it is time that we spoke of this."

He shoved his hair aside to gaze down upon her hand with the ring as she extended it towards him.

"Is—is there some other step you wish me to try?" Sir Theo asked. "I can skip side to side if you wish, but my feet get tangled when we do that turn with our palms together. Lady Ronwen gave me a fierce scolding when I stepped on her toes."

Isabel had forgotten that he had danced with Ronwen all night. She had thought of nothing for hours except her own happiness and how completely content she had been dancing with Lucian. No quarreling, no intolerable commands, no dark blond brow arched in an ironic *I told you so.*

She waved her hand at Sir Theo, suddenly impatient to have the decision made. "No, Sir Theo, I speak of the ring you sent me."

"The ring—*I* sent you?"

He had not. She saw it on his face. He knew nothing of the ring she wore. Relief washed through her, chased by the obvious question: *Then who?* The thought rose on a wave of panic. Agnes had been right; Isabel had been too hasty in donning the ring, too eager to show that she had moved beyond her past with Lucian by choosing herself a husband

165

right under his nose. She would have done anything at that moment to be able to cast the ring back into the apple tart where she had found it.

A sudden wild hope engulfed her. Perhaps no one but Lucian had observed the ring. She had danced most of the night with it hidden in his broad palm or beneath his strong fingers. Except for the claps and when they had spun palm to palm. Hope turned to a sour puddle in her stomach. The sender would surely have been watching for it on her hand. Oh, why had she let pride overrule the sound judgment that usually guided her? She had 'til Epiphany to satisfy her father's ultimatum, twelve days yet to choose a husband by careful weighing rather than this impulsive throw to fate.

"There has been a misunderstanding," she murmured to Sir Theo. "Forgive me, sir."

Useless as she knew the action likely was, she turned the ring with the stone to her palm. Perhaps the sender had not seen. Perhaps no one had save Lucian.

How now to fill this awkward silence with Sir Theo? She glanced to the side of the circle opposite where she envisioned Ronwen laughing and spinning with Lucian's aid and saw Agnes ignoring Sir Gavin's outstretched hands with her arms crossed over her breast and a fierce little frown on her lovely face. Had Sir Gavin been unwise enough to say something that belittled Agnes's astuteness?

"Are you very good with sums, Sir Theo?" Isabel asked abruptly.

"Sums?"

"Numbers. Arithmetic."

"I—I have never bothered much about such things. I leave my accounts to my clerks. I am an excellent hunter, though, and my swordsmanship is above respectable."

She caught the rare thread of energy beneath his boast. So, 'twas martial pursuits that stirred his passion, not the dull work of business or the awkward courtship of dancing.

Isabel found herself smiling. "My father will say we have danced like heathens tonight. I will command the musicians to make the next song more sedate. And I think my sister Agnes might be glad of a new partner."

She took Sir Theo's arm and guided him across the floor, sent Sir Gavin off to fetch her a cup of wine, coaxed Sir Theo to ask Agnes to take his hand for the next dance, and was about to leave them to speak to the musicians when she heard Lucian's voice carry across the chatter and music of the circle.

"Pray, Lady Ronwen, I will be but a moment. I must speak just a word to the Lady Isabel."

Isabel stood frozen as Sir Theo led Agnes to another point along the circle, smiling bashfully at her. Had Lucian observed Sir Theo's dismay when Isabel had curtsied to him and how, after they had spoken, Isabel had swiveled the ring on her finger? He could not possibly guess the truth, for he knew not the source of the ring. Did he come to mock her nonetheless, thinking Sir Theo had changed his mind after observing the forward way she had taken control of the dancing? She knew she had annoyed Lucian. It had not been the first time she had seen that exasperated look on his face. Fie on the man! She would not pretend to be stupid to satisfy his or any man's vanity.

She heard a footfall behind her and lifted her chin. She had a few complaints of her own she meant to throw in his teeth if he intended to renew their quarrel.

She pivoted about on her heel, then gasped as her eyes met, not Lucian's challenging blue gaze, but the sultry, dark eyes of Sir Eustace. He took her hand in his and raised it to his lips, allowing his kiss to linger against her white skin. Then with a slow, sensual touch that caressed more than the yellow stone, he turned the gem outward once more on her finger.

"I have waited all night to thank you, my lady, for accepting my token."

167

"You?" she whispered.

"Indeed. I knew you would remember I wear a topaz signet ring and hence would know that this—" He rubbed his thumb across the yellow stone. "—came from me. I shall be honored to make you my wife, and I assure you, I shall make you a most—zealous—husband."

She heard murmurs as she stared into his saturnine face and knew his resonant pronouncement had reached the ears of the other dancers. A movement jerked her gaze to the space over his shoulder. Lucian had stopped a mere two feet behind Sir Eustace. His eyes held the same bleak look they had the day she had sent him away. He gave her a curt little bow, then returned to Ronwen's side.

The Oak Tree

Sir Eustace glanced down dubiously at the snow beneath the barren branches of the great oak where judgment had been passed on Lord Stephen's manor since the days of the Conquest.

"This is not what I had in mind when I agreed to a moonlight tryst," he said.

Isabel raised her brows at him, knowing he could see her frown perfectly in the glow of the full moon set in a winter sky, so cold and clear that the stars glistened like tiny crystals in the midst of the silky black heavens. "Have I agreed to marry a man so tame he is afraid to dampen his tunic in the snow?"

Sir Eustace ran a hand down his sleeve to the jewel-encrusted cuff. "'Tis a very fine tunic, purchased new for this Christmas feast."

The garment of forest-green wool, adorned with three bands of jewels about the neck, fell in flowing folds to his ankles, allowing the curling points of his red slippers to peek out. She did not know why she remembered the more conservative points on the half-boots that had graced Lucian's feet in the hall, or the fashionable way Lucian had drawn the sides of his tunic up through his girdle to expose the muscular calves beneath his straw-colored hose, or how his blue tunic had made his eyes look like vivid chips that had fallen out of a summer's sky.

Sir Eustace's voice broke through her lovely vision. "There are better ways for a man and woman to pass their time on Christmas Eve than to stand shivering apart in the cold. Let me warm you, my lady." His arm passed slyly about her waist, but Isabel slipped away before the caress could become an embrace.

"You should have called for your cloak while I fetched mine from my chamber." She felt quite cozy in her cloak's plush lining of squirrel fur.

"Have pity on me, my lady. Your beauty overwhelms me. I came out here promptly at your bidding, trusting in the love betokened by the ring you wear. Give me but one small pledge of your affection, and I shall be your slave forevermore."

She knew from the way his gaze fastened on her lips that he hoped for a kiss. And from the heat in his eyes, she knew he would not be satisfied with just one. In spite of her cloak, she shivered a little, but blamed it on the breeze that swirled up to nip her cheeks.

"There shall be neither pledge nor reward until you have assisted me with my quest, sir. Help me gather some mistletoe to decorate the hearth and then—we shall see."

His desire thus rebuked, the sultry gleam died from his eyes. He stomped his feet in the snow and blew on his naked hands. "Let us go sit by the Yule fire and send a servant for your task." He barely bothered to conceal his petulance.

"We shall sit there soon enough," she said. "'Tis a small enough thing I have asked of you, sir. But if you are so vain that you fear for your tunic . . ."

170

"I assure you, my lady, I am not so frivolous," he said, even as he tenderly stroked his other sleeve. His topaz signet ring flashed like a tiny flame in the moonlight. He cast another longing glance at her lips, then raised his gaze to the branches which reached like spectral tentacles towards the sky. "Are you sure there is mistletoe? I can see nothing but barren branches."

"That is because the upper branches are too high to see distinctly in the dark, and the lower ones are hidden in the shadows of the upper ones. But I saw some growing here a week ago. If you will only let me climb on your shoulders, I am certain I can pull myself into the limbs there . . ." she pointed to a branch she judged that she could reach from his shoulders if he knelt in the snow ". . . and achieve a perch that will allow me to knock down a cluster with this sword."

Sir Eustace looked startled when she drew her father's war blade from beneath her heavy cloak. Weapons had not been permitted at the Christmas feast, so she'd had to borrow Lord Stephen's from his chamber.

"Does your father know you have that?" Sir Eustace asked. "I cannot imagine Lord Stephen would be pleased to know you are carrying his sword about this way."

"He will not be pleased that I am gathering mistletoe, either. It is banned by the Church, though few people outside of the priests themselves observe the proscription." She had been one of those few until tonight, not out of concern for the plant's pagan connotations, but merely because she had never thought it worth the trouble of gathering it when holly and ivy were so much easier to obtain. She had a purpose tonight, though. "Does it trouble you, Sir Eustace, to defy the Church this way?"

"It troubles me only that I might displease you," he said with a promptness that should have gratified her, had she not been hoping for another answer. "However, I cannot allow you to climb the tree yourself, much less wave a sword about once you are sitting in the branches. Hand me the blade, and I will endeavor to fetch the mistletoe for you."

Everything in Isabel rebelled at his offer. She had no choice but to marry him now that everyone at the Christmas feast had seen her wearing his ring, but it was not in her nature to permit another, man or woman, to perform a task she knew herself perfectly competent to perform. She knew this obstinacy in her had driven Lucian away. She had hated herself for weeping at his loss, and deplored the moment of springing hope she had felt this night that he might have forgiven her pride and wish to try again. The joy she had known whirling about with her hands in his still glowed inside her, even now.

One man is very like another, she had said to Agnes, but dancing with Lucian had exposed those words for the lie they were. No man had ever made her feel like Lucian, and after being with him again this night, she knew that no other man ever would.

Her impulsive determination to punish him for the quarrel that had left her so miserable and alone had resulted in binding her to Sir Eustace. She knew perfectly well that despite a flattering tongue, Sir Eustace wanted her only for the pleasure of her beauty. Lucian might have been aggravating beyond bearing, but their heady exchange of kisses had been interspersed with laughter and the sharing of hopes and dreams, and even sweet stretches of silence.

She knew she could never reclaim those days. She had seen Lucian return Ronwen's smile as he'd led her in the sedate dance she had commanded the musicians to begin just before she had invited Sir Eustace to join her in the moonlight. Lucian had found himself a more docile love to fit his temper. Isabel had rashly chosen herself a husband as well. Having once accepted Sir Eustace's ring, her father would never allow her to return it.

Still, she had yet one test to pose to Sir Eustace. If it caused him to request the ring back, well, her father could not fault *her* for that.

"That is good of you, Sir Eustace, but you confess you cannot see where the mistletoe is, while I recall its position from daylight hours. You may hold the sword for me, if you wish, until I am in the branches, then hand it up to me. Now, if you will please kneel as I requested . . ."

She trailed off, bracing for another protest while gathering her arguments to parry it. A nice, brisk quarrel, followed by his demand for the ring . . .

Sir Eustace glanced at the snow again. "Perhaps I could boost you up thus." He bent over and linked his hands together, forming a stirrup for her foot.

Isabel sighed. That he preferred to capitulate to her unorthodox request, rather than seek to resist it, suggested that his ring would remain firmly planted on her finger right through their wedding day. At least, she consoled herself, a man who would sooner bow to his lady's wishes than sully the skirts of his tunic should be easy enough to govern in marriage. She blamed the sour lump in her throat on an unidentified dish from the feast that disagreed with her, leaned the sword against the trunk of the tree, placed her foot into his waiting hands, and let him lift her into the branches.

She had climbed this tree as lithe as a cat when she had been a little girl and had scrambled over the shoulders of a cooperative stable boy. However, lack of recent practice, the weight of her now-adult body, and the cumbersome folds of her winter cloak threatened to frustrate her project for a moment, but a panted command for Sir Eustace to boost her higher enabled her to finally heft herself onto one of the lower branches. It took a deal of bouncing, swiveling and swishing of her skirts to arrange herself into a sitting position of some modesty.

The breeze that had chilled her cheeks on the ground blew more briskly at this height, gusting her braids away from her neck and imparting a sudden surge of freedom that echoed a bittersweet memory: the rush of air against her face, her hair whipping in the wind, the powerful muscles of the stallion Abatos pounding beneath her as he galloped headlong down the forest road while she had embraced an almost mindless burst of triumph . . . then the ache of her shoulders, the reins beginning to slip through her fingers, and the uprooted tree blocking the road, cast down by a summer's storm . . .

She shook away the awful aftermath of that day and devoted her concentration to scrabbling her feet beneath her and pulling herself up into a standing position along the branch.

"Now, Sir Eustace, if you will hand me up the sword."

"Are you sure you are steady, lady?"

His belated words of concern only made her cross. "Quite steady. The sword, please."

She grasped a nearby limb as she leaned down to take the hilt he held up to her, and then she straightened. The sword was much heavier to lift over her head with one hand than it had been with two, but she was not foolish enough to entrust her balance to her feet alone. She shifted her supporting grasp to a limb nearer the height of her face, and on the second swing, succeeded in stabbing the blade into the branches above where she had seen some mistletoe clinging earlier that week.

"Great heavens, man! Are you mad?"

Isabel looked down at the ringing tones she knew like the beat of her heart. Lucian and Ronwen came striding, hand in hand, through the snow. The same wind that tossed her skirts and shook the limbs around her blew off Lucian's acorn cap. He made an absent grab for it then let it swirl away without breaking his forceful advance. The moonlight bathed his dark blond hair as silver as Ronwen's and revealed an expression in his eye that made Sir Eustace step back as Lucian halted before him.

"She has her heart set on some mistletoe," Sir Eustace said. "I offered to go up for her—in fact, I insisted, but she is a headstrong lass and clamored up into the branches before I could stop her."

Isabel snorted the same instant that she heard Lucian do the same.

"Headstrong I know her to be," Lucian said, "and sly enough to defy a direct prohibition as soon as a fellow's back is turned, but I doubt even she could reach a branch of that height on her own. Thank the Saints I arrived in time to put an end to this farce of a betrothal before she left you with a corpse to marry. She is determined to break her neck one way or another, and you are imbecile enough to abet her."

Sir Eustace spluttered a protest, but Lucian shoved him out of the way with one hand.

"Come down from there, Isabel. *Now.*"

Isabel glared at him, though she suspected he could not see it from that height. "You, Sir Lucian, forfeited the right to command me six months ago."

Lucian gave a harsh, ringing laugh. "Had I ever had the power to command you, you would be my wife today. Don't make me come up there and get you."

"I will come down as soon as I have dislodged some mistletoe." She made another jab into the branches above her head.

"Lucian, pray let us go," Ronwen begged. "I meant no harm, and it has all turned out for the best. Sir Eustace will make her a splendid husband. Why, I would give my eye teeth to have you look at me with the passion that he bestows on her."

A growling sound startled Isabel into glancing down again. She saw Lucian release not Ronwen's hand, but her wrist.

"He'll bestow his passion on her over my dead body—but not, Isabel, over yours. Now are you coming down, or am I coming up?"

"Neither," she said. "I do not need your help with the mistletoe any more than I needed it with Abatos."

Her heart hammered as the falsehood slipped from her lips. Why could she not confess the truth they both knew?

A white band of anger formed around Lucian's mouth. Isabel braced herself for a blast of fury, but his look must have frightened Ronwen, for she made a half turn as if to run back to the castle, which distracted him.

"Stay where you are," Lucian snapped at her. "You are the reason I suspect she is standing in that tree, and— Great heavens, Isabel! Is that a sword?"

The weight of the blade had begun to sag in her hand, so she had lowered it to her side to rest. "What if it is?" she said, jutting up her chin.

He reminded her just how much taller he stood than the other men she knew by grabbing hold of the branch she perched on without even lifting onto his toes.

"This limb will not hold both our weights," she warned. She did not know if it was true, but her words checked him.

"Blazes, Bel, what is it you're trying to prove?"

Isabel did not know the answer. She had never understood what drove her to try to command every situation. It had hovered as a barrier between her and Lucian from the first, barely noticed by either in the beginning, but gradually stirring some measure of annoyance in Lucian as their courtship had progressed. Even knowing how it nibbled away at the edges of their trust in one another, she had not been able to subdue her need to control, to confirm a degree of independence within herself, even at the risk of losing at last his patience and his love.

"I don't need you, Lucian," she repeated, though something cracked in her heart as she said it.

Her avowal seemed to refresh Sir Eustace's confidence. He stepped between Lucian and the tree. "You heard her, Sir Lucian. Take your lady back to the hall and leave me to deal with my betrothed."

Lucian made a guttural sound of rage in his throat. Isabel had heard it the day he had wrestled her from Abatos' back, when the stallion, sensing her waning strength, would have dislodged his unfamiliar rider by jumping the fallen tree.

"She is not your betrothed," Lucian growled. "That ring she wears on her hand is mine, not yours."

The statement hit Isabel so hard that she swayed on the branch. "*Yours?*" she repeated. "Lucian, *you* sent me the ring?"

Shock collapsed her into squatting down on the branch. Relief, followed by a heady burst of joy, extended the sword to the hand he held up.

"No, he sent the ring to *me*," Ronwen's voice huffed. "That was *my* tart you found it in."

Isabel jerked the sword back before Lucian's fingers could close around the hilt. Her gaze shot over his head at Ronwen, who stood, smirking with her hands on her hips.

"Agnes and I overheard Lucian bidding his squire to take the ring to the kitchen and persuade Marjory Cook to place it in a tart and mark it just for me," Ronwen said. "But Agnes, the little traitor, must have told Marjory to send the tart to you instead. As soon as I saw the ring on your hand, I guessed what had happened. The way Agnes smiled as she watched you dance with Lucian confirmed it. She must have hoped when you donned the ring that it would trap Lucian into marrying you after all, but I could tell that you failed to guess its origin. I saw Sir Eustace's signet ring and the hungry way he looked at you, so I told Sir Eustace to claim it."

Isabel glanced at the topaz on her hand. She did not need to ask if the story was true. The stone agreed too well with Ronwen's gown, while Lucian—Lucian had said he would drape Isabel in rubies.

"You should thank me, Bel," her cousin continued. "You wanted a husband you could rule, like you have ruled your father. I have given you one. And you know I will suit Sir Lucian much better than you. He wants a meek wife, not one who absconds with that ferocious destrier he brought back from the East and scrambles about in trees."

Isabel stood back up. Thankfully, she could not see Lucian's expression through the tears that swam in her eyes; his silence was condemning enough. She pushed the sword under her arm, pulled the ring from her finger, and hurled it over Ronwen's head.

"Take it, then. And take your tyrannical betrothed back to the hall. As soon as I have my mistletoe, I shall announce to my father that Sir Eustace and I wish to be married by Epiphany."

"Tyrannical?" Lucian exclaimed. "You call me a tyrant merely because I wish to safeguard the woman I love?"

"Then do so," Isabel said. "Safeguard Ronwen to your heart's content, because I—"

"Do not say it again," Lucian said. "Don't you dare say you do not need me while you stand in that tree, the wind tangling your skirts around your feet, a sword you can barely lift tucked under your arm, and a temper so proud you think it mere foolishness to hold on to a branch to steady yourself." Lucian jerked his head disdainfully in Sir Eustace's direction. "Do you think *he* has wits enough to catch you if you fall?"

Isabel realized that to pull off the ring, she had released her hold of the supporting branch. As right as she knew Lucian was about her carelessness, she could not bear to give him the satisfaction of clutching at the branch again.

"I am perfectly steady, as I told Sir Eustace," she said, praying no powerful gust of the wind would prove otherwise.

"Oh, bother!" Ronwen cried. "What were you thinking to throw the ring like that, Bel?" Her cousin knelt, digging in the snow. "Lucian, Sir Eustace, help me find it."

Sir Eustace joined her like an obedient puppy. Had the man no backbone at all? Apparently he did, but only where his vanity was concerned, for he attended his hems and carefully bent from the waist to join Ronwen in the search.

"Go help them," Isabel said when Lucian continued to stand where he was. "I have a task to finish here." As soon as he would turn away, she would grab the branch again and swing the sword back up to knock down the mistletoe.

"And leave you to topple out of that tree?" Lucian said. "I don't think so."

"I am not going to topple out."

"Like you would not have lost your seat, and broken who knows how many bones, had I allowed Abatos to jump that tree with you still on his back?"

Aha! She had known he would bring that up. She answered defiantly, "I would not have fallen! I can ride as well as you, even that brute you found in the East."

She recognized the frustration that twitched his lips. "So you have told me a dozen times whenever I forbade you to try. I have seen you ride, Bel, I know what a skilled horsewoman you are. But Abatos surpassed your strength, as I warned you he would. I saw the fear in your face when you realized he meant to make the leap. You knew I was right, yet you refused to admit it then, just as you do now. If I had not caught you in time and pulled you from the saddle—"

"I would have landed safely on the other side."

"Blazes, Bel! I vow you are the most contrary woman in England!"

She ground her foot against the branch to prevent herself from stamping it. "Go help your meek little love find the ring you intended for her. Let her fawn and pet over you, let her declare you her lord and master. I won't bend for you, Lucian de Warrene. I won't bend for any man."

"I haven't asked you to bend, only to listen—"

Rage erupted from a tender core pricked to bitter life by his words. "I will not be dutiful and complaisant when I can think for myself. I will not be my mother!"

"What has the Lady Felicia to do with this?"

"She listened to the men who told her to be quiet and submissive. She played the simpleminded wife when she was three times as clever as my father or any of the men who served in our house. It was she who made all the decisions that allowed their lives to run smooth as the pebbles beneath the stream, but always she was careful to make them think the shrewdness was theirs. She had the eye and aim of a hawk with her bow, but took care to miss the mark so she would not put my father's aim to shame. At chess, she could see the way to corner a queen in five moves, when it took my father twenty, but always, always she let my father win. I watched her weep over books she could not read and refused to learn, even when my father would have granted it, because she said a woman should not be more knowledgeable than her husband. She smiled for my father, but the frustration ate her up inside. Before she died, she told me . . ." Isabel stopped and pressed a hand to her lips. Where had those memories come from? She had scarcely thought about her mother's suppressed longings for years.

"What did she tell you, Bel?"

The gentleness of Lucian's voice shook her almost as much as the sudden vision of her mother's forlorn face.

"She said—" The vision blurred, smeared by Isabel's tears "—she hoped God would have mercy on the minds of women and let them read in heaven."

Another anguished memory bubbled up. The little girl peeking through the door of her mother's chamber, watching her cry, hearing a panicked plea for forgiveness from Heaven for the stubborn desires of her heart. Small though she was, Isabel had vowed to embrace the life her mother had shunned, at whatever the cost. In time, the memory had faded as her father deferred to Isabel's every request, so long as she kept his life running smoothly. His yielding nature had allowed her to become this horrid, arrogant creature who must command every detail of her family's life and prove to herself that she could match any man, Lucian most of all, for only he had ever tempted her to wonder if the cost might be too high.

"Oh, there it is!" Ronwen's voice rang out. "Sir Eustace, do you see it? It is gleaming there in the snow."

Lucian pivoted and dove for the spot where Ronwen reached. Isabel saw him scoop a palm full of snow. His fingers brushed the white dusting away until all that remained was the ring.

Ronwen sprang to her feet, her face aglow with excitement. "Silly, you did not need to hide it in an apple tart. You had only to ask me. Yes, Sir Lucian, I will marry you gladly."

Ronwen held out an eager hand and waited for Lucian to place the ring upon it. Isabel closed her eyes to shut out the scene. At the first sound of Ronwen's voice, he fled back to the woman who would happily play her mother's meek role without suffering her mother's silent grief. Isabel never could. However she had come to be what she was, she could not change herself now, even if it left her heart as empty as her mother's, albeit in a different way. Just now, she felt more desolate than that day when she first sent Lucian away.

"Bel?" The voice came from so directly beneath her that Isabel knew Lucian had moved back to the tree. She slitted her eyes open to look narrowly down at him.

"Lucian, what are you doing?" Ronwen's voice quavered.

"Sir Eustace, will you please escort the Lady Ronwen back to the Yule fire while I fetch the Lady Isabel safely down?"

Of course he would not leave her standing in the tree. He was too obstinate for that.

Sir Eustace stiffened in his stance near Ronwen. "I beg your pardon, Sir Lucian, but you heard the Lady Isabel say that she wished to be my w—"

Lucian turned his head towards the other knight. Isabel knew the sort of look he used to cut off Sir Eustace's protest. He had quelled Isabel with it a handful of times, though afterwards regret of her cowardice always drove her to an act of rebellion to reassert her mettle.

"Ah . . . er . . ." Sir Eustace stammered. "Lady Ronwen, your fingers must be chilled from sifting through the snow. Let us thaw them out by the fire, as Sir Lucian suggests."

"But Lucian—" Whatever Ronwen saw in Lucian's face silenced her, too. She sniffled loudly, but let Sir Eustace draw her hand through his arm and lead her away.

Lucian turned back to the tree and stared up at Isabel for a long, silent moment. She felt him trying to search her face as she sought to search his. She wondered if her features were easier to read in the height of the branches than his were with the shadows that snaked across them. His fingers fidgeted together uncharacteristically.

"Bel . . . I know it is not your color . . ."

The ring. He still held the ring! Her heart jumped high as the elusive mistletoe. Fear that she had misunderstood led her to repeat Ronwen's question. "Lucian, what are you doing?"

"Asking you to marry me."

Her heart threatened to explode, but indignation laced her euphoria like the stars that meshed across the sky. "With another woman's ring?"

"I will trade it for a ruby if it will please you better."

"That is not the point. Just a few moments ago, you wanted to marry Ronwen."

"That was hours ago, not moments—before I heard you laugh at dinner, before you danced with me, before I remembered . . ." His words suspended her breath where the wintry air had failed.

"Before you remembered?"

"How much I love you."

Her motions became a blur. She remembered letting the sword fall into the snow, and then somehow she was off the branch and in his arms, face buried against his neck as he held her tight against him, her toes dangling in the air.

"What about Ronwen?" she whispered.

"I was lonely, Bel, and hurt. You said you did not love me anymore. You said we were a mistake—"

"I—*I* am the mistake. Oh, Lucian, I can never be the meek, obedient wife you wish. I stole Abatos when you commanded me not to ride him. I was ever so relieved when I saw you cutting through the woods on my father's big bay, and even when I heard the way you growled when you pulled me from the saddle, just as I felt the reins slipping from my fingers, and I knew how I should have listened . . . even with all that, I cannot promise I will never do anything like it again!"

"I never wanted a meek wife, Bel. I never wanted to change you. I only wanted to keep you safe from your own headstrong ways. And so I will, if I have to fight the fiends of Hell and your own silent demons to do so, for I want to live to a very old age with you."

She wondered if he minded her soaking his neck with her tears. "Oh, Lucian, how can you? I broke your nose!"

She would never forget the awful crack at the back of her head snapping into his face when he pulled her free of Abatos. She had squirmed her way out of his stunned hold to land on the ground, whirling about to deny her need for the rescue she had so fervently prayed for only moments before. But her words had choked off at the sight of blood streaming from his nose and tears from his eyes. Mortified at the consequence of her act of defiance, she had run sobbing through the woods all the way back to her father's castle. The next time she had seen him, with two black eyes and a crooked nose, she had sent him away with frigid words to conceal the shame that still shuddered in her heart. How could he want her now?

He laughed into her hair. "You did me a favor. I was altogether too handsome before. My face has more character now. There, Bel, if you squeeze my neck any tighter, I won't be able to breathe."

She loosened the stranglehold of her arms and drew back to search the face she could now see clearly, bathed as it was in the light of the moon.

He must have seen the fear in her eyes, for he said, "This does not feel like a mistake, Bel. Nothing has ever felt more right than holding you in my arms. If you love me—if you have the courage to try—we will find a way to make us work."

"A challenge?" She grinned. "You know I cannot resist a challenge."

They were well lost in a kiss before she realized she had not answered the first part of his question. It did not seem very urgent just now to free her lips to tell him that she loved him. They had not needed words that summer day when he had held her almost exactly like this and kissed her beneath this same oak tree. When they had sat afterwards together in the sweet-smelling grass, her head on his shoulder, his cheek pressed to her hair, their hands tangled together in the promise of the oneness she had thought their future held. A promise she saw renewed in his eyes when he set her feet in the snow and ran his chilled thumbs along the high bones of her cheeks.

"Ronwen told me your father was eager to be rid of you," he said. "I think Epiphany is altogether too long a wait to satisfy him, don't you think?"

"I cannot simply abandon him," she said, even as she felt her center melt in the warmth of Lucian's gaze. "I must find him a wife before I let you carry me off."

"He has Agnes."

"Who will very soon be wed herself."

His brows shot up. "To whom?" he asked, then almost immediately guessed the answer. "Sir Theo? It'll take six months to loosen his tongue enough to court her."

"Then I must find a way to hurry him along."

Exasperation mingled with laughter in Lucian's face. "I've no intention of waiting six months to make you my wife, nor even twelve days. This is one time, Bel, that you will listen and obey me."

She felt the rebellious cloud fall across her brow. "Lucian—"

His cocked his head cut her off. "Do you hear that?"

She thought for a moment that he meant the beating of her heart. Then she heard it too—the lilting sound of a flute and bright rhythm of a drum.

"It is my father's serfs," she said. "They like to dance caroles on the green."

"Do they spin with hands clasped like you taught us to do?" He caught both her hands in his and whirled her in the snow as he'd done in the hall.

Her laughter rang like a bell on the winter's air. "No, I made this step up."

"I do not know which makes me dizzier, this spin or your kisses."

She knew her own answer. She would trade dancing for kissing any day, as long as the kisses were Lucian's.

He stopped and caught her against his side, holding her there, steady and strong, safe until her senses steadied.

Safe, as he'd promised always to do. Perhaps it would not be so bad to lean on his steadiness and strength just once in awhile. Perhaps it would not be so bad just this once to listen.

"Shall we go watch them, or shall we return to the Yule fire to hurry Sir Theo along?"

Had it not been for the serfs and their caroles, she would not have danced with Lucian tonight and everything would be the same as the day she had sent him away. She knew if she watched them now, singing and skipping and clapping, the joys of this night would flood her again, and she would be Lucian's wife before the week was out.

She slid her hand into his. "Let us go down to the green."

ABOUT JOYCE DIPASTENA

Joyce DiPastena moved from Utah to Arizona at the age of two and grew up to be a dyed-in-the-fur desert rat. She first fell in love with the Middle Ages when she read Thomas B. Costane's *The Conquering Family* in high school. She attended the University of Arizona, where she graduated with a degree specializing in medieval history.

Joyce loves to play the piano and sing for her own amusement, and she sings in her church choir. Other interests include reading, spending time with her sister, trying out new restaurants, and, unfortunately, buying new clothes. The highlight of her year is attending the Arizona Renaissance Festival, which she has not missed once in its twenty-four years of existence.

Joyce enjoys hearing from her readers and may be contacted at jdipastena@yahoo.com. You can also visit her on her website at www.joyce-dipastena.com, keep up with her latest news on her JDP NEWS blog (http://jdp-news.blogspot.com), or follow along as she researches her novels at *Medieval Research with Joyce* (http://medievalresearch.blogspot.com). Visit her Facebook page at http://www.facebook.com/AuthorJoyceDiPastena.

A Winter's Knight

by Donna Hatch

Other Works by Donna Hatch

The Stranger She Married

Queen in Exile

Mistletoe Magic

Constant Hearts

The Rogue Hearts Series

Regency Hearts

Chapter One

England, 1813

Clarissa Fairchild stared out of the coach window at the forbidding fortress crouched atop the bluff. Dark clouds closed in around it as if to echo the evil lurking inside the grey stone castle, a castle teeming with secrets Clarissa longed to discover.

Next to her, Great Aunt Tilly shivered. "Do close the curtain, Niece. That cursed place gives me the chills. Filled with murderers, you know." She waved a gnarled hand at the window and shifted as the carriage hit a particularly large rut in the road.

Fascinated, Clarissa couldn't tear her gaze away. All her life, stories whispered furtively about Wyckburg Castle and its terrifying lords had captured her imagination—a dark and terrible place with an equally dark and terrible earl. What a grand adventure it would be to explore the forbidding castle, a gothic novel come to life. If only she could find a gothic hero of her own.

Clarissa tapped her chin absently. "I wonder if they hid their wives' bodies inside the castle, or if they buried them in the churchyard to make it appear as if they died naturally."

Aunt Tilly pulled her cloak more tightly around her and shifted her feet. The warming bricks had cooled since they left the village, leaving the floorboards cold. "You'd have to be foolish to venture amid murderers to view the headstones."

Tired from shopping, they fell silent as the carriage bumped along the country road. Again, Clarissa considered Wyckburg Castle, where, for generations, the mysterious lords were born, lived, married, and killed their wives. Of course, no one ever proved the wives had been murdered. After all, who would have the audacity to accuse an earl of murder? Yet, for generations, every Countess Wyckburg had met an untimely death shortly after marrying each successive earl.

Clarissa conjured all sorts of possibilities, each more wonderfully frightening than the last. The current lord had been reclusive even before he married, but had made no public appearances since his wife's death. What manner of man was he? Openly evil? Slyly sinister? And what manner of woman had dared marry him, knowing the family's reputation?

A new thought hit Clarissa and she drew in her breath in horrified delight. Perhaps the earls abducted maidens and forced them to wed. Or maybe the earls were so darkly handsome, no lady could resist them.

How delicious! She shivered. "I wonder if any of those poor women knew of their doom before they were murdered, or it if it happened suddenly."

"It's not proper for a gently bred young lady to dwell on such morbid thoughts," Aunt Tilly said primly. "You should be thinking of finding a nice young man and settling down. After all, you'll be twenty soon. You don't want to be an old maid, do you?"

"Oh, Aunt, all the men I've met are so dull." Murderous earls were so much more fascinating than real men wearing bored expressions while playing polite social games. Her gaze wandered back to the castle. "What would drive generations of men to kill their wives?"

"Oh, for Heaven's sake, child!"

"Sorry, Aunt." Clarissa laughed at herself and her obsessive thoughts. Perhaps she did read too many Gothics. "I won't speak of it again." But oh, she could imagine.

Moments later, wind shook the carriage, and swirling whiteness overtook them, forcing the coach to slow. The castle and bluff blurred into shapeless dark masses.

"The storm has caught us," Aunt Tilly gasped.

Alarm tightened Clarissa's stomach as the very real danger of the storm finally sank in. She put an arm around Aunt Tilly. "I'm sure all will be well."

Aunt Tilly's lips moved in silent prayer. Clarissa opened the compartment inside the coach where they kept writing implements. She dug around, looking for the food or drink it occasionally contained, but found nothing. Not surprising; their shopping trip to town was only supposed to take a few hours. With a sigh, Clarissa closed the hatch and leaned back. The carriage followed a curve in the road and began climbing a steep incline.

Aunt Tilly let out a gasp. "We must be going to Wyckburg Castle! I'd rather freeze!"

The castle? Dizzying excitement swept over Clarissa. After all this time, would she really see the inside of the castle, or even steal a glimpse of the earl? She should have been frightened, she really should, but oh, going inside the castle at last!

She patted Aunt Tilly's arm. "Surely the driver wouldn't take us there if he thought we'd be in danger. And the storm is a more immediate threat."

Aunt Tilly prayed vocally, asking for protection from both the storm and the evil that awaited them in the castle.

A terrible groan splintered the air. The coach lurched sharply to the side, throwing them both out of their seats. Clarissa slammed against the side of the coach as it fell sideways. The carriage continued to roll, then tottered, groaning, before it rocked onto its other side, where it lay still. Outside, horses screamed and tack jangled. Then all fell silent except for the moaning wind. Next to Clarissa, Aunt Tilly lay in a motionless heap.

Taking a shaky breath, Clarissa pushed herself onto her knees. "Aunt Tilly?"

Her aunt's eyes fluttered open. "Clarissa? Are you hurt, dear?"

"No, I don't think so. You?"

"Just shaken, I think." But already a bruise was forming on Aunt Tilly's head. She tried to sit up, but let out a cry and crumpled. She lay, gasping, her lined face twisted in pain as she gripped her wrist with her other hand.

"Lie still, Aunt." Clarissa spread both carriage blankets over her aunt. Where was the coachman? Had he been injured? "I'm going for help." She fumbled with the door latch.

From outside the carriage came a voice. "Miss Fairchild?" A face appeared in the window above them. Though respectful to her, the coachman always appeared ominous with his teeth sharpened to points to aid him in whistling to the horses. "I have to get the team out of the weather!" he shouted over the wind. "We're about a mile from shelter. You can ride on one of the horses."

"My aunt is injured," Clarissa called up to him. "I won't leave her here alone." Not even with the lure of the castle singing to her like a siren's song. Would her trip to Wyckburg prove as treacherous as sirens were to sailors at sea?

The driver's head bobbed. "Stay inside. You'll be protected from the wind. I'll return with help."

"I understand. We'll be fine until then," she said confidently.

"Here's some light." He opened the door to hand down a carriage lamp. Snow blasted inside and bit into her cheeks like shards of glass.

Standing as much as possible in the cramped quarters, Clarissa took the lamp and offered him an encouraging smile. The coachman closed the door, shutting out snow. Outside, wind howled and rocked the carriage. Her teeth chattered, and her body shook.

"So cold," her aunt mumbled.

Clarissa removed her woolen cloak, lay next to Aunt Tilly, and laid the cloak over them both like a blanket. Cold crept in like icy fingers burrowing to her bones. Sleepiness drifted over her. She battled it back but never banished it, only driving it off for a moment before it returned. She drifted in a haze of gray. Wind screamed like ghosts demanding vengeance.

"It's going to be all right," she whispered, as much to herself as to her aunt. "We'll be rescued soon, and then we'll be safe and warm."

The carriage door flew open. A dark form appeared in the doorway above them. "Miss Fairchild? Can you stand?"

She ordered her limbs to move but could barely lift her head. The coachman spoke to someone outside her line of sight, then lowered himself into the carriage.

"Help is here." He slid his arms underneath her shoulders and knees, and lifted her. Standing, he raised her and transferred her to another pair of arms which cradled her against a hard chest.

"Good heavens," muttered a male voice.

Clarissa floated into darkness.

Chapter Two

Christopher de Champs, Earl of Wyckburg, stared at the young woman in his arms. His breath left him as quickly as his wits. To say she was beautiful would have been a tragic understatement. For the first time in three years, his dormant heart awoke and took a good look.

No. He wouldn't make that mistake again. He wouldn't condemn another woman. Too many former Countess Wyckburgs filled the family crypt, his own sweet wife among them.

He tore his gaze off the woman in his arms and carried her to the waiting coach where he promptly bundled her into a blanket. He pulled off her half boots and rubbed her feet to restore the circulation before he placed her feet atop a rag-wrapped brick. He put another brick against her back. She mumbled, pushing at the hot bricks. After ensuring they weren't burning her, he wrapped her again, holding her against the sources of warmth.

His gaze drifted to her face—lovely, delicate features and full lips, framed by a dark green hood. A light dusting of freckles over her nose and cheekbones revealed her propensity to spend time outdoors without a bonnet. Judging by her fine clothing and smooth hands, she was a well-bred lady of quality. Because he never attended society functions, he had no idea as to her identity.

One of his footmen, Hobbs, arrived with an older woman about half his size. A bruise spread over her wrinkled forehead. They bundled her in warmth, and Hobbs cradled the old woman as if she were his own grandmother.

The strangers' coachman stuck his head inside the carriage. Icicles clung to his beard, and his lips were purple. "All set?" the driver asked through chattering teeth.

Christopher motioned. "You get in too. You've been out in that weather too long."

"'Twouldn't be right, milord."

"Get in, man, before you freeze to death. This weather leaves no room for propriety."

The driver climbed in, his shaking hands struggling with the door. Once they were seated, the coach lurched forward. With one arm holding the unconscious young lady, Christopher reached into a compartment and withdrew a flask wrapped in cloths to keep it warm.

He handed the flask to the coachman. "Mulled wine. Drink up."

"Thankee kindly." He drank deeply and passed the flask back.

"Where were you headed?" Christopher asked.

"Birchwood Manor, the Fairchild place down the road."

Christopher choked. "Fairchild?"

"Yes milord. Storm didn't look that close when we left town, or I wouldn't've risked it."

Fairchild. The woman in Christopher's arms descended from the very witch who had cursed his family generations ago. Though tempted to open the carriage door and throw out the witch's spawn—or run a blade through her—he gritted his teeth and remained still. As his gaze strayed back to the unconscious young woman, all thoughts of revenge faded to impotent wishes. He couldn't very well condemn a lady for a crime her ancestor committed. Besides, no one believed in witches anymore. He hardly believed in them himself. He was an educated, enlightened man, but five generations of family history, not to mention his personal loss, left no room for doubt.

As he looked into the young woman's angelic face, thoughts of retribution melted like snowflakes on a flame. Besides, Christopher was no murderer, and seeking revenge wouldn't bring back his wife. No, he'd keep his distance and rid himself of the chit as quickly as the storm allowed.

"My thanks for your aid, milord," the driver said. "We wouldn't have lasted long in that weather."

Christopher nodded numbly. The woman in his arms mumbled, her eyes fluttering but not quite opening. Christopher pressed the flask to her mouth and ordered her to drink. She swallowed and coughed, her eyes still fluttering. Twisting against him, she pushed back her hood, displaying a halo of abundant auburn hair.

He might have known. A redheaded witch like her Irish ancestor. It was just his luck that his foe would fall into his hands, leaving him with the dilemma of what to do with her.

As the coach rolled to a stop, Christopher gathered up the unconscious woman and hurried inside, followed by Hobbs carrying the old woman, and the coachman following.

Christopher thrust his bundle at the nearest footman. "Take them to whatever room Mrs. March prepared for our . . . guests." Guests. He almost snorted. There hadn't been guests in the castle for years. His housekeeper was probably having an apoplexy. "And see to their coachman."

A footman motioned to the coachman, who stood holding his hat awkwardly, and they left together. After discarding his snow-covered overcoat and hat, Christopher stalked to his study. Pouring himself a cup of mulled wine, he sipped the hot liquid and stared into the fire.

The door burst open, and his sixteen-year-old brother-in-law charged in. "Is it true?" Henry asked urgently, his eyes wide. "She's a Fairchild?"

"So their coachman says."

"And with red hair, too, just like the witch . . ." Henry trailed off then fixed a piercing gaze on Christopher. "Are you going to kill her?"

Christopher choked. "Henry!"

"Well?"

"One doesn't go about murdering hapless young women in their sleep without bringing the law down upon one's head. Not to mention, I have no stomach for it."

"Your enemy has been delivered into your hands. This is your chance to break the curse."

"I have no way of knowing if killing the ancestor of the witch will lift the curse. And as I said, I've no stomach for murdering anyone, especially not a woman."

"If she were a man, you could challenge him to a duel."

"When did you become so bloodthirsty?"

"The moment I saw that red hair and heard the name Fairchild. You and your family have been dealt a sore injustice. As have I." The lad clamped his mouth shut and blinked rapidly.

Christopher sank into an armchair near the fire. "Indeed."

"I don't suppose *my* killing her would lift the curse, but it would serve justice."

Alarmed, Christopher leaped to his feet and went to him. Placing his hands on the boy's shoulders, he peered into Henry's eyes and waited until their gazes met. Solemnly, Christopher said, "Henry, that girl upstairs did not kill your sister. You cannot even think of harming her. What you are suggesting is morally wrong."

Tears filled Henry's eyes. "It's not fair. Jane didn't hurt any of them. And she died such an unnatural death."

"You're right; it isn't fair." Christopher stared unseeing at the dark window, reliving every labored breath his beloved wife took before her last. He curled his hand into a fist. "Promise me you won't hurt the Fairchild girl."

Silence.

"Henry."

The young man heaved a sigh. "I promise I won't hurt her."

Satisfied, Christopher sat once again and stared into the fire, his thoughts consumed by the beautiful, fiery-haired enemy upstairs.

Chapter Three

*D*ressed in the clothing she'd worn yesterday, including her cloak, Clarissa stood by the crackling fire in an unfamiliar bedroom. Though sore all over, she didn't seem to have suffered injury from the accident or the cold. Besides, she was inside the castle at last. No injury could keep her from exploring.

The room smelled closed in as if from disuse, but it had been recently cleaned—a bit hurriedly, judging from the dust in the corners. The lavish furnishings might have been found in any great house. Nothing in the room gave any clues as to the secrets of the castle and its inhabitants. Disappointing, really.

Outside, the snowstorm rattled the windows. She sighed. It was the first day of Christmas. If she didn't get home, she'd miss the festivities. She'd never been away from her family on Christmas. Homesickness arose briefly. And yet, at last, she'd been handed a coveted chance to investigate

Wyckburg Castle. Since she couldn't control the weather, she may as well explore the inspiration of her most vivid fantasies.

She'd found a washbasin to aid in washing her face, a hairbrush to tame her unruly hair and twist it into a simple chignon, and a clean toothbrush, but of course had no change of clothing. She longed to venture out in search of breakfast, but first, she ought to find her aunt and learn whether she was well. Then she'd explore the castle. Perhaps she'd even meet the terrible Lord Wyckburg. Excitement thrilled her at the thought. As she moved toward the door, wind howled outside, and a cold draft blew across the room like the icy touch of a phantom.

The door opened, and she jumped. A plump woman with gray-streaked hair entered, carrying a tray of covered dishes. As the woman's gaze flicked over Clarissa, she wrinkled her nose as if she smelled something unpleasant. She set the tray on the small table by the hearth.

"Breakfast." She spoke in a flat tone, not entirely rude, but without any friendliness.

"Thank you, but my aunt . . . I'm concerned for her well-being. She was injured."

"She is your aunt, then, and not your mother or grandmother?"

Taken aback at the inquisitiveness of the servant, Clarissa summoned a smile. "She's my great aunt—my mother's aunt on her mother's side."

"I see. She's resting in the next room."

"I'll check on her before I eat, then."

The woman paused a moment. "This way." She led her to the room next door.

Inside, Clarissa found her aunt sitting in bed propped up by pillows. "How do you feel, Aunt?"

"Well enough, child. My head hurts, and my arm, but nothing seems to be broken." Aunt Tilly held up her hand

and wiggled her fingers. "It hurts to put weight on it, but I'm certain it's just a sprain."

Clarissa kissed her aunt's cheek, resisting the urge to smile at the pieces of hair sticking up at odd angles from Aunt Tilly's head, making her look as if she'd suffered a fright. "I feared you were truly injured."

"Just shaken, it appears." She patted Clarissa's cheek. "You, dear?"

"A bit sore all over, but I'm well enough." Turning back to the servant, who eyed the entire exchange more boldly than a servant ought to, Clarissa said, "I'd like to thank those who came to our aid yesterday."

All she remembered was a strong, gentle pair of arms. Surely they couldn't belong to the frightening recluse who'd murdered his wife.

"Lord Wyckburg is a very busy man. However, I will convey your gratitude." The woman turned and left, leaving Clarissa to stare after her.

"Impertinent," Aunt Tilly sniffed. "No way for a servant to treat a lady."

Clarissa smoothed the counterpane on the bed, fingering the rich fabric. Surely there must be some way to meet the mysterious, murderous earl . . . or at least see him.

"Perhaps I ought to arise and find the necessary." Aunt Tilly's gazed darted around as if she expected to see a murderer appear. "Your parents will have servants searching for us as soon as the weather improves. The last time it snowed this much, the roads were impassable for three days. They had to dig out the mail coach."

"Three days?" Clarissa didn't try to hide her dismay. Her lust for exploration of this long-forbidden castle evaporated in the face of missing so much of Christmas with her family. "We'll miss the feast and the lighting of the Yule log tonight."

Aunt Tilly gave her a sympathetic smile. "Then let us hope the weather clears soon. I really must find the necessary." She threw back the counterpane and stood. After testing her balance, she disappeared into the next room.

Clarissa tried to remember how far it was to her family manor from the castle. Her bedroom window provided a view of the castle, but she'd never walked the distance. In the summer, she could probably walk there in a few hours, but tramping through snow would take all day, and she had only her half boots and cloak to keep her warm. No, she didn't dare risk it.

Aunt Tilly reappeared and used the washbasin to splash her face. At her aunt's request, Clarissa took up a hairbrush lying on the bureau and brushed out her aunt's gray hair. She coiled it at the back of her head and pinned it.

The inquisitive servant appeared again, carrying a tray identical to the one she'd brought to Clarissa. After depositing the tray, she turned to Clarissa. "Shall I bring your tray from the other room?" Her expression and tone made it clear she'd rather not.

Clarissa drew herself up. "Yes, thank you." She drew up a chair opposite her aunt's.

With a sigh, the servant retreated, then returned and placed the tray in front of Clarissa.

Clarissa gave her a brilliant smile. "Thank you, Mrs. . . . ?"

The servant blinked, clearly taken aback, but only eyed her in disapproval before she left.

"Odd creature," Aunt Tilly murmured.

"I don't expect murderers have an easy time retaining quality servants." Clarissa turned her attention to the delicious array of food and a steaming cup of chocolate. "I think after I eat, I'll seek the library."

Aunt Tilly eyed her shrewdly. "You're just looking for an excuse to go exploring. Your curiosity is bound to be your end someday, mark my words."

Grinning unrepentantly, Clarissa sipped her chocolate. "Perhaps. But one always finds such interesting things when one indulges in a bit of curiosity. Maybe adventure awaits us here."

The wind blew harder, like the moaning of ghosts of murdered wives. Clarissa shivered in horrified delight. They finished breakfast, and Aunt Tilly dozed by the fire. Clarissa's lure for adventure sang. After a lifetime of looking up at Wyckburg Castle and wondering about it, she was finally inside. Now was her chance.

She tiptoed out of the bed chamber and stopped, staring breathless at the ornate carvings and gold leaf that graced the high ceiling, the rich carpet running the length of the long corridor that cushioned her feet. She had expected to see cobwebs and disuse, but everything was clean, orderly, and well cared for. Nothing seemed sinister. Vaguely disappointed, she moved down the corridor. She passed pastoral paintings, tapestries, family portraits, crystal candle sconces, and sideboard tables bearing vases and figurines, all revealing wealth dating from a bygone era.

Gripping the gleaming mahogany banister, she descended a large, winding staircase, the thick carpet runners making her footsteps soundless. The stairway ended at a great hall with a polished floor and four dark fireplaces.

So far, the only thing unusual about the castle besides its beauty was a lack of Christmas decorations.

Standing in the middle of the great hall, Clarissa admired the splendid room with its arched ceiling. Several doors led off to the sides, with no clues as to what might be found beyond. Only one way to find out. She chose a door and moved to it.

With her heart pounding in excitement, she pushed open the door. The hinges creaked ominously. A cavernous room enshrouded in darkness met her eyes. Only gray light filtering through the windows provided any illumination. She stepped inside and paused until her eyes adjusted to the gloom. As her vision sharpened, she caught her breath. She stood in a grand ballroom, more glorious than any she'd ever seen during her four seasons in London. Crystal sconces graced the walls, and enormous chandeliers hung from the ceiling which might have been painted by the great Michelangelo.

Caught up in the beauty of the room, she imagined herself dressed in a glorious ivory ball gown, greeting a foreign prince. She sank into a deep curtsy and let her imagination take flight. "Why yes, Your Highness, I'd be delighted."

Humming a waltz, she put her hands into waltz position and gave herself over to the rise and fall of the rhythm. Across marble tiles she danced, humming and spinning, imagining other dancers around her, their voices and laughter mingling with the musicians. When her tune came to an end, she sank into another curtsy toward her imaginary prince.

"It was my pleasure, Your Highness."

"Pardon me for asking, but do you have permission to waltz?" a male voice echoed through the room.

Startled, Clarissa whirled around and stumbled backward. A dark figure blocked the doorway. Her heart thudded in her ears, and heat crawled up her neck to her face. Who had caught her in such a childish display? Inwardly laughing at her own silliness, she fought off her embarrassment, and faced the consequence of her lapse.

The figure strode toward her in the long, confident strides of a man of authority. This was no servant.

She held her breath, peering at him. Was this the mysterious earl? She offered a sunny smile. "I didn't mean to intrude, but your ballroom is exquisite. I just couldn't resist."

The man gestured toward a space in front of her where her imaginary partner had stood. "I don't think His Highness minded."

Surprised at the humor he'd just displayed—or was he mocking her?— she let out a strained laugh. "Er, no, perhaps not."

The stranger stopped his approach within arm's length. Her head barely reached the bottom of his chin, and the breadth of his shoulders surpassed those of other men of her acquaintance. In the dim light, she couldn't see his face clearly and got only an impression of strong features framed by dark hair. But his clothing was of the finest cut and fabric. No doubt she stood in the presence of the terrifying Earl of Wyckburg. Although at the moment, he didn't seem terrifying. Surely a murderer wouldn't tease her about dancing.

He gazed at her with curious intensity. "You didn't answer my question."

She blinked. "Question?"

"Do you have permission to waltz?"

"Oh." She laughed nervously again. "Yes, actually I do. The patronesses were kind enough to give me permission to waltz during my first Season in London a few years ago."

He continued to look her over carefully. She wanted to retreat inside her cloak. Instead she smiled up at him, despite his lengthy scrutiny, and wished she could see him better.

She cleared her throat. "We haven't been properly introduced."

"No." He said nothing more.

"I'm Clarissa Fairchild." She sank into a proper curtsy.

"Yes, I thought so. Your father is Sir Richard Fairchild, is he not?"

"Yes." Smiling, she waited.

He continued his grave appraisal. Something in his face bespoke abiding sadness.

"I presume you are the Earl of Wyckburg?" she prompted gently.

He drew in a breath. "Yes, of course, where are my manners?" He bowed. "Christopher de Champs, Thirteenth Earl of Wyckburg, at your service. This room is freezing. Do come into my study where I have a fire. I'm sure you'll be more comfortable there—if you can bear to leave the prince, that is." One corner of his mouth lifted so slightly she might have imagined it.

He offered her an arm, and she took it, still smiling up at him. He didn't seem terrible at all, just sad. Perhaps he was lonely. Could everyone have been wrong about him? About his family? It was too early to tell, of course, but nothing about the castle or the earl had been what she'd expected. And he smelled wonderful! Mulled wine and bay rum mingled in a heady blend. She drew in a deep breath and resisted the urge to lean closer.

His gaze slid her way. "I trust you've been made comfortable, Miss Fairchild?"

"Indeed I have. The room and meal were both lovely. I went in search of a library, but found your ballroom instead. I hope you don't mind."

He paused. "Not at all. I'm gratified to see you've not suffered any ill effects from yesterday. You were barely conscious when we brought you here."

She nodded. "It was terribly cold, but as you can see, I'm unharmed."

"And your companion?"

"Only minor injuries."

They crossed the main hall to a cozy study. A fire roared in the hearth, and lamplight illuminated the room. She looked up at the mysterious Lord Wyckburg—handsome in an austere sort of way, with sharp, stern features. His face was decidedly patrician, and his hair pure black. He was younger than she expected, probably not yet thirty. He looked down at her, and she blinked at the startling pale blue of his eyes. Strange, but she'd expected them to be as dark as night. Those light blue eyes should have been as clear as a brook, but harbored such brooding sorrow that she caught her breath. He stared at her as if he hadn't anything else to do. Then, visibly swallowing, he stepped back, severing all contact.

"Do try my selection of books here in my study before you brave the frigid air of the library." He paused. "I seldom have guests, so I don't heat rooms I don't frequently use."

"Of course." She moved to one of the bookshelves on either side of the hearth and pretended to peruse the titles, but all her attention remained fixed on the man in the room. As he started to leave, she called out, "Do you have any recommendations?"

He paused, eyeing the door as if he'd hoped to escape through it. He turned to her, tension rolling off him. "That depends on what you enjoy. This section is mostly poetry, this is philosophy—"

"Are those your favorite things to read?"

Again he paused, as if taken aback by her question. "I suppose, on occasion. I read the newspaper the most."

"You may think me terrible, but I love novels." She smiled.

"No, not terrible." He paused, looking her over in that careful assessing way. "Is your red hair a family trait?"

She stiffened. Whatever charm she'd thought she saw in him evaporated in the face of his condescending question. "My hair is not red anymore, it's auburn."

His lips twitched upward. "Sensitive about it, are you?"

Folding her arms, she eyed him coolly. "You would be too, if you were subjected to the names I've endured."

"I suppose your father's a redhead too?"

His insistence on calling her a redhead made her grind her teeth. But as she relied upon both his hospitality and his mercy, she felt obligated to reply. "No. It appears to be a feminine characteristic in our family, but it frequently skips generations."

"Fortunate."

She gasped at the slight. Her mother had assured her that her once-red hair had deepened to an envious shade of auburn, but apparently, men still thought it a flaw. At least, this man did. Reminding herself that she'd received numerous offers of marriage, she squared her shoulders and told herself she didn't care one whit for his opinion. Despite how lovely he smelled. Or how beautiful his eyes were. And how, the rare times he almost smiled, his face softened and became quite handsome. She shook herself. She meant to discover his secrets, not rhapsodize on his looks.

He rested an arm on the mantle, his curiously light blue eyes focused directly on her. "You are a direct descendant of Sir Reginald Fairchild and Aislynn McGregor?"

Her mouth dropped open. How did he know? "They are my grandparents five generations ago. How do you know so much about my ancestors?"

Grimly, he said, "I ought to, considering how much our family histories are intertwined."

"What do you mean?"

He frowned. "Surely you know about the curse?"

Fascinated to meet someone superstitious, she leaned in. "Curse?" Was he was making fun of her? She let out her breath in annoyance "No, please, do not tell me my hair color is a curse."

He blinked, then slowly, a smile curved his mouth, transforming his stern face into an extraordinarily handsome one. A dimple appeared on his left cheek, giving him boyish charm. "No, not your hair. It really isn't that bad."

"'Not that bad,'" she repeated. "Not a direct insult, but not exactly a compliment, either."

He chuckled softly, but the sound seemed to come from the surface, as if he never felt enough joy to truly laugh. "No,

Miss Fairchild, the curse I refer to is the one your grandmother Aislynn placed upon my third great-grandfather William."

She stared in horror. "Sir, that is a terrible thing to say."

"It was a terrible thing to do. She cursed him and all future earls and countesses of Wyckburg." No trace of humor touched his face. He fully believed his words.

Clearly, she stood in the presence of a madman. How delicious!

Chapter Four

As surprise and curiosity sparkled in Clarissa Fairchild's eyes, Christopher realized she had no knowledge of the curse. Perhaps Aislynn never confessed her act of vengeance and took her secret to the grave.

Miss Fairchild focused clear, emerald eyes on him. "Curse?"

Christopher took a breath. "When my great-great-great-grandfather, William, told Aislynn he'd been forbidden to marry her, she said if he loved her, he'd defy his parents."

"That would have been the act of a deep and abiding love."

He issued a short, mirthless laugh. "Love. Love brings only heartache." As he well knew.

She cocked her head to the side and peered at him in rapt attention.

"My family has a deep sense of honor and duty; we seldom let emotion rule our decisions. Therefore, William refused to go against his family's wishes. He married the lady to whom he'd been betrothed. Aislynn flew into a rage and placed an Irish curse upon him; after the birth of his first son, his wife would die."

She drew in her breath sharply.

He focused on the fire, unable to look at her as he laid out the ugly truth about her ancestor. "At the time, he discounted it as the ranting of a broken heart. To his surprise, a few months after his marriage to his betrothed, she wedded your ancestor, Sir Reginald Fairchild."

"Oh, dear. How awkward to have her as a neighbor."

"More than awkward. A few days after his wife gave birth to their first son, she died."

"Murdered?" She stared at him wide-eyed as if equally fascinated and horrified.

"Not in the natural way. At least, not as far as anyone could tell. The doctor said her death was due to a poor recovery from childbirth. But it gets worse; a few years later, he married again, and she, too, died—a few months after the birth of their first son."

"You don't believe their deaths a coincidence."

"Such a curse has traveled from father to son. Each time, the new countess died of something different—a fall, an illness, consumption, a hunting accident, an unexplained illness. But the results were the same; within a year of giving birth to a son, each countess perished."

"So they *weren't* murdered by their husbands." She put hand to her forehead, and her eyes took on a faraway look.

"No. Despite what people say, none of my ancestors murdered their wives."

She studied him as if she meant to open up his mind and his heart and uncover all his secrets. "You didn't murder your wife, either."

Her words hit him like a blow to the stomach. "No. I would never have harmed her. I loved her." For all the good it did him. It would have been better if he hadn't.

Deep, poignant sorrow darkened her eyes. "I'm so sorry. Truly I am."

Old grief arose and choked him. He looked away and curled his fingers into a fist.

"Let's imagine I believe in your curse," she said. "Aislynn suffered from a broken heart and an Irish temper, but surely she wasn't a monster. Perhaps there is a way to lift the curse."

He couldn't resist saying, "My brother-in-law believes murdering you will do it."

She took a step backward, glancing around as if she expected to be attacked.

At her expression, he smiled ruefully, feeling wicked for teasing her. "Don't worry. I don't uphold the practice of murdering maidens, nor of harming houseguests."

Her ready smile banished the gloom in the room, and a place inside his icy heart began to thaw. "Very gallant of you, sir."

He effected a courtly bow. "But to answer your question—though many have searched, no one has found a way to lift the curse."

She sank into a chair, her brow furrowing in concentration, and tapped a long, slender finger against her shapely lips, a hypnotic gesture that tied his stomach into knots. "Perhaps the curse is attached to the castle. Has anyone tried leaving?"

He dragged his gaze from her lips. "Many. My father took my mother to Ireland. Despite the war, I took my bride to Italy. They all died, no matter how far from the castle."

"Were any daughters born?"

"Yes, a few, but each time a countess delivered a son, she died within a year."

She turned her green gaze upon him. "So, you have a son?"

The door opened, and Henry burst in. "When—" He stopped as his gaze landed on the Fairchild girl. "Saints above."

All the wind seemed to have been knocked from him as he stared at Clarissa Fairchild. Visibly taken aback at Henry's stare, she looked to Christopher for help.

He gestured. "Miss Fairchild, my brother-in-law, Henry Seton."

Henry lifted his nose and curled his lip as he stared at Miss Fairchild. "You have a lot of nerve coming here."

Miss Fairchild took a step backward, bringing her closer to Christopher.

He couldn't explain the surge of protectiveness toward the girl, but Christopher stepped forward to stand shoulder to shoulder with her. "She had nothing to do with it, as you well know." To Miss Fairchild, he explained, "Henry's sister was my late wife. He is my ward, home from Oxford for Christmas. He, er, blames your family for his sister's death."

Henry's eyes narrowed as if he gazed upon the Corsican Monster instead of a beautiful young lady. "She was my only family in all the world. You—your family—took her from me."

She held up a hand in a helpless gesture. "I'm sorry for your loss, Mr. Seton, truly I am. Until moments ago, I was unaware of any such curse."

Briefly, Christopher wondered if she truly believed the tale of the curse, or if she thought them all mad and had decided to play along until she could make her escape.

Henry drew himself up and looked down his nose at her. "Ignorance is no excuse."

Christopher let out his breath in frustration. "Henry . . ."

Miss Fairchild's voice broke in. "If there is a way to lift the curse, I vow I will find it. I'll ask all my relatives and search our library."

Henry eyed her dubiously. "You would help us?"

"Of course. As Aislynn's descendant, it's my duty." She glanced up at Christopher with a wry smile that did odd things to his breathing. "I don't suppose you have any records which may hold the answer?"

"We have an extensive history of our family as well as a number of old tomes on folklore and legends. But my ancestors have searched them already."

"My father taught me to speak Gaelic, so maybe I can find something your forefathers overlooked due to the language barrier."

"It may be a complete waste of time."

She held up her hands in a slight shrug. "I have nothing else to do, and it will help take my mind off the fact that I'm here on the first day of Christmas instead of with my family."

Christopher nodded. Of course. Christmas. He'd forgotten. Very well, to help her pass the time until she could return home, he'd help her search his library.

"Very well. Let's begin our quest." Christopher gestured to Henry to lead the way so he could keep an eye on his charge. Henry probably wouldn't try to hurt the girl, but his pain and lust for vengeance was real, and his tumultuous sensibilities made him unpredictable.

Inside the library, after lighting several candles and building up both fireplaces, they began searching. Christopher climbed the ladder to the section he thought would be most helpful and began handing down ancient books. He couldn't believe he'd committed to spending the afternoon with the Fairchild chit, contrary to his earlier vow to avoid her. But perhaps the search would help Henry overcome his animosity. And for some strange reason, this lovely girl, who smiled so easily, made him want to please her if for nothing other than to win another smile. She was such a bright spot amid his normal gloom that he couldn't resist staying near her. Besides, if she really could find a way to lift the curse . . .

No. Even if she found one, the only way to test the cure would be to marry and risk another woman's life—something he refused to do.

Hours later, after skimming a dozen volumes of family history, they were no closer to solving the problem. Miss Fairchild had started on books of folklore and sat reading, her lips curving charmingly, and her face alight. His housekeeper brought in tea with sandwiches and biscuits. They consumed the repast while they read.

Finally, Miss Fairchild sat up. "Here's something. It's written in Gaelic. 'How to Lift an Irish Curse. Enter a sacred place under the moon's full light. Fill a bowl of water. Add salt, sage, lavender and chamomile. Light thirteen white candles . . .' Oh, wait, someone wrote in the margin next to the incantation, 'ineffective.' It looks like one of your ancestors already tried it." Her mouth turned down in a pretty little pout.

Christopher pushed back his book. "I'm certain William and his sons tried everything. *I'd* be willing to try it. But there's no way to know if anything works unless I marry some poor girl and father a son with her. I won't put another woman at risk."

Her eyes softened. "Did she believe the curse? Your wife?"

He let out a labored breath. "I told her, but she thought the deaths all tragic coincidences."

Henry spoke up. "I didn't believe either, to tell you the truth. It sounded too fantastic."

Miss Fairchild gestured to the book in front of her. "There's no way of knowing who wrote this notation. It might have been someone else, and for an entirely different purpose. Perhaps you should try it."

"It doesn't matter. I won't remarry."

She smiled gently. "But if you tried it, it might work for your son."

Christopher drew a breath. "My son died shortly after I lost my wife. I have no heir except a very distant cousin."

She watched him with enormous, sad eyes. Silence hung heavy in the room. Outside, the wind wailed like a banshee. To give himself something to do, Christopher picked up another tome and thumbed through the pages.

Henry pushed his book away. "This is pointless. We're wasting our time." He got up, glared as if he thought Christopher had defected to the enemy, and left.

Miss Fairchild watched him leave, her expression thoughtful, then returned to her study.

When the gray of the day waned to the dark of night, he glanced at the clock. "Dinner will be served shortly."

Miss Fairchild pushed back the book and rubbed her eyes. She marked her place with a sheepish smile. "Perhaps someday you'll decide to try it."

As they crossed the main hall to the stairs, she gestured at the room. "You don't celebrate Christmas on a grand scale, do you?"

Christopher swallowed. "No." His word came out harsher than he'd intended. She couldn't know what Christmas meant to him, of all he'd lost.

"I've never been away from home on Christmas," she said softly.

Her forlorn expression and the sadness in her voice moved him to a compassion he never expected to feel for a Fairchild. He searched for a way to apologize. Awkwardly, he asked, "I suppose your family has a grand celebration? Tell me."

Her eyes lit up. "Family comes from all over to celebrate, and they stay all twelve days. We bring in the Yule log and light it, and we put evergreen boughs all around the house, decorated with big, red bows. It's very festive. We hang mistletoe underneath the doorways, and the boys all try to steal kisses from the girls who pretend they don't want to give them." She giggled. "I'm not sure why it's acceptable to kiss under the mistletoe but not at other times."

Silently, Christopher watched her animated face and the light in her eyes as she spoke.

She gestured as if seeing it all before her. "Then we decorate a fir tree with candles and almonds and raisins in papers. We also hang toys and fruit on the boughs, all tied up with bright ribbons. On Twelfth Night, we exchange gifts we've placed under the tree."

He envied her joy. In a strained voice, he said, "It sounds perfect."

"It is." Her face clouded over again. "I'll miss the First Day of Christmas Feast."

The thaw in his heart spread outward, and he found himself searching for a way to banish her sorrow, to return the bright smile to her face. He came up with nothing but the hard truth. "I'm sorry you're stuck here instead."

As they ascended the staircase, she smiled, but it was forced, more like a grimace. "I wish to thank you for your hospitality, my lord."

"No thanks necessary."

As she looked up at him, he was struck by the trusting innocence in her eyes. "It *is* necessary. You've been most kind, especially since you consider me the enemy."

"Yes, well, you know what they say: 'keep your friends close and your enemies closer.'" He smiled to soften his words.

"How close do you keep your friends?" Again came that probing stare.

He offered a pained smile. "These days, very far away, indeed."

"Don't you get lonely?"

He stiffened, unwilling to confess the truth. "I keep busy."

"I would be dreadfully lonely if I didn't have family and friends around me."

He stopped at the door to her room. "I'll have one of the maids bring you a bath if you'd like. And perhaps we can find you some clean clothing. I can't promise the fit or style, but—"

She put a hand on his arm. "I would consider it a kindness."

She smiled again, and he found himself smiling in return. Christopher couldn't remember the last time he'd smiled so much in one afternoon. It was a wonder his face didn't crack.

And all due to the smile of an enemy.

Chapter Five

After Clarissa bathed, a maid fastened, tied, and pinned her into a borrowed gown. Despite being at least two years out of date, her ivory gown trimmed with gold lace made her feel elegant and lovely. With her hair tamed into a cascade of curls down the back of her head, Clarissa strode, head high and smiling, to the drawing room to gather with the others. Instead of being home for Christmas, she'd found herself among those who viewed her as the child of the enemy.

But she'd finally realized her dream of entering Wyckburg Castle. And what an expected delight she'd found in Lord Wyckburg. He couldn't be a murderer; his words and sorrow had been genuine. Something terrible had happened to this man—to his family—and she was determined to discover the truth. And if it turned out that this curse was indeed real, as she was beginning to believe, then she'd discover a way to lift it. There had to be a way.

In the drawing room, Aunt Tilly, dressed in a gown as out of date as the one Clarissa wore, sat sipping a sherry.

Henry stalked around the room like a caged animal. Lord Wyckburg stood quietly, so utterly still that he might have been a statue. When his gaze flicked to Clarissa, his eyes widened, and he looked her up and down.

"Lovely," he said in a hoarse voice. Haunting vulnerability entered those pale eyes.

Clarissa paused. Was she wearing his late wife's gown? Her breath left her. Lord Wyckburg was no murderer. He was a sad, considerate man who'd shut himself away from the world out of grief, not because he hid generations of crime.

He recovered quickly, but his smile was strained. "May I offer you a sherry?"

"No, thank you."

The woman who'd brought Clarissa her breakfast tray announced dinner. As Clarissa placed her hand on Lord Wyckburg's offered arm, he pressed his mouth together in a thin line. He led her to a dining room and seated her at his right. Henry silently escorted Aunt Tilly to Clarissa's side then took a seat opposite them.

Very gently she asked Lord Wyckburg, "Am I wearing your late wife's gown?"

He nodded.

"I'm sorry. The maid who was helping me—"

"I told her to find something she thought might fit."

"Oh." Humbled by his gesture, she lowered her gaze. "It was very kind of you to see to my comfort. Thank you."

"You do look lovely."

"Despite my hair?" she said, hoping to tease him out of his somber mood.

Those beautiful eyes swept over her, resting on her hair. "It makes me think of sunset on the water."

Clarissa wanted to throw her arms around him. After years of torment about being a redhead, his romantic description made her glow.

As they dined, Henry couldn't seem to decide if he should ignore her or watch her every movement. His behavior hadn't changed, despite having spent all afternoon with her. Would she ever prove to him she was not his sister's murderer?

Clarissa smiled at her host. "A delicious meal, my lord."

His mouth twitched. "Probably not the Christmas fare to which you are accustomed."

"No, but I expect everyone has their own traditions. Are you having a Christmas pudding?"

He took a moment to reply. "Miss Fairchild, when I said we don't do much for Christmas, what I meant is that we have never celebrated it."

Clarissa dropped her fork. "Not at all?"

"No. Not in five generations." A distinctly haunted expression overcame him. As if realizing he'd lost his mask of cool reserve, his expression closed, and his features took on the same stern, unyielding look as the first moment she saw him.

She wanted to reach out and touch him, ached to comfort him, but knew he'd probably rebuke her efforts. Besides, she'd only met him this morning. Yet she longed to bring him out from behind all the barriers he'd built around himself and show him what a grand adventure life offered if one would only step outside his invisible walls.

Softly, she said, "Perhaps if you replaced bad memories with good ones . . ."

"No." His tone suggested no room for argument.

Her appetite fled. How could one not celebrate Christmas? And worse, how could she stand to be here in this dismal castle, with its equally dismal lord, on what was supposed to be the most joyous time of the year?

He continued as if unaware he'd completely dashed her spirits. "The storm stopped, so I sent a messenger to bring word to your family that you're here."

Through the lump in her throat, she managed, "Thank you. I'm sure that will bring them peace of mind." But it wouldn't bring her home in time for the Christmas Eve feast, the lighting of the Yule log, or any of the other family customs. Nor would it reunite her with those she loved.

Aunt Tilly squeezed her hand, a comforting, familiar gesture. Clarissa swallowed and pushed back her disappointment. She had her beloved aunt and a kind host. That would have to be enough for now.

Lord Wyckburg's voice gentled. "I had the carriage brought into the coach house so the wheel could be repaired. Do you need any of the parcels from inside the carriage?"

Clarissa shook her head. "No, they were Christmas gifts."

He nodded, then looked past her with a faraway look in his eyes. Shame at her selfishness wound through her. Missing Christmas with her family mattered little compared with the losses his family had suffered over the years. Besides, she'd fulfilled her lifelong dream of meeting Lord Wyckburg. Though he hadn't been the monster she'd feared—hoped?—he would be, he'd been a fascinating diversion. His being handsome didn't hurt, either.

After dinner, Lord Wyckburg and Henry excused themselves, leaving Clarissa and Aunt Tilly to amuse themselves in the drawing room partitioned off to serve as a sitting room. A fire and an abundance of candles cheered the room. In one corner sat a pianoforte and a harp.

Clarissa moved to the harp and caressed the carved column. "What a lovely instrument. Do you think he'd mind if I play?"

"I'd mind if you didn't," Aunt Tilly said with a sniff, settling by the fire.

Smiling, Clarissa ran her fingers across the strings in an arpeggio. Though out of tune, it had a lovely, rich tone. After painstakingly tuning it, she sat, brought the soundboard to her shoulder, and played. The soothing tones washed away her woes, and her mind drifted. Lord Wykburg's face, one moment stern, the next soft, danced before her eyes. How could anyone suspect him of being a murderer? He was too honorable, too kind, too sad.

And that curse. If there really was a curse—and it was getting harder to deny the possibility—there had to be a way to lift it. If only she could return home and question her relatives, search out old family journals, seek out any sign that might help her discover what really happened. As her mother's aunt, Aunt Tilly wouldn't know. Her father might, or Great-grandmother Fairchild.

But first she had to get home. Even her sense of adventure stepped back in favor of the cheer of home and family during Christmas.

Chapter Six

Christopher stood outside, his breath puffing in great clouds as he looked up at the likeliest-looking fir tree near the castle. Illuminated by faint moonlight filtering through clouds, the tree seemed to hold its breath in anticipation. A cloud drifted over the moon, obliterating its light. At least the snow had stopped. Christopher gripped a lantern in one hand and an ax in the other. Hobbs eyed him patiently.

Why was he doing this? Christmas meant nothing but grief and sorrow and loss. Yet here he stood, considering chopping down a tree and bringing Christmas into the house for a girl he'd only known a matter of hours, and the daughter of the witch who'd cursed his family, at that. He was about to betray his family—his wife, mother, grandmother, his ancestors. Henry in particular would hate the idea of doing anything kind for Miss Fairchild.

Yet, how could he not? The loss in her eyes when she spoke of her longing to be with her family for Christmas tugged at his heart. When he'd informed her that his family never celebrated Christmas, she'd gone white with dismay and nearly burst into tears. If this simple gesture of a traditional Christmas Eve would bring another of her enchanting smiles to her face and make her day bearable despite her separation from her family, then so be it.

He glanced at Hobbs. "Think this one will do? It's the only fir tree in sight."

"Ye'd haf' ta go deeper into th' forest to find one better, mi'lor'."

"I'm not that mad. This one will do." Christopher set down the lantern and hefted his ax.

They swung their axes, and within moments, the tree fell. Standing on either side, they grabbed the tree by a large, lower branch and began hauling it back to the house, tramping through knee-deep snow. The thaw in his heart warmed further at the thought of her smile. As they returned to the house, he scanned every tree they passed, looking for mistletoe.

Christopher stopped underneath an oak. "Is that mistletoe?"

Hobbs held up his lantern. "I think so, m'lor'."

"I'll take a look." Christopher jumped for the lowest branch.

"Oi, m'lor', lemme get it. We can't have ye fallin' and hurtin' yesself."

"It's been a while since I've done this, Hobbs, but I'm not exactly an old man."

He climbed upward, surprised at how exhilarating it was to climb a tree, the danger and the pleasure of anticipating Miss Fairchild's happiness mingling into a heady euphoria. Calling himself a great fool, he reached one of the top branches and examined the plants hanging from it.

He let out a satisfied grunt. "It's mistletoe, all right."

With a small knife, he cut several bunches. They plopped in the snow as they fell. After sheathing his knife, he carefully climbed down, grateful his sturdy boots had good soles and that he'd worn a pair of leather gloves to aid his grip.

Hobbs gathered up the bunches. "That's a lot o' mistletoe."

"Take some. Maybe you can coax a kiss out of some of the maids."

"I migh' at that." Hobbs grinned.

Once inside, they dragged the tree to a corner of the great hall where the servants waited.

A maid curtsied and held out a box of bright ribbon. "'Twas all we could find, milord. And these are the smallest candles we found." She gestured to a box on the floor.

Mrs. March, the head housekeeper, shook her head in confusion. "I don't understand, my lord. Why now?"

"Because we have pair of houseguests who are missing their family. If we can give them a Christmas of sorts, it might help."

Mrs. March shook her head again. "She's bewitched you."

"Perhaps. Or perhaps it's time to end the hatred."

Just then, Henry crossed the hall, glanced their way then halted, staring. "You aren't."

Christopher drew himself up. "I am. You can either join us and remember what Christmas is about, or you can sulk in your room, but you aren't to do anything to make our guests unhappy."

Henry stared at him, aghast. "No, not after—"

"This topic is not open for discussion."

Henry clamped his mouth shut. As he stalked away, he said, "As you wish. My lord."

Christopher stared after him, wanting to call him back. He'd probably handled that badly, and he knew how traitorous a Christmas celebration must seem to Henry, but he couldn't explain why he felt so compelled to do this for

Miss Fairchild, how happy she made him, and how he couldn't wait to see her beautiful smile.

He addressed the servants in the hall. "When I give the signal, come in and bring all this—" he gestured to the boxes "—with you. Build a fire in every hearth and light all the candles."

Christopher moved to the drawing room. Sweet harp music floated through the air to him, coaxing him near. In the doorway, he stopped. Miss Fairchild sat at the harp, her hands floating gracefully over the strings, her lovely face serene. She played with such beauty, such passion, that his soul stirred. The scene took his breath away. How long he stood there, drinking in the peace and beauty of the music, entranced by the angel who created such loveliness, he couldn't say, but when she stopped and set the harp upright on its base, he wanted to beg her to continue.

"Exquisite," he breathed. "I seldom hear such passion in music."

Standing, Miss Fairchild smiled. "I hope you don't mind."

"I am rewarded many times over just for the pleasure of hearing you play."

Her smile brightened, and she inclined her head in acknowledgement rather than pretending to be demure. Drawn to her, he moved to her side. His hand lifted as if it had a mind of its own, and he had to fist it and bring it back to his side. Her lips drew his gaze, and his cravat seemed to strangle him.

"Are you betrothed, Miss Fairchild?" he heard himself ask. He nearly cursed out loud. What had possessed him to ask such a thing? He'd sworn off marriage. Such a thing would only lead to death for the unfortunate bride. And he couldn't bear to lose a wife again.

Her eyes opened wide in surprise. "No, my lord. I haven't found a man to whom I am willing to pledge myself."

She chuckled. "My aunt fears I'll die a spinster if I don't choose someone soon."

Her aunt let out a grunt. "She's turned down half a dozen offers."

He grinned at Miss Fairchild. "A spinster at what, eighteen? Nineteen?"

In exaggeratedly mournful tones, she said, "I'm nearly twenty, my lord."

"Ah, yes, quite in your dotage."

She laughed, the sound seeping into him like the warmth of a soft blanket. Again came that terrible urge to touch her face, her lips.

He cleared his throat and stepped back. "I have something for you. A poor substitute for your family, but I hope it will make your stay here more pleasant."

He nodded to a servant who hovered at the open doors. A footman dragged in a log. Two more brought in the fir tree. Others carried boxes. She stared as if she didn't quite comprehend.

He made a grand bow. "For you, my lady." Grinning, he glanced at the girl's aunt who had arisen and stood with tears shining in her eyes.

A servant approached. "My lord, Cook says it's time to stir the pudding."

Christopher glanced at Miss Fairchild to watch her reaction. She didn't disappoint. She looked at him first with surprise and then delight. Her smile lit up the room more brightly than the fire in the hearth.

"A Christmas pudding? Truly?"

He grinned. "Yes. Should we go stir it and make a wish?"

"Oh, yes!"

He chuckled at her enthusiasm. How gray his life had been until she came. Now his world exploded with color and joy, with Clarissa Fairchild in the middle of it. It would be a dark day, indeed, when she left.

After stirring and wishing on the Christmas pudding, they spent the remainder of the evening decorating the drawing room until it looked more festive than the castle had been in his lifetime. Miss Fairchild directed all the servants, who lost their hesitation of helping a Fairchild, and scurried to please the lady whose contagious enthusiasm and smiles spurred them on. When all was done, they stood back and admired their handiwork.

"It's perfect," she whispered as if she stood on holy ground. Her eyes shone.

"It is, indeed." He turned to her. "I'm sorry there are no gifts for you on the tree."

She touched his arm, her eyes alight with the purest joy he'd ever beheld. "You have given me a wondrous gift. A knight of old could never have been more chivalrous or more generous." She stood on tiptoe and kissed his cheek, so softly and gently, it might have been the touch of a snowflake.

Tingles spiraled outward at her touch, and the last of the ice inside his heart thawed. If he didn't watch himself, he'd tumble irrevocably in love with this Christmas angel who'd brought light into his dark world. "Is there anything I've overlooked?"

"No, nothing. Unless you have musicians, that is, for dancing." Her eyes twinkled.

"Dancing. Er, yes. Well, I suppose we could. Do you have a suggestion?"

She smiled impishly. "The waltz comes to mind."

"May I? Unless you prefer your imaginary prince." He grinned back.

She laughed. "No, I gladly accept you over him."

Her aunt went to the pianoforte. "I'd be happy to play for you." She began playing a slow waltz.

Christopher took Miss Fairchild into waltz position and lead her the steps. She followed beautifully. How could he ever let her go? In a few short hours, she'd transformed him

231

from a brooding recluse with no hope into a man who smiled, laughed, danced—and the biggest surprise of all—a man who celebrated Christmas.

When the tune ended, they stopped but he didn't release her. Her fingers tightened on his arm, and her gaze searched his eyes. A current crackled between them.

Hobbs sidled up to him and cleared his throat. Grinning, he held a sprig of mistletoe over Miss Fairchild's head. "It *is* traditional, m'lor'."

Christopher didn't know whether to laugh or run in terror. He watched the emotions play on Miss Fairchild's face—surprise, embarrassment, expectation, hope.

She glanced up at him from beneath her lashes. At his hesitation, she blushed but made no move to step away. "You needn't feel obligated, my lord."

"No." He drew a steadying breath and put a finger underneath her chin. Gently, he lifted her face upward. His heart thudded as he leaned downward. Her eyes widened, and her pulse throbbed in her neck. Her fragrance of winter roses mingled with the unique scent of her wrapped around him in a sweet cocoon. He leaned closer. Her lips parted and she closed her eyes. He kissed her. Her velvety lips grew soft and pliant under his, and she followed his lead as instinctively as she'd followed him in the waltz. Years of emptiness, sorrow and bitterness melted away as her kiss healed him. He poured his heart into that kiss, hoping she'd feel what he couldn't tell her.

And knew he'd never be the same.

Chapter Seven

*I*n all the books she'd read, and in all the whispering, giggling conversations Clarissa had shared with her married friends and sisters, nothing had prepared her for the intensity, the passion, the purity of Lord Wyckburg's kiss.

Her heart soared, and she knew, at long last, she was home. The man she'd sought among the suitors in London was here, kissing her as if he'd never let her go. He slid his arms around her and pulled her against his solid chest. She clung to him, praying he'd never stop. Warmth and tenderness swept over her.

"My lord," Aunt Tilly's voice broke in. "Really, I must protest!"

Clarissa swallowed a moan. Lord Wyckburg ended the kiss, but his lips moved first to her eyelids and then her forehead. With a sigh, he drew back. Cold air rushed in where his warm body had been seconds ago.

Christopher's eyes glowed with quiet joy and tenderness. "I should apologize, but I'm afraid I'm not sorry, not one bit."

Neither am I, she wanted to say, but instead summoned a playful smile. "We could blame the mistletoe."

He brushed a finger over her cheek. "I've wanted to do that all day." Sorrow returned, and he closed his eyes. "What am I doing?" He stepped back and cleared his throat.

Everyone in the room stared. Clarissa's face flamed. That kiss had gone way beyond the acceptable mistletoe kind and had bordered on impropriety. But she didn't care. She wanted more. Much more.

Christopher cleared his throat again. "Forgive me. I am not in the habit of assaulting young ladies, not even under mistletoe."

"Isn't mistletoe wonderful? It's resilient and verdant even in the darkest winter. Perhaps we can learn something from it."

He turned tortured eyes on her, and her attempt at levity crashed to the floor. "Miss Fairchild, you must know that you've touched my heart in a way I thought I'd never feel again. But I cannot offer you a future. I refuse to bury another wife."

Clarissa gaped. He'd as good as told her he wanted to marry her, but the curse stood in the way. She considered a life with him. What had seemed restrictive and dull with other men now appeared bright, with endless new discoveries and beautiful possibilities—only with him. In but a few hours, this man had captured her heart as none other. No wonder his late wife had been willing to take a chance.

Now more than ever, she had to find a way to break the curse and convince him to take another chance on love. With her.

She squared her shoulders, raised her chin. "Then we must double our efforts to find a way to end the curse."

"Even if we do, I won't risk your life testing whatever solution we find. The danger is too great." He turned away.

She rested a hand on his back, and he tensed, but didn't step away. She whispered, "Christopher."

His shoulders heaved. "I had my carriage modified to a sledge. Tomorrow, unless it's stormy, I'll take you home so you can celebrate the rest of Christmas with your family." He nodded to Aunt Tilly and strode out of the room.

Clarissa let her hand fall as his rejection fully sank in. He wasn't just denying himself; he was denying her. Her throat thickened. Servants drifted out, bidding her a joyous Christmas. The footman with the mistletoe gave her a cheeky grin.

The housekeeper, whose name she'd learned was Mrs. March, stopped next to her. "Thank you, miss, for bringing a smile to my lord, and for bringing Christmas back the castle." Her mouth curved into an awkward smile before she strode quickly away.

Moments later, Clarissa and Aunt Tilly were left alone in the festive room.

Aunt Tilly stared at her. "Curse?"

Clarissa related everything she knew about the curse. "Do you think it possible Great-grandmother Fairchild knows anything of it?"

Aunt Tilly put her hand on her head. "A curse? Impossible."

"Then explain why every countess has died only months after bearing a son."

"The lords murdered them." But her voice lacked conviction.

"I don't believe that. Not anymore. Do you really think Lord Wyckburg is a murderer?"

"I admit, after meeting him, he seems gentle and kind. Not sinister." She heaved a sigh. "I suppose a curse isn't any more difficult to believe than a legacy of murder."

"Something is going on. And I refuse to leave Chri—er, Lord Wyckburg to face a lifetime of loneliness. I must help him."

Aunt Tilly tilted her head. "What, exactly, do you feel for him?"

"Oh, Aunt Tilly, I've never felt this way before. Of all the suitors I've had in London, none has made me feel this way." She gestured around her. "And look what he did for us. For a man who'd never celebrated Christmas before in his life to have gone to so much trouble . . . it's beyond kind and generous. It's heroic."

"It is, indeed. Clearly, he's a good man."

Clarissa sat down and took Aunt Tilly's hand. "I love him, Aunt. I know it's mad, and I know we've just met, but I vow I'll have him and no other."

Aunt Tilly drew in a breath. "Your father will have something to say about it, considering what everyone believes about the Wyckburg lords. And it sounds as though Lord Wyckburg may be equally hard to convince."

"Leave that to me."

Aunt Tilly chuckled and kissed her cheek. "I know that look. Come, off to bed."

They crossed the main hall toward the stairway. The metallic scraping of a gun cocking sent chills down Clarissa's spine. She froze. Aunt Tilly gasped.

Standing in the shadows, Henry pointed the barrel of a pistol at her. "I cannot kill the original witch who cursed this family and my sister, but I will take vengeance on you."

Stunned, Clarissa stared in disbelief. The surreal scene came straight out of a gothic novel. This couldn't be happening. Too shocked to be afraid, she fell into a state of unnatural calm.

She moistened her lips. "Shooting me won't bring back your sister, Henry." She used his Christian name in the attempt to reach him in a personal way.

"It will avenge her death."

Very softly, she said, "Perhaps, but will it help you find peace?"

He hesitated. "My sister will be avenged."

"Are you truly prepared to kill?"

The determination in Henry's face faded, and the gun lowered an inch.

"Henry!" barked Lord Wyckburg. Christopher! Again, her knight had come to save her.

Henry flinched but put a second hand on the gun to hold it steady. "Stay back, Christopher. This is something I have to do."

"No, you don't." Christopher raised his hands and walked slowly toward Henry.

Henry glanced at him. "You do it, then. It could lift the curse."

"It might." Christopher took another step toward him. "But what if we kill her and the curse remains? What then?"

"We will have justice!"

"It won't be justice or even vengeance. It will be murder."

Henry flinched. Christopher leaped. He sailed through the air and landed on Henry, knocking him down. The gun flew from his hands and slid across the floor. Henry struggled against Christopher, who held him tightly. Then Henry went limp. All the fight seemed to leave him. He started weeping. Christopher gathered Henry in his arms and held him. Clarissa stood in shocked silence. Unable to think of anything else to do, she picked up the gun, eyeing it as if she'd never seen one. This weapon had nearly taken her life. It might have harmed Aunt Tilly or Christopher. Lives could have been shattered if the gun had gone off. If someone had been killed, Henry would have been haunted all his life. He would have faced possible deportation or execution.

All the gothic novels she'd read made this type of event seem thrilling. But it wasn't. It was horrible. A sob lodged itself in her throat then forced its way out.

Christopher sat talking softly to Henry. After a moment, they both stood. Henry came to Clarissa, head down and shoulders slumped. She couldn't decide if he was horrified over his actions, or angry he'd failed.

"I'm prepared to face the law for what I tried to do." He spoke in quiet monotone.

Clarissa gulped back her tears and glanced at Christopher, whose impassive face gave her no clue as to his thoughts. Briefly, his control slipped, revealing grief and inner turmoil. If she turned Henry over to the law, Christopher would have no family. He'd be alone in the world. And Henry was only a grief-stricken boy who hadn't been thinking clearly.

She handed the gun to Christopher without taking her gaze off Henry. "That won't be necessary. I can't pretend to imagine what you've lost, but I can see how you must view me as the one responsible for your sister's death. I won't swear out a warrant for your arrest."

Henry drew in a labored breath. "Thank you," he mumbled. "I'm in your debt. I hope someday you can forgive me."

"I already have. Just please know I'm not your enemy."

Henry nodded without looking at her, then mounted the stairs as if each step pained him.

"Good heavens," Aunt Tilly said. "I didn't think my heart would survive that." She pulled Clarissa into a rough embrace and kissed her cheek. "You were so brave."

Lord Wyckburg let out his breath slowly. "How can I ever apologize for that?"

Clarissa touched his arm. "You needn't apologize. He's young, he's hurting, and he's trying to make sense of it all."

He put a hand over hers. "You are remarkably compassionate."

"I did it for you as much as for him."

Their gazes locked, and he brushed a finger along her cheek. "Thank you."

"Thank you for saving me. He may not have pulled the trigger, but I'm grateful for your intervention. Once again, you are my knight. All you need is the shining armor." She rose up on tiptoe and kissed his cheek. Then, seeing his arrested expression, boldly kissed his lips.

He returned her kiss as if he were starving. Then, as before, he pulled away. "We cannot keep doing this." He glanced at Aunt Tilly, who stared at them with a thoughtful expression.

"Young man, if you insist on kissing my niece, I demand to know what your intentions are toward her."

He heaved a great breath and closed his eyes. "I'm afraid I cannot act on my desires. My intentions must be nothing more than providing shelter until I can return both of you safely home. Good night."

He left Clarissa standing alone, more determined than ever to save him.

Chapter Eight

*C*hristopher glanced at Clarissa Fairchild sitting next to him in the sledge, then back at Henry and Aunt Tilly in the back seat. Their faces barely peeked out over the mountain of blankets he'd piled on them; their cheeks and noses were pink from the chill wind. Aunt Tilly teased Henry about girls who no doubt set their caps for him, and he was actually smiling. Considering the debacle last night, his mood came as a surprise, but some of the weight seemed to have been lifted from his shoulders.

Storm clouds closed around them, and a few flurries of snow flittered down, but he still had time to bring Clarissa—Miss Fairchild, he reminded himself—home. Then he'd return to his solitary existence, which seemed lonelier than ever now that he'd seen what a bright spot Clarissa would be. If only he could make her a part of his life. But he didn't dare.

Clarissa's eyes sparkled, and she smiled in recognition. "There's the driveway to our manor. Oh, you've done it!

We'll be home in a few minutes, and I'll get to spend the rest of Christmas with my family, after all." She kissed his cheek again. "Although last night was so lovely! I cannot thank you enough for making it such a wonderful First Day of Christmas. I'm afraid the other eleven will seem rather dull in comparison."

Looking into her shining face, Christopher's pleasure at making her happy bubbled over. "It was a long overdue event. Although, I'm sure we could have all done without the little incident in the great hall."

"Never mind that. And I want you to know, I understand it was a great sacrifice for you to celebrate Christmas with me."

He wanted to throw down the reins and take her into his arms but settled for smiling softly. "You were right; replacing bad memories with good memories was a wise thing to do."

"Why hasn't your family celebrated Christmas? I realize with all the tragedy, it might have seemed wrong to celebrate, but still . . ."

He drew a breath. "Because every countess died during Christmas."

She fell silent and sat staring ahead as if dazed. "Oh, Christopher, I can't imagine. No wonder."

He inwardly gloated over her use of his Christian name. It felt so intimate, so right.

Her breath caught, and she visibly swallowed. "I didn't realize last night what a wondrous gift you gave me. I thought I knew, but now . . . how can I ever thank you?"

He smiled, his heart lighter than it had been in years. She didn't know it, but she'd given him a priceless gift he would always cherish. "Your enjoyment was thanks enough."

She smiled at him, a playful gleam in her eyes. "I must warn you that my family will prevail upon you to stay and spend the rest of Christmas with us. Do you think you can stand eleven more days of holiday cheer?"

"I wouldn't dream of imposing."

"It would be my—our—way of thanking you. They'll probably insist on sending a servant to your house for enough clothing for an eleven-day visit."

He couldn't decide if he should be pleased or pained. Eleven days bathed in her light. Eleven days of the torture of knowing she would never be his.

They reached the manor. As Christopher helped his passengers out of the sledge, the front door burst open and a group of people swarmed out of it, falling all over Clarissa and her aunt. One attractive, elegant woman in particular hugged and kissed Clarissa repeatedly. Her mother, perhaps. Christopher stood apart, decidedly out of place among so much affection, and envious of the love surrounding Clarissa.

She drew him into their midst and made the introductions, adding, "Lord Wyckburg went to great effort to make us comfortable."

Clarissa's father, Sir Richard, a distinguished older gentleman with silver hair at his temples, offered his hand. "I am in your debt, my lord."

Christopher shook his hand. "It was a delight, sir. They brought a long-absent cheer to Wyckburg."

The elegant woman who'd been kissing Clarissa sank into a proper curtsy, and, with a wide smile identical to Clarissa's, bounded forward and kissed his cheek. "How can we ever thank you? We were frantic when they didn't come home. We are so very grateful to you."

Clarissa pulled Henry into the circle. "And this is Henry, brother of the late countess."

"Welcome, Henry." Lady Fairchild said warmly.

Henry flushed as if recalling that he'd held a gun on the man and woman's daughter only last night.

Lady Fairchild swept a hand toward the door. "Please come in. You are both most welcome. We have plenty of food and hot drinks."

"I'll have your team seen to." Sir Richard motioned to a servant.

As Christopher entered, Clarissa introduced more relatives than he ever would remember. If he counted correctly, there were seven siblings, a dozen aunts and uncles, a plethora of cousins, and a swarm of children too numerous and mobile to count. The happy cacophony rolled over him. Though a bit overwhelming, love and joy permeated the scene, and he found himself grinning and trying to answer the questions they fired at him.

Clarissa led him to a settee near the fire in a small, comfortably furnished drawing room. He let his gaze drift over the room, noting the decorated fir tree, boughs of greenery, and ribbons, just as she'd described. She took a seat next to him, admiration shining in her eyes as she related to her family his great efforts to bring Christmas to her.

She was so lovely, so full of life and cheer. He wanted her in his life, not just today, not just during Christmas, but forever. But he couldn't marry her. Life without her stretched out in endless, bleak emptiness. How could he ever return to that? He leaned back and crossed his legs as if to provide a protective barrier. No, he couldn't stay. He'd be forever lost if he did.

When the furor died down, a wizened woman in the corner raised her crooked hand and motioned to him. In her crackly voice, she commanded, "Come here, young man, and let me get a look at you."

Sir Richard glanced at Christopher in apology and addressed the woman. "Grandmother, this is Lord Wyckburg. One doesn't ask him to come."

The woman let out a scoff. "I know who he is, Richard, why do you think I need to get a look at him?"

"It's all right," Christopher said to let Sir Richard know he took no offense.

He knelt before the woman and looked her in the eyes. Though her wrinkled face and pure, white hair showing beneath a lace cap revealed her advanced years, her green eyes, faded versions of Clarissa's, were clear and alert. She peered into his face as if she could read all his thoughts, leaving Christopher feeling decidedly exposed.

She patted his cheek. "You are a good man, I see, unlike public opinion, and my great-granddaughter seems quite taken with you. But I see hopelessness in your eyes."

Christopher broke eye contact and glanced around, embarrassed at her intimate assessment, especially in view of the entire family. The others made a point of either leaving the room or conversing. Loudly.

She patted his hand. "I've made you uncomfortable, and for that I'm sorry, but at my age, I need to act quickly. I'm eighty-seven years old—I never know when I'll draw my last breath. Unburden yourself. Grandmama keeps many secrets." She tapped her head.

Why he felt the need to reveal himself to her, he couldn't say. Maybe she held some mystical power, but he wanted to share his burden with someone else. "I daren't remarry."

She nodded. "The curse."

He lifted his gaze hopefully. "You know about that?"

"Grandmother Aislynn told me all about it."

He rocked back. "I see."

"She also told me on her deathbed how the curse might be lifted."

Her words hit him like a bolt of lightning. "Lifted?"

She patted his arm. "It's very simple. A direct descendent of the man she loved must fall in love with and marry one of *her* direct descendants." She motioned to

Clarissa, who sat watching them with rapt attention, her mouth opened into an O.

"Clarissa is a direct descendent of Aislynn, and the only one of marriageable age in the family. To lift the curse, you must marry her."

He swallowed. He must marry Clarissa to lift the curse? It seemed too good to be real. Too simple. Too wonderful. Hoarsely, he said, "Are you certain?"

"Do you love my great-granddaughter?"

"More than I ever imagined possible—especially in such a short amount of time. But I won't condemn her to the same fate as every other Countess Wyckburg."

"Grandmother Aislynn might have been hurt and bitter, but she was honest. If she said that this is the way to lift the curse, you can count on it being true."

He looked back at Clarissa, who smiled softly. The room had fallen silent, even the children were quiet. All eyes were trained on him.

Could he do this? Did he dare the risk? Surely Aislynn wouldn't let the curse fall on one of her posterity, but still, he had only the word of an old woman who claimed to have heard the deathbed promise of the witch who'd cursed his family. What if he did marry Clarissa, and she died? What if they broke the curse, but she died from something else? Could he bear the heartbreak of burying another wife? For any reason?

And yet, here was his chance. He might have love and happiness again. He could have children, not only heirs to pass on his title and lands, but the joy that comes from family. He might enjoy Christmases like this his whole life. Bright hope shone in front of him like a star piercing dark clouds.

Looking back at the old woman, he took her frail hand in his. "Are you absolutely positive there's no risk to Clarissa?"

She smiled. "Not from the curse. As to what fate has in store, we are all ignorant of that. But you will never truly live if you are paralyzed by fear of death."

Clarissa watched him with tears in her eyes and a tremulous smile curving her lips. She nodded. Lastly, he looked at Henry, who appeared more serene than he'd been since his sister's death. Smiling a little, he shrugged.

Christopher cleared his throat. "Sir Richard, may I have permission to court your daughter?"

Sir Richard smiled. "You may court her. Slowly."

Christopher understood his point and wondered how quickly he could ask for her hand in marriage and still meet the criteria of "slowly."

Lady Fairchild smiled. "Why don't you and your brother-in-law remain here during Christmas, Lord Wyckburg? We'd be pleased to have you spend time with our family. Besides—" She gestured to snowflakes falling gently outside the window. "—I think you may be here a while."

Christopher grinned at the chance she handed him. He would ask permission to marry Clarissa on Twelfth Night. "My lady, I can think of no place I'd rather be." Returning his gaze to the old woman, he kissed her hand. "You've given me hope. Thank you."

"Thank me by taking care of that girl. She'll be good for you."

"Yes, I believe she will." He moved to Clarissa, who shooed a child out of the seat cushion next to her. Unable to take the grin off his face, he sat next to her, took her hand, and kissed it. Under his breath, he said wolfishly, "Where can I find a sprig of mistletoe?"

General laughter filled the hall, and once again, happy conversation flowed around him. Home and family, first with Clarissa, and later of his own; he couldn't think of a better Christmas gift.

Epilogue

Seated in the family parlor of her childhood home, surrounded by her family, Clarissa smiled at her husband. Christopher removed their tiny daughter, Tilly, from Clarissa's arms and handed her to his eight-year-old son, Christopher the Seventh. With a gleam in his eye, Christopher reached into his pocket and withdrew a sprig of mistletoe. Holding it over her head, he kissed her until the children groaned and begged them to stop.

Great-grandmother Fairchild winked at them from a chair in the corner. Six-year-old Emily, named after Clarissa's mother, climbed onto his knee, battling three-year-old Richard for the same spot. Henry, tall and handsome, laughed in the corner with a cluster of Clarissa's cousins as he regaled them with tales of mischief during his years at Oxford before becoming a barrister. Evergreen boughs graced the mantle over the Yule log burning in the hearth.

Christopher wrapped his arms around Clarissa. "I'm happier than a man has a right to be."

Clarissa let out a contented sigh. "I'm always happy when I'm in your arms."

She looked out the window at Castle Wyckburg perched on the top of a nearby hill, no longer shrouded in mystery, only filled with love. A snowflake fell. Then another.

"Looks like we'll be spending another night here instead of returning home."

He tightened his arms around her. "As long as I'm with you, I don't care where we are. Besides, we can help your family take down all the Christmas decorations tomorrow. It's bad luck to leave them up after Twelfth Night, you know." She heard the grin in his voice.

Wrapped contentedly in her husband's arms, Clarissa smiled. "I don't believe in bad luck. I only believe in love." Love, which had finally broken the curse.

Surrounded by those they loved most, they sat holding one another and looking forward to many more joyous Christmases to come.

ABOUT DONNA HATCH

Author of historical romance and fantasy, award-winning author Donna Hatch is a sought-after speaker and workshop presenter. Her writing awards include the Golden Rose and the prestigious Golden Quill. Her passion for writing began at age 8, when she wrote her first short story, and she wrote her first full-length novel during her sophomore year in high school, a fantasy which was later published. Between caring for six children, (7 counting her husband), her day job, her work as a freelance editor, and her many volunteer positions, she still makes time to write. After all, writing *is* an obsession. All of her heroes are patterned after her husband of over 20 years, who continues to prove that there really is a happily ever after.

A Fortunate Exile

Heather B. Moore

Other Works by Heather B. Moore

Finding Sheba

Heart of the Ocean

The Fortune Café

Esther the Queen

The Aliso Creek Novella Series

The Newport Ladies Book Club Series

Chapter One

New York City, 1901

"Are you pregnant?"

Lila stared at her father, her eyes focusing on his stiff collar, stark white against his carefully shaved, red face. Her mouth opened, but nothing came out.

"By all that is holy, if you are with child. I will—" His hand came up too swift to stop and struck her across the face.

She stumbled back, knocking against her mother who sat prim-faced on the settee.

"James," her mother yelped, half-hearted as it was.

Lila scrambled away from the settee as her father turned his wild eyes on his wife. "I will not have our daughter behave like this, Annabelle! Not in my house."

Her mother's face paled even more, if that were possible, as she clenched her already clenched hands tighter. Her mouth closed into a pinch.

Making her way behind the settee, Lila spoke in a raspy voice that had already spent hours crying. "I am *not* pregnant. We did not . . . I am *not* compromised."

Mr. James Townsend looked from daughter to mother, his face darkening, disbelieving.

The knot in Lila's stomach twisted until she thought she'd be sick, right there, on her parents' talk-of-the-town Persian rug. *Now I will be the talk of New York. Either by a sudden marriage, or worse, a suspicious departure.* But how could she explain to her father that she was not defiled, that the things she and Roland had done may have been touching the fire's flames, but not *that.*

Her eyes brimmed with tears—tears she thought were already spent. They weren't from her father's slap, but because she'd sent a letter to Roland early that morning, and there was still no reply. It was now well past the ninth hour, and had been dark for three. The blizzard that had hit the upper coast the day before had just reached New York City. The snow fell swiftly outside the floor-to-ceiling windows. No one in their right mind would venture out in the face of the storm.

"Can you swear this over your sister's grave?" her father asked in a steely tone.

Her mother gasped at the mention of their younger daughter, and Lila straightened, lowering her hand from her stinging cheek. That her father had brought little Charity into this ugly argument was momentous indeed. "I swear," she whispered.

The room was quiet for a moment. It seemed as if the tick of the grandfather clock in the corner had faded with the silent falling snow. Her father turned away as if he could no longer bear to look at his only surviving daughter. He stood with his back to the women and stared out the massive windows.

Finally, his pronouncement came. "She will leave in the morning for my sister's estate. There she will stay until this whole business is completely forgotten." He scrubbed his balding head. "What will the society papers say tomorrow? There has already been enough speculation, since any woman who associates with Roland Graves is ruined, and our . . . daughter . . . has more than associated with him."

Her mother whimpered and brought a handkerchief to her mouth.

Lila's head throbbed. Her father's sister, Mrs. Eugenia T. Payne, was as austere as her name. She'd worn nothing but widow's black since her husband's passing, and her eldest daughter had converted to Catholicism and gone into the nunnery.

Who goes into the nunnery in 1901 America? That was the thing of gothic novels.

Aunt Eugenia's younger daughter, only one year older than Lila, had made a boring and dull marriage to the local parishioner. Lila had attended the wedding in Connecticut the year before, which was the first and last time Lila ever planned visiting their "estate"—which was in reality nothing more than a farm.

I can't leave the city. What if Roland comes to propose? She stared past her father into the driving snow. *Surely he wouldn't send me out in such a storm.*

Lila's father turned from the window, and she lowered her gaze. "She'll leave first thing in the morning with a letter of explanation to Eugenia. Send Fay up to pack her things. As far as society will know, our daughter is spending the holidays with her widowed aunt."

Her mother murmured assent; Lila wanted to crumple up on the floor. Instead, she turned and slowly walked out of the room then up the stairs to the second floor. Her heart hammered as she thought desperately for some sort of plan. *Should I send another letter? Could I bribe our driver to deliver it in the storm?*

Tears started immediately after shutting her bedroom door. Not tears of shame like another girl would shed at being discovered with the most notorious bachelor in the city, but tears of anger. How dare her father send her away? She was certainly not the only woman in the world to make a mistake. Her father had made plenty of his own.

His own sister refused to come visit their home because of the corruption in the city—at least that's what she called it. *I know otherwise. Aunt Eugenia doesn't approve of my father, or his associates, or his business practices. I'll admit that I'd been pretty innocent before meeting Roland—innocent of all things. But no longer. He taught me a thing or two about the ways of men, and I'll never look at my father, or any other man, the same way again. What will my aunt think when she learns about Roland?*

Lila sat at her ivory painted dressing table and absently moved the trinkets and perfumes around. Everything in her room was ivory and gold, patterned after a distant cousin's bedroom in Paris. When Lila had visited France in the summer, she'd fallen in love with the opulent décor. Her father had ordered furniture from as far as India to achieve the right ambience, and now she'd be trading this divine room for one of splintered furniture and moldy linens.

A light knock sounded at the door. Lila didn't have the voice to answer, so she wasn't surprised when Fay opened the door anyway.

Fay shut it with a firm click before turning to Lila. The sorrow in the maid's eyes about did Lila in. Fay was her oldest friend and confidante. Only she had known about Lila's secret escapades. Fay might have been twenty years Lila's senior and would never live life beyond a personal maid, but she never judged Lila.

The tip of Fay's nose was red, and her pale blue eyes watered. "This came for you, Miss Lila, when you were in with your parents."

Lila stared at the folded envelope in Fay's hand. "Someone delivered it to the door?" She'd heard nothing. Even over her father's yelling, she would have heard if someone had arrived in the front hall.

"It was delivered to the stable boy. He brought it to me."

Lila held out her hand. She'd have to thank Tim later, since he'd done the proper thing with this sort of letter. But when she took it from Fay, her heart stuttered. It was the same envelope she'd sent Roland. Had he returned it unopened?

Lila turned it over and saw the broken seal. Her heart thundered in her ears as she slid the letter out. She knew without opening it that it was the one she'd sent. Her throat pinched as she skimmed her note, then read his answer below.

> *Dearest Roland,*
>
> *Do I dare believe the words you spoke to me this fortnight past? I know there have been other women for you in previous years, but I hope that I was different. My feelings are true, and I can only hope that yours are too. My father wants to send me away. Probably someplace like Africa to live among natives and to grow crops in the dry dirt.*
>
> *I didn't mean for us to be discovered, and I'm sorry that it happened this way. To be forced upon you when you've lived in bachelorhood for so many years. But I hope you do not feel forced and will consider my father's request. I would be most honored to accept your offer.*
>
> *Affectionately Yours,*
> *Lillian Beth Townsend*

Below her carefully constructed letter were the scrawled words:

L—.

I depart on the next steamship to England and will be gone for an undetermined time. My deepest regrets to you and your family. You knew who I was when you involved yourself with me, and I never gave you any promise. Your expectations are your own.

Best wishes in Africa,

R—.

Lila read Roland's note a second time, then a third. Disbelief pulsed through her, then sorrow, anger, more disbelief. He was leaving for England. He was leaving *her*.

Her face burned, the heat spreading down her neck, to her chest. The things he had whispered to her, *promised* her, and the way he had kissed her . . .

"Fay," she croaked. "Tell Collings to have the carriage ready at midnight. I'll be paying a visit to Roland."

"Your father—"

"Shh! He'll know nothing!" Lila hissed. "I deserve a better answer than this." She held out the scribbled letter. "Roland didn't even use his own stationery."

Fay's face paled, and she peered at the letter, although she couldn't read it.

"We will pack just as father ordered," Lila said in a hurried whisper. "But my things will not be going to Connecticut to reside with my suffocating aunt. We'll be taking the same ship as Roland to England."

"There will be many expenses," Fay cut in, her eyes wide with horror.

"Roland will be sponsoring our fare." Lila's voice sounded confident, final, but inside, her heart was breaking.

"But, miss, everything I know is here."

"Then you'll stay here. I'll go alone," Lila said in a sharp voice. "I'll be a married woman soon enough, and I won't have to answer to you or anyone." She closed her eyes against

Fay's stunned expression. *I hurt my only friend, but it has to be done.* She went behind her dressing screen if only to get away from Fay's gloomy face.

Once Roland saw her again, he'd remember how much he loved her. How perfect they were for each other. How she made him laugh, and how when they kissed, everything transformed into the most beautiful dream.

Chapter Two

When the midnight bell chimes came through the window, Lila was dressed in her heavy cloak. She pulled on her warmest gloves as Fay tiptoed inside her room.

"Everything's ready," Fay whispered.

Behind her, Tim entered. The twelve-year-old's eyes were huge in the near dark. He and Fay silently picked up the trunk together and carried it out of the room.

With a final glance at her ivory and gold bedroom, Lila slipped into the hallway, closing the door behind her. If Lila had been a religious woman like Aunt Eugenia, she might have realized that sneaking out of her home with a large trunk, without being detected, was a miracle. But Lila had only one worry on her mind—how to convince Roland to marry her.

Roland Graves was the most notorious bachelor in New York City. He broke women's hearts like a spoiled toddler broke a trinket, with little thought, knowing another would be handed him. But Lila had refused to believe he could break *her* heart. Even during that first waltz they'd danced on All Hallow's Eve only six weeks previous, Lila hadn't intended to fall in love with him. After all, he was a man twice her age, and he'd made it more than clear in society that he never intended to marry.

Lila slipped through the back kitchen door and walked around the side of the house, where the carriage waited. The snow had accumulated to several inches, and Fay and Tim already stood next to the carriage, shivering. Lila gave Fay a quick embrace and handed Tim a few coins then patted him on the head. She didn't dare meet Collings' stern gaze. She could very well guess what he thought—that this was a charade. Even the horses looked put out. As it was, she'd given Fay all of her spending money to keep quiet with the promise if they were caught, Lila would take complete blame. Pushing back the guilt of involving so many people in her plans, Lila climbed into the freezing carriage and pulled a thick wool blanket over her.

The rug did nothing to warm her feet, and her Italian high-button boots were no match for the snow. As the carriage lumbered down the middle of the avenue, her toes started to ache from the cold.

It seemed ages before they reached the corner house Roland had rented for the past two weeks—*To be closer to you,* he'd said. The lower bank of windows was bright, shedding a welcoming glow onto the snowy lawn. Lila's heart leapt. He was awake. Most likely packing for England, but the timing couldn't be more perfect.

Lila rapped on the carriage window, and it slowed. She wanted to speak to Roland without Collings serving as audience. The carriage stopped about half a block down, and Lila climbed out. She hiked up her long skirt and trudged through the snow-covered walk. The Italians knew nothing about warm boots.

Just as she reached the edge of Roland's property, a buggy came around the opposite corner. It pulled to a stop in front, and the bundled driver gave a whistle.

Lila froze in place. Was he signaling *her*? Or Roland? She looked back at Collings, but he seemed lost in his wool muff.

Roland's door opened, and a woman stepped out, followed by Roland. He wore a white shirt, unbuttoned, and his feet were bare. His sandy blond hair looked mussed up, his jaw darkened by a day's growth. The woman's hair was a deep brown or perhaps black, left down and reaching her narrow waist. She turned with a smile and gazed up at him. Roland grinned in that lopsided way of his and leaned toward her.

Lila's breath halted. If she hadn't seen the kiss for herself, she never would have believed it. She'd heard rumors of course of Roland's escapades; he'd been a bachelor for a long time, but when a man's eyes were all for you, it was hard to believe gossip. Roland kissed the woman longer and deeper than one would kiss any relative, so that couldn't be an explanation.

The woman pressed against him, then quite possessively pulled him closer until there was no distinction between their bodies.

Heart thundering, Lila looked at the buggy driver who'd whistled. He didn't seem to be paying attention, as if it were the most natural thing in the world for a woman to come out of a man's house at midnight then garishly kiss him in a manner definitely not fit for public viewing.

What irked Lila even more was that she'd been in Roland's arms just two days before at their secret rendezvous place at a reclusive café. He hadn't wasted a moment finding another love after sending back Lila's letter with his reply. Or was this woman someone he'd been seeing all along, even when he was with Lila?

She wanted to scream, but mostly she wanted to close her eyes and make the image disappear. She wanted to arrive again at his house and for the door to open, but this time only Roland would be standing there. No one else. Especially not a woman who did not hesitate to wrap her arms around him and kiss him like a—

"Lila?" It was his voice. He'd seen her.

She turned away, her feet blistering with cold as she stumbled back to the carriage.

A woman's muffled laughter sounded, and Roland called out again. "Wait, Lila!"

He was coming after her. Lila's heart skipped. Roland would tell her that he'd made a terrible mistake. He'd propose, and they'd elope to England. He'd . . .

He grabbed her arm and spun her around. "What are you doing here? Your father will have my head if he finds out."

Lila blinked up at him. Somewhere in the back of her mind, she heard the buggy pull away, the horses' hooves growing fainter, a woman's voice laughing and calling out good-bye.

"Who is she?" Lila said above the sob choking her throat.

His eyes narrowed, and she literally felt his animosity. Lila had never seen him like this, angry at her. His grip tightened. "Didn't you get my letter?"

"You mean the scribbled note you returned on top of mine?"

He pulled her toward the carriage. "You need to get home."

Lila tugged away. "What about that woman? Is she your . . . lover?"

"That's none of your concern, Lila." He grabbed for her again.

"Am I nothing to you then?" The tears refused to stay put, and her voice shook as it rose. "When you kissed me—it meant *nothing*?"

Roland stared at her as if she was his worst nightmare. "I explained in my letter. You knew who I was when we met." His voice was fierce now. "You knew who I was when you agreed to see me. I never lied about it."

"You said you loved me," Lila whispered, tears streaking down her face.

"I love women. Nearly everything about a woman . . . except for this part." His face twisted into a half-smile, pitying her.

Lila took a step back. "You used me. You didn't care."

"Of course I cared," he growled. "But just because we shared a few kisses doesn't mean I'm obligated to marry you. You can't be idiotic enough to believe that. I knew you were a starry-eyed innocent, but this is ridiculous." He paused, his voice softening. "Any woman would be miserable being my wife. I wouldn't ask it of anyone."

"What about that woman?" she asked with a sniffle.

"She's not looking for marriage."

Lila stared at him. She'd thought she'd been the exception. She didn't understand how he could act one way, and now another.

"If you really want to know, that woman has been my lover for years. We have a mutual agreement." There was a twisted amusement in his eyes, and his voice dropped a notch. "In fact, she's married. And if that doesn't convince you to leave my property, she's not the only one."

Lila staggered back, his words like icy shards through her. "You . . . you're a scoundrel. You're a cheater. You—" Her voice broke off into a sob. She turned away and stumbled to the carriage. She grabbed the handle, using it to hold herself upright as she tried to catch her breath.

"I warned you that you'd hate me," Roland said.

Her body felt as if it had been wrenched inside out. The memories flooded through her. His immaculately tailored tux and her favorite ocean-blue gown complemented each other in such a way on the dance floor that it had been raved about in the society column the next day. Lila remembered Roland leaning toward her at the Gallivans' ball, that lopsided grin on his face, saying, "All the women hate me. If you spend enough time with me, then you will too."

She'd laughed and taken another sip of champagne. She'd never seen a man so handsome as he'd been that night, and she'd been determined to never hate him. Her father had been in Chicago that week, and her mother home with one of her headaches. Lila's chaperone had been Widow Godfrey from down the street. That was also the night Roland had kissed her for the first time, a slow and startling kiss on the Gallivans' terrace, the music floating all around, and every possibility stretching out before them.

By the time her father had returned and her mother had recovered, it was too late for Lila. She had fallen in love with the notorious bachelor.

Now, it seemed her father had been right. Roland Graves was the worst man possible for her. She yanked open the carriage door then turned to look at him once more. This time she saw signs of aging along his neck—the lackluster eyes, his too-thin lips. An aging man who would be forever alone. By his choice.

"You may have told me that I'd hate you." Her voice trembled in the white stillness. "But I didn't believe you. Until now."

Chapter Three

The snowstorm lasted two days, and it took two more days before the roads were passable. Lila spent every minute in her bedroom, all the lamps off, covers pulled over her head. The night she'd come home from Roland's, her father had been waiting for her. He hadn't said a word, and neither had she.

Fay brought her meals up, and when she tried to give Lila any news, she shushed Fay. It didn't take a notice in the newspaper to tell her that Roland had truly sailed to England; her father had informed her through the closed door of her room. His voice had been soft, matter-of-fact, and for a moment, she believed he might actually feel compassion for her.

But that didn't change the plans to leave for Connecticut. And even worse, her father was now determined to travel with her, saying he wasn't taking any chances.

The fateful morning dawned cold and gray. Lila's mother came to her room early to bid a feeble farewell. She had another headache and wouldn't be seeing her off at the carriage.

"Time with Aunt Eugenia will sort all of this out," she said, twisting the handkerchief in her pale hands.

"I'll be sure to write home about which nunnery I choose."

"Lillian!" Her mother's voice was sharp, which would bring on an even greater headache now.

"What else is there for me, Mother?" Lila asked, not repentant at all. "Father says I'm ruined, and I'll be spending who knows how long on a chicken farm."

"It's not a chicken farm."

"Father doesn't even like his sister. Why would he send his only daughter to live with her?"

"It's temporary, Lillian, and only until—"

"I *know*, the society papers. It's all that you and Father really care about anyway." She knew she was being cruel, but the pain of her broken heart had dulled her sensitivity to lesser infractions.

When her mother left in tears, Lila closed her eyes and berated herself. How had she allowed herself to step so low as to make her mother cry even more? Deep down she knew her parents were right, but the anger of Roland's betrayal was still fierce, and she didn't want to trust in anyone or believe that things could ever get back to normal.

There would certainly be no balls at her aunt's farm. Her father had told her to pack her plainest clothing, but she'd slipped in two of her favorite ball gowns, even if the only time she could wear them would be in the middle of the night by herself in her room.

With her mother returned to the recesses of her rooms, Lila took a final look at her bedroom. She was leaving everything behind except for the clothing she was taking with her. The brocaded drapes, the guilt-edged furniture, and the massive canopy bed with its silk coverings, would all soon be a distant memory.

She made her way downstairs, gazing at the square portraits lining the walls—her grandparents and great-grandparents. Lila stopped at a miniature perched on the hall table, showing two girls, Lila and her sister. They were six and eight, and the artist had set them against Greenwich Village, with the ocean in the background. Charity's deep blue eyes seemed to sparkle from the picture. Next to her, Lila's violet ones seemed dull. Even then, perhaps she knew that her love life was doomed. Lila slipped the miniature into her satchel.

Chapter Four

"Help me, Lila," Charity squealed. She splashed at the water's edge. There was no real danger, but Lila walked toward her sister anyway. Just as she reached the sand bar, a man darted in front of her and scooped up Charity.

Roland! He'd come for her. Lila was about to call out to him when she realized Charity wasn't laughing with delight, but screaming in fear. Moving quickly, Roland carried Charity out to the sea.

Lila picked up her skirts and started to run after them, but her gown was too heavy, and her feet wouldn't move. She screamed for Charity.

Something jolted Lila from the side, and she blinked her eyes open.

"We're here," her father said, his voice cutting through the haze left from her dream.

She'd dreamed about Charity's drowning over and over, but never had anyone else appeared in them. As Lila's mind transitioned to the reality of her father leaning forward and opening the curtains of the carriage, she exhaled.

Roland wasn't coming for her. And Charity was gone forever.

"It looks like Eugenia has gone to bed for the night," her father said, disappointment plain in his voice.

Lila couldn't see much past her father's head—only that it was dark outside. The carriage came to a stop, and her father swung the door open, then climbed out. Lila hesitated as the cold air curled around her, penetrating through the blanket across her lap.

Stepping out of the carriage, she looked toward the house. It was completely dark, the only light coming from the two lanterns hanging from the carriage. Lila dreaded surprising her aunt, but there was no way a letter would have made it through the storm before them. Their visit would be twice the surprise this time of night.

Collings was already at work unloading the trunks, two for her, and a smaller one for her father. He'd stay one night then leave her to her doom. Her father strode toward the house, across the rutted drive and up the porch steps. Lila hesitated between staying with Collings or joining her father on the porch.

"Go on, Miss," Collings said.

Lila picked her way to the house, a plain two-story stone construction. It might have appeared quaint now, but she couldn't forget the horrible smell of manure used to fertilize the surrounding fields in the spring. Thankfully, it wasn't spring now.

Her father knocked on the door again as Lila joined him, standing off to the side. The door creaked open, and a faint light spilled out.

Aunt Eugenia wore a dark robe over a white nightgown, her eyes wide and dazed above the flicker of the candle she held in one hand.

Lila wanted to ask if the electricity was out, but didn't dare speak first. Her aunt stared at them for a few seconds. "James?" Her eyes narrowed as they landed on Lila. "Lillian?" Her hand came to her chest. "What's happened? Is it Annabelle?"

"No, nothing like that," her father said. "I've brought Lila to stay with you for a short time. Sorry we weren't able to get word to you before our arrival."

Her aunt's full attention went to Lila. "What is it?" Her tone rose, bordering on panic.

"Let's go inside and talk, shall we?" her father said.

Eugenia backed away from the door, opening it wide.

"Are the electric lights out?"

"No." Eugenia turned on a hall lamp. She threw Lila a furtive glance as she became her bustling self, so different from Lila's mother, who moved like a whisper about the house.

Without a fire laid, the parlor was freezing. Lila wished she'd brought in the wool blankets from the carriage. As it was, she sat on the edge of a loveseat that had seen better days. She wouldn't be surprised if it was handed down from a grander home.

Aunt Eugenia had no qualms being the object of charitable acts.

Lila had spied her father's ledger once and seen money drawn and sent to his sister. Of course, she was a widow, and it would be impossible for her to maintain the farm by herself and pay for hired laborers . . . Lila wrinkled her nose as a spoiled scent reached her. Something brushed against her legs, and she nearly cried out.

It was only her aunt's little pug—an ugly dog, much too affectionate for Lila's taste. But dutifully she reached down and scratched the top of its head while Eugenia kept her mouth in a firm line as her brother delivered the unwelcome news.

Once her father ended his recitation, followed by the request for Lila to stay at the farm, she waited for Eugenia's shocked pronouncement, then the inevitable, I will do my best to salvage your daughter's soul.

But Aunt Eugenia did nothing of the sort. She stood, pulling her robe tightly about her, chin lifted and said, "Absolutely not."

Both Lila and her father stared at Eugenia.

"W-What?" her father sputtered.

"My dear husband's cousin's son is staying with me—a Yale man," Eugenia said with a disdainful sniff. "Peter Weathers."

Lila reeled as she tried to understand who her aunt was speaking about.

"Larson's boy?" her father asked.

"No, Ruth's son. From Vermont."

"Ah," her father said, his thick brows drawn together. "You've become quite the abode of hospitality. How long has this Weathers fellow been staying with you?"

"He arrived for fall term and was planning on taking up residence at the University after the holidays, but it seems to have fallen through. He'll stay on until something opens up." Her appraising eyes darted in Lila's direction. "So you can see, with all his comings and goings, sometimes with a whole group of friends, it would be quite inappropriate for Lila to stay here, especially while she is trying to salvage her reputation. It simply won't do to have her in one of the spare bedrooms."

Lila vaguely remembered that all of the bedrooms were on the second floor of the farmhouse. There were three or four. A larger bedroom at one end of the house, and the other, smaller ones grouped together at the other end.

The barely concealed triumph on Aunt Eugenia's face made Lila's stomach turn over. Her aunt was positively gloating.

"Eugenia," her father said in a measured tone. "I'm surprised that you allowed Ruth to put her son upon you for so long."

Eugenia's hands flew up. "You're one to criticize my hospitality, barging into my home in the middle of the night—"

"Lila," her father called.

She jumped at her father's voice.

"Please wait in the other room while your aunt and I discuss arrangements."

Eugenia looked as if she might boil over like a teapot at any moment, and Lila was more than grateful to escape the impending storm. She rose from the loveseat and left the parlor, shutting the door between rooms. Her father's low tones resumed, mellow, but firm.

Lila decided to step outside, although the air was freezing. She could do with a bit of fresh air. She opened the front door and stepped onto the wide porch.

"Collings, you must be frozen," she said to the man silhouetted against the cold moonlight.

"Pardon me?" a deep voice said.

"Oh." It was definitely not Collings. "I thought you were our driver."

The man turned around fully; this man was anything but their driver. He was at least a head taller than she, which was saying something, as Lila had always been tall. It was hard to make out his features in the dark, with his back was to the moon, but she could almost see inquisitiveness in his eyes.

"I let your man in through the kitchen. Told him to make himself comfortable." His voice washed over her, and curiosity consumed her—she wanted to see his features clearly. "And you are . . . an acquaintance of Mrs. Payne?"

"Her niece. My father is her brother, James Townsend." Lila bit her lip. Who was this man? Then she realized that it had to be the relative spoken of. Peter something . . .

His hand extended toward her. "Pleasure to meet you. I'm Peter Weathers, from—"

"Vermont," she said, taking his hand.

His fingers wrapped around hers, and she suddenly felt small, an unusual feeling.

"Your hands are cold," he said, his tone soft and deep.

"So are yours." Lila realized she was still holding hands with the man and quickly withdrew hers.

"It's an unusual time of night to pay a visit to your aunt," he said. She thought she detected a bit of amusement in his voice.

"I'm here to visit for a couple of weeks," she said, although she didn't know exactly how long she'd be there. By the time New Year's hit, she hoped the society papers would be on to grander and more scandalous topics. Her heart fell just thinking of spending the holiday season in this dreary place. *If I'm allowed to stay here at all.* The man in front of her had superseded any welcome that Lila might have had.

"Welcome to the farm," Peter said, with a mock bow.

He was definitely amused now. Lila smiled and curtseyed right back, as ridiculous as doing so was under the circumstances. "Interesting you should call it as such. My parents don't care for that description."

Peter folded his arms and leaned against a post as if he had all the time and was most interested in what she had to say. "Oh? What do they call it?"

"An estate."

The moonlight caught the edge of his grin, and again Lila felt the urge to see what he looked like in broad daylight. His voice was certainly pleasing, most unlike Roland's, which was a bit feminine, if she was to own the truth of it.

Why are you comparing this man to Roland? Lila chastised herself. *You are one step away from a nunnery, and after all the tears and heartache, a quiet nunnery far away from any good-looking bachelor is just what I need.*

"Well, then," Peter said. "Shall we go inside? Or shall we stand here until we can no longer feel our toes?"

Lila's heart thumped. "I quite value my toes; let's go inside."

Peter moved past her and reached for the door, but not before she caught his scent of musk and earth blended into something decidedly masculine and natural. Roland preferred expensive imported colognes. In a room full of people, the combatting scents could be overwhelming.

Peter would probably fade in the background in a room full of socialites—such as a ball. Did he dance, and if so, how well?

"After you, Miss," he said, breaking into her thoughts.

What am I thinking now—dancing with this man? Fool. She moved past him, ignoring the way his scent once again touched her senses and spun her thoughts.

The low murmur of voices continued from the parlor. Nothing sounded hysterical, so that was a relief on Lila's part. It wouldn't do well for Peter to overhear an argument between her father and Aunt Eugenia. Lila turned to face Peter as he shut the front door. Her breath caught as she gazed into the darkest eyes she'd ever seen. In the light of the single entry lamp, she realized his hair was lighter than she'd first thought—more of a medium brown—but his eyes . . . they were the sort a woman could get lost in.

His cropped sideburns reached to mid-cheek, and his strong jaw was shadowed with several days' growth. Perhaps Yale was lax about such things. He shrugged off his overcoat, his height becoming even more apparent. His narrow vest did nothing to minimize the breadth of his shoulders.

Lila flushed when she realized Peter was watching her appraise him. When her eyes roamed back to his, he smiled. At that instant, she knew that Peter would never go unnoticed at any ball.

She opened her mouth to say something, to say anything, but found herself at a loss.

Peter tilted his head, as if waiting for her to come up with a speech. When she said nothing, he offered, "How will society ever do without Lillian Townsend this holiday season?"

As unattractive as it might have been, she gaped at him. "How do you know—?"

"I've heard about you, of course. When you told me your father's name, it all fell into place."

Does this University man read the gossip columns? Dread pulsed through her at what he might know about her.

"Please accept my apologies. I didn't realize I was in the presence of such an esteemed lady." He bowed dramatically, and she didn't know what to make of it.

Was he funning with her? His eyes were so dark when they once again settled on her, that she couldn't decipher his intent.

"There's nothing to apologize for. We are— I am—" She cut herself off with embarrassment. If he really had heard about her, it couldn't be good, especially if it was from the society papers. And her Aunt Eugenia would be an even worse source. She broke her gaze from his just as the voices from the parlor rose to a crescendo.

Her aunt was apparently not in the least pleased, and her voice rang clear. "There will be no chances, James. If she but does one thing that I deem inappropriate in my household, she'll be sent back immediately!"

Lila's stomach clenched. Not only had her aunt made threats, but Peter had just overheard her. She couldn't meet his gaze now, so she stared at the floor, wishing one of them would disappear.

Something tugged at her hand.

"If it were up to me, I'd let you stay," he whispered. "In fact, I'd move Mrs. Payne into a smaller bedroom and give you the largest room all to yourself."

Lila blinked up at him, her eyes burning. Was he teasing her? But when she met his gaze, it appeared full of concern.

He brought her hand to his lips and pressed a kiss against her skin.

"I hope to see you in the morning, Lila." He released her and turned away.

Before she could respond, he'd gone up the stairs, out of sight. Her hand tingled where he'd kissed it, and she swallowed against the lump in her throat. What had that kiss been about? But she didn't have time to consider the events further because the parlor door flew open.

Aunt Eugenia stood there, her chest heaving, her eyes blazing. "Your father will speak to you now."

Lila walked into the room, feeling as if her aunt were pricking her in the back with knives.

Her father didn't waste a moment. "Your aunt will allow you to stay here. In the morning, she'll have a list of agreements for you to sign. The first sign of trouble . . . which you undoubtedly overheard . . . will be cause for sending you home." His gaze faltered, and for a moment, she saw the concern in his eyes. "It will take a few weeks, maybe longer, for things to be cleared up at home."

Then he was all business again.

Chapter Five

*P*eter paused on the second-floor landing, just out of view from the main hall of the house. The voices floating upward were easy to distinguish. Mrs. Payne's high-pitched nasally tone, and the lower bass of what had to be Mr. James Townsend. He strained to hear Lila's, but there was nothing.

The young lady had looked like an ethereal fawn with those doe-eyes when she stepped out onto the porch earlier, the light spilling out behind her. Although she had been quick to reply to his questions, he sensed a naivety about her. She had seemed a bit unsure around him, which didn't make sense.

Surely she was used to conversing with the upper crust of New York. A simple man such as Peter shouldn't prove to be any sort of challenge for a woman skilled in the art of conversation, especially now that he lived in reduced circumstances. His dear widowed mother had been in for the shock of her life when he went through his father's financials. Father had significant business debts that neither Peter nor his mother knew about.

Peter had offered to leave Yale, though he had only one more year left, but his mother wouldn't hear of it. She'd insisted they sell most of their furnishings and pay down the debts as much as possible. The creditors had allowed her to stay in their home for one more year. Half of that time was gone now.

The three came out of the parlor. Mrs. Payne's face was drawn and tight-lipped, but Mr. Townsend looked calm despite his flushed complexion. It was Lila's expression that tugged at something deep inside him. She looked like she was at a funeral. What could have possibly happened in the young lady's life to make her look so dismal?

It's none of my concern. Courting one high-brow society woman is enough to last me a lifetime, Peter decided, yet he couldn't leave his hiding spot. Lila seemed different than Dannelle. They were both well-bred ladies of society and came from wealth, but their looks, mannerisms, and conversation were vastly different. Where Lila seemed innocent and vulnerable, Dannelle had been cold and calculating. Lila was tall and willowy, Dannelle compact and fierce. Lila was fair like a bright star, while Dannelle had been olive-skinned with hair as black as her nature.

It was with some trepidation that Peter accepted her advances and eventually proposed, making his mother exceedingly grateful. They'd planned to live on one of Dannelle's family estates, so his mother would always have a place with him.

Then Peter discovered that Dannelle's interest in him was only to anger her family and get what she really wanted—a chateau in France, to live near her French lover and, most likely, have the opportunity to entertain many more admirers.

Peter drew back farther into the shadows as Lila turned toward the stairs. Her chin lifted, and he saw a tear drip onto her cheek. He had to clench his hands to stop himself from moving onto the landing and asking what was wrong.

With a grimace, he hurried down the hall to his bedroom and slipped inside. He was suddenly glad he didn't have the funds to live on Yale's campus. Shutting the door quietly, he ran a hand through his hair. It would do no good to get involved with another high-brow lady. They were nothing but trouble. He climbed in bed and tried to sleep, but instead, he listened for any sound that might be coming from Lila.

Chapter Six

I will not fraternize with any men, single or married.

I will not speak to any male guests or visitors.

I will complete all chores in a timely manner.

I will read from the Good Book twice daily.

I will complete samplers for the Ladies Auxiliary.

I will only speak when addressed and not refer to anything personal.

Lila stared at the list in the early morning light, her heart turning cold as Aunt Eugenia leaned over her left shoulder, reading each item out loud. Her voice grated on Lila's nerves until she wanted to scream and rip the paper into tiny bits.

Her father had left just a few minutes before, and that was when Eugenia produced the list with a triumphant smile. Peter was nowhere to be seen this morning, and now it seemed that Lila was forbidden to even speak to him if they met again.

Her eyes burned with frustration. She'd slept poorly on the lumpy farm mattress. What had been in it? Stone eggs?

A voice came from the doorway of the kitchen. "And what if the house catches fire, and Lila needs to warn me to get out?"

Lila's heart about jumped out of her chest. She looked up and wanted to laugh, or at least smile gratefully, at Peter. Seeing him the in light of the day, his intense black eyes no lighter than the night before, she realized it was good that she hadn't had such a full view of him. He would have certainly invaded her dreams—which was the complete opposite of what she wanted. If she couldn't return to her parents newly minted, she'd have to suffer in this creaky place for far too long.

One night here had been plenty.

She pursed her lips together, because, officially, she wasn't allowed to fraternize with this man of men. Maybe her aunt really was inspired, since it was true that the Lila of last week would have not held much back. But, the new Lila was refined, restrained, and focused on restoring her reputation.

"Peter, you are still home?" her aunt said.

Lila didn't need to see the woman's face to sense that she was more than flustered.

"I overslept. Classes are finished, and my final exams don't start until the afternoon." His gaze landed on Lila, and she wished she knew what he was thinking.

"Oh," Aunt Eugenia said. "Would you like breakfast?"

"I'll eat in town," Peter said, his eyes going to the paper Lila was about to sign. He crossed to the table. "Well, what should it be, Mrs. Payne? Will Miss Townsend be able to warn us of our eminent deaths?"

Lila would give anything to see the expression on her aunt's face, but she didn't dare look.

"Of course." Aunt Eugenia's voice was quietly controlled. "In any sort of emergency like that, she may speak to you."

"So this line needs to be nixed." Peter took the pen from Lila's hand, their fingers brushing. He leaned over and made a bold line through: I will not speak to any male guests or visitors.

That musky male scent was back, although it was lighter this morning. Lila nearly shivered as bumps broke out on her arms. She was grateful for her heavy shawl that concealed them. Peter seemed to be taking an inordinately long time leaning over her to cross out the single line. He was so close that she felt his warm breath against her cheek.

I should rewrite that line, she thought. Fire or no fire.

With the pen, Peter then crossed out the top line: I will not fraternize with any men, single or married.

"There. That's more reasonable and something we can all live with." He straightened and moved around the table so he was facing both women. "I'll see you this evening, ladies."

Lila and her aunt were silent after Peter left. Warmth spread through Lila at the way he'd taken command over her aunt's unreasonableness. She hid a smile as she touched the pen to the list of agreements and signed her name.

"First chore of the day is to make the bread dough and set it to rise," Aunt Eugenia said in a tone that must have been what sent her older daughter to the nunnery.

The warmth dissipated as Lila followed her aunt to the pantry to measure out flour. She was about to ask if they had to grind the flour as well, but kept her lips pressed tightly together. She didn't want to give her aunt any ideas.

Lila followed her aunt's direction as best she could, but soon she had flour and bits of dough in her hair, underneath her fingernails, and on various spots on her face and arms. As a little girl, Lila had watched her parents' cook make bread. Lila had always been fascinated with the process, but she hadn't realized how much muscle power kneading took.

As she pushed back a pale strand of stray hair for the umpteenth time, Aunt Eugenia said, "I'll be dining at Phyllis and Pastor Wallace's tonight."

Lila thought it odd for her aunt to refer to her son-in-law as Pastor Wallace, but she supposed the position demanded it.

"How is Phyllis doing?" Lila asked.

"Oh, splendidly," Eugenia said, the pride obvious in her voice. "She's expecting late spring."

"So soon?" Lila said then clamped her mouth shut. Phyllis had been married only that summer.

"Pastor Wallace believes family is the most important institution on earth." Her tone was back to its usual sharpness.

"Yes, of course," Lila said. "I didn't mean—"

"I'll be going alone. You'll have to stay in your room while I'm gone. I can't rightly say when Peter will return or whether or not he'll be alone." Her aunt scraped bits of dough from the bowl and patted them onto the mound she was kneading. "And you must lock your door."

"Lock it?" Was this another thing to add to her list of duties? Stay home from dinner invitations and lock herself in her room?

"There's no telling who Peter will bring back. Sometimes his gentlemen friends are a bit on the rowdy side. Fortunately he's never included lady friends in his party, and he hasn't spoken a word about any particular lady since the engagement."

"Peter's engaged?"

"Not anymore." Her aunt pursed her lips together and laid a length of cheese cloth over the loaf, then took the ball of dough Lila had been kneading and started to rework it.

Lila waited for Eugenia to continue, curiosity burning through her. But she was quickly realizing that, after spending the morning with her aunt, too many questions had caused her to clam up. So Lila began to clean the mess of flour and dried dough.

Her reward came a moment later when her aunt said, "High society girl she was."

Lila found herself met with a narrow-eyed gaze from her aunt.

"Much like yourself, I suppose. My cousin Ruth said the lady's father was opposed, but he allowed the spoiled girl to have her way with most things." Eugenia carried one of the loaves to a shelf above the stove, motioning for Lila to follow with the second. "It was all hushed up before the society papers could get much information, and the lady apparently left for France. Of course, that left Peter in quite the lurch back home."

Lila paused by the window and looked out at the frozen fields. She wondered what the woman who'd steamrolled Peter was like. Something unpleasant tugged at the back of Lila's mind—did Peter see her as the same? He'd been quite courteous and amused to make her acquaintance last evening, and this morning . . . well, he certainly had his own ideas of what her restrictions should be.

He was a gentleman, it seemed; the fact that he attended Yale attested to that. But money was another matter, of course. If Roland had had any honorable intentions toward her, her father would have accepted him as a son-in-law, for Roland could well afford to live in style on more than one continent.

Eugenia continued to prattle on, and Lila listened only with half a mind as she scrubbed the kitchen table and chairs, lorded over by her aunt. By noon-time, she was worn to the bone. It seemed her aunt had waited until her untimely arrival to do any chores. She'd never spent a day with so many physical demands, and all she wanted to do was rest.

"I should probably read from the Good Book; I missed it this morning," she said, as she dusted the parlor while her aunt sat reading. Normally Lila preferred novels, the more adventurous the better, but reading the Bible was better than sneezing from dust every half minute.

Fortunately her aunt agreed, and Lila took the heavy book into the kitchen, away from her aunt's speculating eyes. Turning to the table of contents, she scanned the headings, stopping when she reached the first Book of Peter in the New Testament. Her stomach flipped as she thought about the way Peter taken over this morning and with two bold strokes of the pen, made her life more bearable.

The only problem with reading instead of cleaning was that her mind wouldn't stay focused. Instead of comprehending the tight verses of prose, she thought of the man with black eyes.

Chapter Seven

"Damnation!" Peter muttered as he pushed through the door and left the classroom where he was sure he'd failed the economics final test. The questions had been in Russian, or maybe German. He wasn't sure. All he knew was that he hadn't been able to concentrate one whit. That blasted woman staying with his mother's cousin had completely drowned out any sense left in his head.

He fished into the inner pocket of his overcoat where he kept the tightly folded envelope that contained Dannelle's letter, in which she told him he wasn't good enough for her after all. Well, not in those words, but the meaning was plain and clear. He wished her all the best with *Monsieur Lover.* Just touching the letter with his fingers reminded him of why he should stay clear of Miss Lila Townsend.

A man like her father certainly had grand plans for his only surviving daughter. Yes, Peter admitted to himself, he'd asked a few questions about campus this afternoon about the

Townsend family to add to his scant knowledge. And the conclusion he came to: *Completely off limits.*

A twinge of hope entered his chest as he imagined securing a prestigious position after Yale, and in a year or two, encountering Lila at some fantastic ball. Their eyes would meet across the room, and at first her pretty little brow would pucker in question. Then a smile would spread across her face as she recognized him. They'd dance, they'd talk, they'd laugh, and by the end of the evening, he'd be courting her.

A cold wind gusted about his legs, which fittingly pulled him from his reverie. He couldn't put his mother through another failed engagement. He'd find a wife eventually, but he could ill-afford one now. He couldn't even keep his mother secure at the moment. If his father were still alive, Peter would have more than a few questions for him.

Peter turned up the collar of his overcoat, shielding his neck against the increasing wind. Today, he'd walk back to Mrs. Payne's farmhouse instead of hiring a carriage, if only to freeze out the image of an alabaster face with violet eyes.

It was twilight by the time he trudged up the porch steps, and only a single light shone from the parlor. The rest of the house was dark.

He stepped inside, expecting to hear voices coming from the parlor, but when he walked into the room, no one was in there. The fire was low, and the room silent. It was barely supper time, so he assumed the women had gone out for their meal. Peter moved to the kitchen. A plate was left on the warming stove, and he peeked beneath the cloth. He'd been right. Mrs. Payne had left him supper and taken Lila with her to dine elsewhere. He realized he was ravenous and without taking off his coat, ate quickly.

Peter bypassed the parlor on his way to the staircase. He planned to go over his economics notes, hoping to discover that he hadn't botched the test as much as he at first thought.

When he reached the second floor, he thought he heard a door shut. Pausing, he listened for any other sound.

Then he noticed light spilling from beneath the door at the far end of the hallway. It was her door. Were the women home after all? It was a bit early for either of them to retire for the night. Curiosity took over, and Peter walked to Lila's room, but then hesitated. The light was definitely on inside her room, but he heard no other sound.

"Miss Townsend? Mrs. Payne?" He heard an unmistakable shuffle.

"Did you get your supper?" a muffled voice said.

"Yes, thank you." Peter stared at the door. "Is everything fine? Why aren't you in the parlor with Mrs. Payne?"

"Oh! Has she returned?" Her voice was clearer. Lila must be standing closer to the door.

"No, I thought . . . Where is Mrs. Payne?"

"She's at her daughter's for supper."

Peter frowned. "She left you here alone?"

There was a pause, and Peter wondered why she didn't just open the door to talk to him. Then he remembered the contract Mrs. Payne had written up this morning. It was about the strangest business ever—Lila was a grown woman being treated like she was a nursery child.

"Mrs. Payne told me to stay home and keep my door locked in case you . . ."

"In case I returned?" Peter guessed. His shirt collar was suddenly too tight and held in too much heat. He loosened his neck tie and undid the top buttons of his shirt. Was he really such a beast of a man that Mrs. Payne had made this lady afraid of him? When Lila said nothing, he said, "I don't know whether to laugh or pound your door off the hinges at the ridiculousness of this. What in the world did you ever do to deserve such censure?"

To his surprise, the door clicked open. A sliver of vertical light spilled out.

"Peter," she nearly whispered.

Bumps rose on Peter's arms at the intimacy of her voice so close to him.

"I'm sorry to seem so impolite, but I dare not disobey my aunt. She is giving me no chances, and I fear that my next stop might be the nunnery if I don't keep her rules." She let out a soft sigh. "No matter how ridiculous they may seem."

"What you're saying is that I must fear for my life, sprint to my room, and barricade the door?"

Lila laughed. The sound reached through the door and warmed him through.

"What I am saying is that I cannot bring more scandal to my name. And if that means staying behind this locked door when I'm alone, with a man in the house, so be it."

Scandal? Surrounding Lila? That only made her more intriguing. "The door is not exactly locked," Peter said, grinning into the darkness.

"Oh." A shuffle, then the door started to move.

But Peter was quicker and stopped it with his foot. "Leave it be. I promise not to barge in and be the cause of your swift dismissal."

Lila's slim fingers curled around the edge of the door, and Peter had the sudden urge to touch them. Instead he moved closer to the opening and said, "I'll just sit out here in the hall, and you can tell me your story. I'll try not to be too *scandalized.*"

She laughed again, and Peter found himself laughing with her.

"Prepare yourself." Her voice was quiet, and he caught a glimpse of her undone hair as it waved across her shoulders.

He sat on the floor and leaned against the wall, turning his head toward her door. Her voice was melodic and soothing as she spoke of her family and how she'd fallen in love with the wrong man. "Wrong in the sense that he would not offer me marriage. I should have known from the beginning because of his reputation, but naively I thought I might be different."

You are different, Peter wanted to say, but he didn't. "Were you in love with him, then?"

Her fingers wrapped around the door again, and he waited for her answer.

"I thought so at the time, but after I saw him with that other woman . . . I guess I realized that he viewed me as another of his . . . flirts."

The pain in her voice tugged at his heart. He wouldn't mind coming face to face with Roland Graves one day and giving him the what for. "I'm sorry you lost what you thought was real," Peter said.

"Thank you," Lila whispered. She cracked the door open a few more inches. "Thank you for acknowledging that. It was very real to me, despite all of the warnings."

Peter couldn't help staring at her. She gazed at him with those incredible violet eyes, and something thawed in his heart—something that had been frozen solid since receiving that rejection letter. Lila did not have the refined looks of some of the women he'd met, but she also didn't have the hardened, calculating ways that they did either. She was innocence at its finest—which had been a detriment to her.

It was plain to see that she'd had her heart broken, her feelings had been truly affected, and now she was simply being punished for falling in love with the wrong man.

Peter exhaled. "Roland is a dastardly fool."

The smile was slow on her face, but when it reached her eyes, Peter had trouble staying on his side of the hall.

"You are being too kind," she said.

"I have never been more truthful in all my life."

Color bloomed on her face, and Peter's gaze went to her mouth. Her lips were slightly full, and her chin perfectly pert. He hadn't had time to become attracted to Dannelle before she homed in on him to be the one to manipulate her father.

Sitting against the wall, next to Lila's door, every detail of her features was new to him. What she would do if he leaned over and kissed her? Slam the door in his face? Confess to her aunt?

He really needed to put some distance between himself and Lila. Peter made a move to stand, when Lila said, "Oh no. You must tell me your story."

Her face grew even pinker. "I—I mean, I shouldn't pry, but I just bared all of my terrible secrets to you."

Peter hesitated. If he knew what was good for him, and what was good for *her*, he should leave this instant and be gone in the morning before she awoke. Instead, he settled back on the floor, and said, "It sounds like Mrs. Payne told you about Dannelle."

Chapter Eight

$\mathcal{T}$he deepness of Peter's voice made Lila want to curl up next to him and listen to him talk all night, even about things that weren't so pleasant. He'd been cruelly tossed aside by his fiancée and had discovered devastating things about his father, a manager at a bank.

As it was, she sat on the floor with her robe tucked around her, as she listened to him. She wondered if their fathers knew each other, then decided it was better not to ask yet. She wasn't exactly well-versed in the business world, but if there was a sullied reputation out there, she suspected her own father would put plenty of distance between himself and the situation.

As Peter talked, his expression was calm, but she sensed the anger and pain in his black gaze. She wanted to reach across the space that separated them, to hold his hand and comfort him. To let him know not all women were cruel and calculating.

It seemed they had quite a bit in common.

Peter went back to the topic of his father. "I'm sure his failures reached every bank in the country—I wouldn't be surprised if your father knew all about it." She could almost see him shaking his head. "If my father had lived, he might have been able to explain the bad investments. But as it stands, he's become the scapegoat for the bank's failure. I will never know the truth."

Lila again had the urge to grasp his hand. "Perhaps things aren't as they seem, and my father could look into it—clear your father's name."

His chuckle was low. "I wish that it were so easy. It's too far gone, and I'm sure a man like your father wouldn't want to involve himself in such a mess."

Peter was right, but Lila's heart tugged for this man who was suffering for a situation not of his own making. She cracked the door open so she could see his face more fully. Her breath caught as their eyes met, and she chastised herself for even allowing herself to unlock her door.

His black eyes bore into hers, and she wished she knew what he was thinking—*exactly* what he was thinking when he looked at her.

"I'm sorry," she said, wrinkling her brow. "I'm sure Yale will give you the chance to redeem everything that was lost by your father."

"It's my last hope," he said in a quiet voice.

Then, before she could stop herself, she lifted her hand and reached across the space that divided them. He clasped her hand, his warm fingers encasing hers, and a shiver trailed up her arm. She hadn't realized how cold her hands were.

"You're freezing again," he said, his voice low and strangely rough. "You must get up off the floor. I'll stoke the fire in the parlor if you want to come down."

She stared at him, thinking how they were in the house together, entirely alone.

The sound of her aunt's arriving buggy snapped Lila back to reality. She was almost breathless with thoughts of

Peter tumbling through her mind. Clinging to his hand wasn't making matters easier.

She pulled her hand abruptly away and held it safely on her side of the doorway. "Forgive me," she said. "I can be too impulsive for my own good."

Peter rose to his feet, looking down at her, his eyes glimmering. "I don't mind impulsiveness."

Before she could reply, he strode down the hall. Lila scrambled to her feet, watching until he turned toward the staircase, before shutting her door and locking it. Leaning against the door, she exhaled.

What is wrong with me?

First Roland, now Peter. I'm acting like a tavern girl who entertains a different man each night. But something deep inside her had stirred, and she knew that Peter was nothing like Roland. She felt that Peter had truly *seen* her and cared about what she'd been through.

He had a sad tale of fate, one that could certainly be repaired, at least she hoped. If not, she couldn't imagine her father being pleased with someone like Peter capturing her affections.

A murmur of voices came from downstairs, but instead of descending to greet her aunt, Lila turned off her light and climbed beneath the cold covers of her bed. She missed her luxurious sleigh bed and piles of damask quilts. She imagined Peter lighting a fire in the parlor and waiting for her to join him. But that would never happen now, not with her aunt in the house. And it shouldn't happen with her aunt absent, either.

Lila closed her eyes, as her body heat slowly warmed the blanket covering her, with thoughts of Peter making the process faster.

❦

When Lila next opened her eyes, her room was filled with winter morning light. Somehow she sensed that Peter had left early, and she didn't blame him. The confessions in the dark hallway the night before seemed too personal in the harsh light of day.

She climbed out of bed and quickly dressed in the near-frosty air. What she wouldn't give for a fireplace in her sparse bedroom. Peter was right; it was freezing. The water in the washbasin had a thin coat of ice on it, and her heart pinged at the thought of the heated water that came through pipes directly to her bedroom back in New York. The farmhouse might have electric lights, but her aunt was a stickler for spending anything on "luxuries," including heated water.

Lila tapped the ice coating, cracked it, then dipped her fingers in and scrubbed her face as quickly as possible. By the time she made it down to where her aunt was waiting expectantly, she was shivering.

"There you are," Aunt Eugenia said. "I expect you up by first light. What happened? It looked as if you went to bed early enough."

How could Lila tell her aunt that she'd been awake well into the night, thinking about her other boarder?

"Pull on your coat; you'll be cleaning the horse stalls today."

Lila stared at her aunt. "What?"

Eugenia bustled past her into the kitchen. "I've saved some porridge for you. Don't want you to be skin and bones when your father comes for you."

"Don't you have a man for the carriage house?"

"Humph. A carriage house? You're not at home anymore, Lillian." Her aunt pulled a bowl from a cupboard. "We have three stalls with barely a roof overhead. Had to sell two horses last summer. Can't very well keep a man to care for just one horse all winter. Only have Barnes around now, and he's away for the holiday."

Lila's mouth fell open. Did her aunt really expect her to clean out a horse stall? What about her son-in-law or Peter? Wouldn't that be more suited to man's work?

She'd ridden horses aplenty when her family had visited her mother's sister in Newport, Rhode Island. But she'd never done anything beyond riding.

Her aunt crossed her arms over her chest, waiting.

"I haven't the faintest idea of how to get started," Lila said, then fell quiet.

The look on her aunt's face told her that she'd learn soon enough. After she gulped down the porridge and pulled on her thickest coat, she followed Eugenia out to the stalls behind the house.

Although the day was clear, the wind was cold and biting.

Her aunt handled the horse and moved him to one of the long-empty stalls. "The pitchfork is propped against that wall."

Lila followed where she pointed, and grabbed the splintered wood handle.

"And you'll find gloves on top of the side table."

The leather gloves dwarfed her hands, but she needed the protection. She took up the handle again and approached the stall.

"Scoop it all out and carry it outside to pile against the outside wall," Aunt Eugenia ordered. "There's more hay in the bin. When you're finished be sure to move Smokey back in."

Lila looked from her aunt to the benign horse; the smell coming from his stall was making her stomach queasy. She was grateful she'd only had a small bowl of porridge.

Her aunt left, and Lila gripped the handle of the pitchfork. The work was slow and freezing. She should have layered two dresses today. She turned up her coat collar to make a barrier between the smell and her senses.

A whistling sounded behind her, and Lila turned. Peter was walking up the road to the house. She took a step back in the shadow of the overhang so he wouldn't see her—she suspected she smelled horrible by now and probably looked even worse.

But instead of turning when he neared the house, he continued along the side of it, coming right toward her. One hand was shoved in a coat pocket, and his other gloved hand carried a satchel, most full of University books and papers.

"Lila?" Peter said, his eyes apparently having no trouble spotting her where she stood inside the old horse stall.

She stayed where she was—there was not much lighting in the middle of the stall. Maybe he'd greet her, then go inside.

He stopped beneath the roof and took one look at the pitchfork she held and reached for it. "What does Mrs. Payne have you doing now? Can you even lift this thing?"

Lila raised her chin. "I've been working here for hours."

"Hours?" A smile touched his mouth.

"Well, maybe *one* hour, or more likely a *half*," Lila conceded. She didn't protest as he took the pitchfork. Just his presence alone made the job seem small and menial.

"You look half frozen," Peter said with a shake of his head. "You should be inside like other ladies."

Lila detected a note of sarcasm in his voice. Was he criticizing or concerned? "Thank you, but I should finish what I started." She reached for the pitchfork, but Peter moved so his back was to her. With a half-dozen swift strokes, he'd finished the job.

"I'm most grateful." She peeled off the heavy work gloves and shoved her hands into her coat pockets, but not before Peter noticed the redness of her hands.

"Those gloves were much too large to do you any good," he said, coming to stand in front of her. He dropped the pitchfork and lifted her arms until her hands came out of their pockets. He pulled off his own gloves and grasped her hands.

His skin seemed almost too hot to Lila, whose fingers had little feeling left. Her heart skipped as he brought her fingers to his mouth and blew warm air on them.

"Are you ever warm?" he asked.

Lila laughed. "I'm afraid I'm doomed as long as I'm living here."

Peter slowly rubbed warmth back into her hands, though it wasn't nearly enough in the cold air. But Lila wasn't going to complain.

"How did your exams go today?" she asked, trying to keep her mind off of his touch, which was sending darts of warmth through her entire body.

"Quite well, I believe." Peter lifted his eyes to meet hers. "I think baring my soul last night helped clear my head."

Lila hid a smile. Nothing he'd said last night had been the least bit amusing, but she was grateful that their conversation had helped him in some way. Relief shuddered through her. Peter didn't seem the least bit put off by her tale either. In fact, he was practically staring at her.

"I'll get the hay replenished, then get you back inside." He shrugged off his coat and set it over her shoulders.

"I'm fine," she started.

"Your teeth are chattering."

"No, they aren't." Her teeth clicked together, quite involuntarily, and he laughed.

Well, maybe they are a little.

It took Peter only a few moments to put the horse stall back to rights; Lila didn't want to think about how long it might have taken her, or how much more frozen she'd have felt. Peter insisted she keep the coat as they walked back to the house. She wondered if she'd ever feel completely warm again.

Once inside, Peter ushered her into the parlor. Aunt Eugenia sat at the writing desk, and she looked up with surprise when Lila entered.

"Finished already? Did you—" Her words died when Peter came in behind Lila.

"Peter helped me with the last little bit." She tried to keep a straight face. Peter was standing very close to her. "Oh, your coat," she said, realizing she still wore it.

Peter took it from her shoulders with a smile then turned to Eugenia. "Miss Townsend was out in the cold a bit too long. She'll require hot broth and warm socks."

Aunt Eugenia opened her mouth, then shut it firmly.

"I'm sure her father wouldn't care to see her indisposed when he returns to fetch her."

Eugenia set down her pen. "O-of course not. I'll get the broth and the . . ."

"Socks," Peter supplied.

When she left, Peter turned to Lila. "Let's get you out of those shoes."

"She's going to be livid," Lila whispered. "You're coddling me too much, and you're a man, you know, so you shouldn't be touching my feet."

"I know that very well," Peter said, leading her to the chair by the fire. He knelt down in front of her and unlaced her boots.

Lila thought she might stop breathing, but miraculously she stayed alive as Peter's deft fingers removed her boots. Even though her feet were practically numb, she felt his touch as if she'd been scorched.

"Better?" He looked up at her with those intense eyes.

She smiled down at him. "Much."

"I only have these wool socks," Eugenia's voice cut in between them.

Peter quickly stood and took them, holding them next to the fire. "These will do fine. And now for the broth."

"Of course," Eugenia said, then disappeared.

When her aunt was gone again, Lila said to Peter, "You're doing too much, you know. It's plain she doesn't like it one bit."

His gaze grew serious. "Someone has to watch out for you, Lila."

She bit her lip. Her parents had watched out for her in their own way, but never so . . . intimately as Peter. She shifted in her seat, moving her toes closer to the fire. "I'm perfectly capable of—"

Peter was at her side in a moment, and he pressed his finger against her lips. "Hush. I'm not leaving your sight until you're completely thawed and your complexion is a healthy pink."

There was nothing she could think of to say. Peter's touch had left her speechless. It wasn't laden with lust as Roland's had been—nor did it come with a long history of other women. And his finger was still against her lips.

She stared at him, and he stared back.

Finally, he seemed to realize what he was doing, and he moved a step back. "You're unlike any woman I've ever met."

"Is that a compliment, Mr. Weathers?"

"Indeed—"

Aunt Eugenia came back into the room. "It's a bit hot, I'll warn."

With great effort, Lila tore her gaze from Peter and accepted the bowl of soup. The steam rose and flushed her neck and face. Her aunt settled back at the writing desk, her lips in a familiar tight line.

Peter moved a chair so that he sat directly across from Lila, a half smile on his face. His feet were so close to Lila's, that if she stretched just a little bit, hers would touch his.

"Now," Peter said with a confident smile. "Would you like me to recite some poetry?"

Chapter Nine

*L*ila placed the final pin into her makeshift coiffure. It wasn't as nice as Fay did it, but Lila had opted for a simple twist and used heated tongs to create soft curls about her face. She took a step back from the old mirror and surveyed her appearance. *It will have to do.* She wore a deep green dress—nearly emerald—that was elegant enough to wear to a parlor gathering, though not lavish enough for any sort of ball.

But it would be perfect for tonight. It was Christmas Eve, and although she was spending it away from home, she was determined to enjoy herself. *Even if Aunt Eugenia serves only cold wassail and stale wafers.* Lila smiled to herself. It wouldn't take too much determination to enjoy herself because Peter promised to stay the night. He'd travel to his mother's in the morning, so it would be their last night together for several days, perhaps until after the New Year.

Music sounded from downstairs. Phyllis and her husband must have arrived, and Phyllis was playing on the pianoforte. That afternoon Aunt Eugenia had told Lila that she'd be expected to perform tonight as well. Peter had jumped into the conversation, offering his talent of reciting poetry. Aunt Eugenia had politely, but swiftly, turned him down. While Lila recovered the day before from her near death of chill—at least that's how Peter had continually referred to it—she'd been astounded when he offered to recite poetry. But she couldn't help laugh when she discovered he knew only nursery rhymes.

Lila smiled to think if Peter were to actually recite nursery rhymes in all seriousness before the gathered Christmas crowd. Her heart rate doubled when she realized she needed to head down to the parlor now. There was no use putting it off. They'd all see her dress sooner or later. Her bare shoulders were a bit chilled in her cold room, but she knew that once she was in the parlor for a few moments, she'd warm up quickly.

She opened her bedroom door, then stepped into the hallway and turned to shut it. A low whistle greeted her, and she spun around.

Peter stood at the top of the landing.

She couldn't help but stare at him. He'd always been dressed neatly enough, but tonight he looked impeccable. Why she had ever thought he'd be just another man at the ball, she couldn't fathom. He wore a fine suit of black that only made his eyes look blacker, and his tie was a deep green—almost as if he'd planned to match her.

He tilted his head as their eyes met, and she forgot to breathe. It was like something was physically pulling her toward him. She knew he'd been hurt before, by a high society woman no less, but did he feel even a measure of what she did now?

A slow smile spread across his face. "You're beautiful."

A blush seemed to start at her toes and rush straight to her face, which was ridiculous, frankly. She'd been told hundreds of times, by many men and boys, that she was beautiful. But this was the first time she'd ever felt the meaning of the word "beautiful" reflected in a man's eyes.

Somehow her legs moved forward, and she walked to his side. She slipped her arm through his, and he escorted her down the stairs. As soon as they came within sight of the parlor, she released his arm and stepped ahead. Aunt Eugenia's eyes about bugged out of her head, but since Lila had done nothing wrong—except wear a beautiful gown— there was nothing her aunt could do. Phyllis was less obvious in her surprise and greeted Lila quite cordially, and none of the assembled neighbors seemed to mind her bare shoulders at all.

The night sped by, of course, just knowing that Pete would be gone before first light in the morning. Time and time again, Lila tried to arrange things so that she'd be standing or sitting near Peter, or involved in the same conversation circles as he. But as the evening came to a close, she realized she'd hardly spoken to him at all.

She bade farewell to the guests, wishing them all a Merry Christmas. Peter was still in the parlor speaking to an elderly gentleman and didn't even glance her way as she passed the open doorway to the stairs. This meant that under her aunt's pointed expression, she ascended the stairs alone.

Once in her room, tears slipped down her cheeks. She couldn't help stop them. It had been a beautiful night, a magical time, but all she could think about was confessing her heart to Peter. Which was what she absolutely should not do, especially while still on probation. Especially since he was destitute. And especially since she couldn't go through another heartbreak.

She lay on her bed, still in her gown, as she listened to the sounds of departure from the final guests. Her aunt would be exhausted tomorrow, and Lila was sure she'd have plenty of extra chores, even if it was Christmas.

Lila had almost dozed off when she heard a faint scratching at her door. She lifted her head and saw a folded piece of paper on the floor. Had someone just slipped it under the door? Her heart hammered as she climbed off the bed and picked up the paper.

Dearest Lila,
Meet me in an hour in the parlor.
—P.W.

Lila bit her lip to keep from shouting with laughter. She wanted to dance and twirl and run around her small room. Instead she climbed on the bed and read the note again.

By the time she crept down the stairs, it hadn't been a full hour, but she couldn't wait any longer. It must have been well after midnight, and the only light in the house was the dim glow of the dying fire in the parlor, its soft orange lighting the stairs.

When Lila reached the parlor door, she realized she still wore her green gown. She probably should have changed into something more sensible—and modest. She hadn't even checked her hair or face; were there tearstains on her cheeks?

Her heart skipped a beat when she saw Peter already there. He sat in a chair, facing the fire, his back to the door. As soon as Lila stepped in, he turned, then rose to his feet. It was as if nothing needed to be said. Lila walked toward him, and before she knew it, she was in his arms.

Chapter Ten

eter inhaled deeply, memorizing the faint lavender scent of Lila's hair as he held her in his arms. *Finally.* He'd never wanted to stay someplace so much in his life, even if it was this freezing cold farmhouse. He knew his days were limited with Lila—she couldn't stay here forever. And with his journey to visit his mother tomorrow, he questioned whether Lila was all just some fantastical dream. What if, when he returned, she was gone?

His heart pounded as they stood together in an embrace. Mrs. Payne could wake any moment, descend the stairs, and catch them together. Their reputations would suffer. Especially with his failed engagement and Lila's entanglement with that wretched bachelor.

Peter couldn't let that happen, yet he had to say goodbye to her. Alone. That was why he'd slipped her the note. But as she had walked across the room and into his arms, his resolve to keep this goodbye to mere minutes began fading.

When he first saw her emerge from her room tonight, wearing that green gown, he knew he was in love with her. It wasn't that she looked so beautiful, like a work of art, really, but because he finally saw her as she'd appear in high society. And he'd felt no reservation as he'd worried might happen. No twinge of concern. No lack of confidence. He realized for the first time since Dannelle that he was not ruined for love.

When Lila's eyes had met his, the emotion in her gaze had struck him to the core. She cared about him, perhaps even loved him. He'd seen it in her eyes—something he'd never seen in his fiancée's eyes.

Lila was pure and real, and now she was in his arms. He drew back and gazed at her. "I miss you already, and I haven't even left yet."

Her eyes blinked as if she'd just realized he'd spoken. Then she smiled that smile of hers and stroked his cheek.

This is becoming too intimate. Too dangerous. Lila touching him and looking at him in this way was perilous indeed. He exhaled. He'd never wanted to kiss a woman so much. But it wasn't only that. He wanted to be with her every moment. To . . . *marry her.* The thought should have scared him. A hundred complications stood in their way, but as her fingers trailed his cheek, then down his neck, he knew he'd overcome every single complication, no matter how long it took.

Chapter Eleven

ow can he stand it? Touching, yet not kissing? Lila wondered.

Peter's eyes closed as her fingers trailed along his neck. His arms were loosely around her, holding her, yet not nearly close enough.

Am I being too forward? Is this because of my former relationship with an experienced man?

No, she realized. Peter was different, and she felt differently about him. She wanted to kiss him, to touch him, but she also wanted to know everything about him. She'd even sit through one of his "poetry" recitations, or let him teach her how to clean out a horse stall. She wanted to meet his mother. She wanted to restore his father's reputation. She wanted to do everything and anything for him.

Peter's eyes opened, their endless depths nearly swallowing her whole.

She didn't know where he got his endurance, but hers had snapped. "Kiss me, Peter," she whispered.

It didn't take long for him to obey; it was less than a second before his lips were on hers. Her pulse throbbed as his arms pulled her close, and her body slowly became inflamed as his mouth moved tenderly against hers as if he savored every moment.

When Lila finally had to breathe, she drew away.

Peter's hands moved to her face, cradling it, and his dark eyes bore into hers. "Come with me in the morning. I want you to meet someone." His mouth brushed hers again, so sweet, so gentle. "And then if you like my mother, I'm going to ask you to marry me."

Lila could only stare at him. Every part of her body trembled. Peter had said *marry*. But she wasn't afraid or confused. In fact, she wasn't really surprised. It just confirmed that Peter felt the same way about her as she did him.

"Don't worry, Lila, I know I have much to accomplish before your father would consent to our marriage." He leaned his forehead against hers. "But will you wait for me?"

She inhaled his scent, then moved her hands up his chest, behind his neck, until her fingers tangled into his hair. "I will wait," she whispered, "but on one condition."

"Anything."

"That you kiss me every day we are waiting."

His mouth turned up into a smile, then, surprisingly, he released her. When she was about to question him, he drew her to the side of the fireplace. He pointed upward, and she saw the mistletoe on the high mantle.

She laughed softly.

"I have no problem with kissing you every day," he said. Before she could respond, he pulled her into his arms again and kissed her cheek. "Is that good enough?"

She smiled and shook her head. "No."

He kissed her other cheek. "Here?"

"Not quite," she whispered.

He kissed her jaw, and she laughed again. "You are terrible."

"Then you leave me no choice." His lips met hers.

She inhaled sharply as his kiss turned hot and demanding. She thought she might melt against him, and the only thing keeping her standing was being held in his arms.

"How's that?" he whispered against her mouth.

"Perfect," she said. "Just perfect."

ABOUT HEATHER B. MOORE

Heather B. Moore is the author of nine romantic historical thrillers, written under the pen name H.B. Moore. She's the two-time recipient of the Best in State Award for Literary Arts in Fiction, and the two-time Whitney Award winner for Best Historical. Heather is also the co-author of the Newport Ladies Book Club series (2012–2014), and the co-author with Angela Eschler of the inspirational Christian book, *Christ's Gifts to Women.*

Heather owns and manages the freelance editing company www.precisioneditinggroup.com. Heather lives in the shadow of Mt Timpanogos, with her husband, four children, and one pretentious cat.

Website: www.hbmoore.com

Blog: http://mywriterslair.blogspot.com

Twitter: @heatherbmoore

Facebook: Fans of H.B. Moore or Heather Brown Moore

More Timeless Romance Anthologies
www.TimelessRomanceAnthologies.blogspot.com

CPSIA information can be obtained at www.ICGtesting.com
Printed in the USA
LVOW06s1550080715

445448LV00021B/1255/P